THE HEIR

A Medieval Romance
Book Two of The King's Cousins Series

By Alexa Aston

Books from Dragonblade Publishing

Dangerous Lords Series by Maggi Andersen
The Baron's Betrothal
Seducing the Earl
The Viscount's Widowed Lady
Governess to the Duke's Heir

Also from Maggi Andersen
The Marquess Meets His Match

Knights of Honor Series by Alexa Aston
Word of Honor
Marked by Honor
Code of Honor
Journey to Honor
Heart of Honor
Bold in Honor
Love and Honor
Gift of Honor
Path to Honor
Return to Honor

The King's Cousins Series by Alexa Aston
The Pawn
The Heir
The Bastard

Beastly Lords Series by Sydney Jane Baily
Lord Despair
Lord Anguish

Legends of Love Series by Avril Borthiry
The Wishing Well
Isolated Hearts
Sentinel

The Lost Lords Series by Chasity Bowlin
The Lost Lord of Castle Black
The Vanishing of Lord Vale
The Missing Marquess of Althorn
The Resurrection of Lady Ramsleigh
The Mystery of Miss Mason
The Awakening of Lord Ambrose

By Elizabeth Ellen Carter
Captive of the Corsairs, *Heart of the Corsairs Series*
Revenge of the Corsairs, *Heart of the Corsairs Series*
Shadow of the Corsairs, *Heart of the Corsairs Series*
Dark Heart
Live and Let Spy, *King's Rogues Series*

Knight Everlasting Series by Cassidy Cayman
Endearing
Enchanted
Evermore

Midnight Meetings Series by Gina Conkle
Meet a Rogue at Midnight, book 4

Second Chance Series by Jessica Jefferson
Second Chance Marquess

Imperial Season Series by Mary Lancaster
Vienna Waltz
Vienna Woods
Vienna Dawn

Rulers of the Sky Series by Paula Quinn
Scorched
Ember
White Hot

Hearts of the Highlands Series by Paula Quinn
Heart of Ashes
Heart of Shadows
Heart of Stone

Highlands Forever Series by Violetta Rand
Unbreakable
Undeniable

Viking's Fury Series by Violetta Rand
Love's Fury
Desire's Fury
Passion's Fury

Also from Violetta Rand
Viking Hearts

The Sins and Scoundrels Series by Scarlett Scott
Duke of Depravity

The Unconventional Ladies Series by Ellie St. Clair
Lady of Mystery

The Sons of Scotland Series by Victoria Vane
Virtue
Valor

Men of Blood Series by Rosamund Winchester
The Blood & The Bloom

PROLOGUE

Blackstone Castle, Sussex—1325

ADELARD DE BLAYS watched his seven-year-old son slip out the postern gate at the rear of Blackstone Castle. Quill took a few steps and then looked over his shoulder, unsure if he should continue.

"Go ahead, Son," the earl encouraged, his heart breaking, knowing it was the last time he would see the boy.

Quill ran back and hugged him tightly. "I don't want to go," he said, his voice quivering.

"You must. I told you why. Go," he ordered. "Now. Before it's too late." The nobleman's voice cracked on the last word.

His oldest child gave him a long look. "I won't forget you, Father. Ever." Quill released his grip and hurried away.

"Goodbye," Adelard said softly as darkness gobbled up the boy all of Blackwell knew as his bastard.

Now, he must do what he could for his other two children before the royal troops arrived to whisk him away to the Tower.

Adelard picked up the lantern and hurried back to the keep. Landon and Katelyn would be in bed now, probably begging Sybil to tell them one more story before she blew out the candle and urged them to sleep. At least she had been a good mother to his other two children, though she'd done everything in her power to make Quill's life unhappy. Still, he owed it to his countess to warn her of his impending arrest.

As he made his way across the empty bailey, Adelard's thoughts turned to Cecily—his true wife. He had loved Cecily Elyot with every breath he took. Each time they'd coupled sent him to the heavens and beyond. He'd been ready to bring his bride to Blackstone Castle when his father's missive arrived in London, informing Adelard of his oldest brother's untimely death. As a third son, Adelard had been quiet and submissive any time he was in the presence of his father. The title and lands would never be his and so he kept his head down and stayed out of sight as much as possible, a shadow in the background who avoided his father's ire.

The missive changed everything.

By the time Adelard arrived at his family's estate, he found the castle's occupants in mourning for not one but two sons. Bardolf, the earl's heir, had died from a sudden fever, which had swept through Blackwell lands and taken a dozen other lives at the castle. Gunter, the middle son, had died in a fall from his horse, the result of a foolish bet accepted while he was too drunk to know any better. Their steward had told Adelard that Gunter had drowned his sorrows from his brother's death in drink. Knowing how close his brothers were to one another, he had wondered if Gunter died on purpose.

And so, Adelard, by default, had become his father's heir.

Immediately, the earl announced that Adelard would wed Sybil, Bardolf's betrothed. The couple would have married in a month's time. With a few adjustments to the betrothal contracts, Adelard's name replaced his brother's. He had no experience in standing up to his father and had obediently gone ahead with the nuptial mass, sick with dread and worry. Shame filled him as he pledged before God Almighty and all gathered to bind himself in holy wedlock to a woman he had never met—thus abandoning his one true love and wedded wife.

Adelard entered the keep, passing the great hall where many had bedded down for the night. He ascended the steep stone steps and paused before the children's bedchamber. His heart racing, he pushed the door open. As he'd expected, Sybil sat next to Katelyn's bed. His false wife looked like a Madonna.

And was the Devil Incarnate.

Sybil de Blays had made his life miserable from the moment Adelard brought Quill home to Blackwell. In some ways, she was more intimidating than his father had ever been. The earl succumbed to apoplexy a mere week after Adelard and Sybil wed. If only he'd been strong and stood up to his father. Told him that he already had a wife he'd gotten with child. It might have made all the difference—then and now.

Regret washed over him anew as he ignored Sybil and moved toward the bed where his daughter slept. Katelyn's dark lashes stood out against her pale skin. Adelard brushed a lock of raven hair from the five-year-old girl's face and then kissed her cheek. He ached, knowing he would never see her beauty blossom, nor see his grandchild in her arms.

Katelyn stirred and blinked. "Father?" Her green eyes lit up.

Of his three children, he favored her most because of her spirit and zest for life. Ever curious, she followed her brothers about and demanded to do everything they did—and usually succeeded.

Adelard bent and kissed her brow. "Go to sleep, my little love."

"Can we go riding tomorrow?" she asked, her eyelids already beginning to droop again.

"Aye," he said, knowing for him there would be no more tomorrows.

"Good," she murmured and grew still. Her small rosebud mouth parted slightly as her breathing became even.

Tucking the bedclothes around her, he looked to the empty bed next to Katelyn's.

"Where is Landon?" he asked his wife softly.

Sybil eyed him with suspicion. "He went downstairs to retrieve his sword. He left it in the great hall. You know how he takes it everywhere with him. I could not get him to climb into bed unless I allowed him to fetch it."

Adelard knew his time drew short and he still wanted to see his boy but he said to Sybil, "I've done something terrible. At least, that's what others will say. You and the children will be the ones to suffer for it."

Her brows shot up and he saw the hatred for him glittering in her dark eyes.

Before she could deride him, he said, "I won't tell you what. The less you know, the better it might go for you. Just know that the king's men are coming for me. They will be here shortly. Do your best to guard the children."

Adelard wanted to slap the satisfied look from her face. Knowing Sybil, she would be like a cat and land on her feet, even if it used up one of her nine lives. He only prayed to the Blessed Virgin that she wouldn't sacrifice Landon or Katelyn while trying to save herself.

"Farewell," he said. "I am sorry I was not a better husband to you—but, in fact, I was no husband at all."

He watched as understanding dawned in her eyes with his parting blow.

"What?" she hissed.

"No one knows, except for Walter," Adelard said, a calm descending upon him as he finally spoke the truth in their last moments together. "He witnessed my marriage to Cecily Elyot in London. Quill is my legal son. Landon and Katelyn are the bastards."

Sybil sprang from her chair and slapped him hard. Before he uttered another word, she raked her claws across his stinging cheek. Adelard grabbed both of her wrists.

"Enough," he said harshly. "I know you will do what it takes to shield our children. No one need ever know."

Her eyes blazed at him. "And your . . . other son?"

"Gone. You'll never find him."

With that, Adelard released her and strode from the room. He hurried down the dimly lit corridor, his heart racing at having finally told Sybil the truth. Returning downstairs, he spied Landon swinging his wooden sword just outside the great hall and stopped to watch him. Already, the boy had an athleticism and grace, moving as one with his toy weapon. Sadness and regret filled him, knowing he would not see this strong, sturdy boy grow to manhood.

Adelard grabbed his son, one he loved as much as his firstborn, and held him close as tears filled his eyes. His actions would cost this boy his earldom and all the Blackwell lands. He released Landon and then knelt, placing his hands on the boy's shoulders and squeezing tightly. Landon winced and tried to pull away, but Adelard held firm.

"You will hear many things about me in the coming years. Some of it even true. But whatever else, there's only one thing you need to remember to the end of your days. I loved you with my last breath."

Landon smiled. "I love you, too, Father." Adoration was plainly written on his youthful face.

"Look after your sister," Adelard urged and then tightened his grip. "And whatever happens, don't tell them about your brother. Ever."

"I promise. I'll never tell, Father. Never."

He withdrew the ruby brooch he'd taken from Sybil's box of jewels and placed it in his son's palm. Shaped as a dragon, it reminded Adelard of the stories his grandfather used to tell him about his pirate days on board *Dragonstar*. The brooch had been Godwin's wedding gift to Melisent, Adelard's grandmother. How he'd loved his grandparents and missed them every day since they'd passed over a score ago.

"Take this," he instructed. "Keep it safe always. When the time comes, give it to the woman you love."

The door to the keep slammed open and the king's men marched in. Adelard kissed the top of Landon's head and rose, a hand still on his son's shoulder. Someone bellowed out orders as soldiers dispersed in every direction, flooding the great hall and racing up the steps. Two knights latched on to Adelard and tore him from Landon.

As they dragged him away and a representative of the king announced the charges against him, Adelard risked a last look over his shoulder.

Landon stood in the midst of the chaos, tears running down his cheeks. His son raised his toy sword high in a final salute. Adelard acknowledged the gesture with a nod and then turned away.

CHAPTER ONE

L ANDON HUDDLED IN a corner of the king's rooms, making himself as small as possible. He hoped the monarch would stay gone for the rest of the day. He'd heard one of the servants say the king and Despenser went hunting. If so, that would give him hours to be left in peace.

He'd been at the royal court four days now but it seemed like a lifetime. The soldiers who'd invaded Blackstone Castle had taken him and his father with them. He hadn't been allowed to tell his mother farewell. Even now, Landon wondered what had happened to her and Katelyn.

And Quill.

Adelard de Blays' last words had warned his son never to mention his half-brother. Landon would keep his promise. If the king and his men treated Landon this poorly, he couldn't imagine what they would do to a bastard son.

That seemed like such an ugly word for such a good boy. Quill was not only Landon's half-brother but his closest friend. Quill had a generous nature and shared anything he had freely with Landon and also Katelyn, when she accompanied them about the estate. Quill was kind and patient. Everyone liked him. Except for Landon's mother. She never allowed Landon to even speak Quill's name aloud. He understood that, somehow, his father had lain with another woman before his marriage and Quill was the result. It still didn't make sense to Landon why his mother would hate Quill so much. When they were together, he made sure they stayed out of her way to avoid her wrath.

He missed his little sister more than he could have imagined. Katelyn followed him and Quill wherever they went. At times, Landon might hesitate trying something, whether it was making his horse run faster or jumping across a narrow portion of a brook. Katelyn proved fearless, no matter what the circumstance, and would bravely plunge ahead. He could keep his silence about Quill but he didn't have a clue how he could protect Katelyn when he didn't even know what had happened to her.

Landon did know what would happen to his father. The earl had done something terrible to offend the king—and Hugh Despenser. The man was always in the king's company, eating with him and telling him stories. Landon didn't like Despenser and the feeling was mutual. He'd humiliated Landon each day in ways small and large. It was why Landon now hovered in a corner. He hoped when the king returned with Despenser that neither of them would see him.

He wasn't allowed to leave. He'd been told to stay. That they would soon decide what to do with him. Twice a day, a servant would take him to the garderobe so he could empty his bladder. Other than that, he had to remain where he was. They had given him something to wear since he'd been in his bedclothes when he arrived. They were filthy after the journey from Sussex to London.

Landon had caught a glimpse of his father after they'd passed through the city gates. Adelard de Blays was bound hand and foot and tied to a horse. He couldn't see his father's face and was glad. The knight Landon rode with had pointed to the earl and told Landon the next time he saw his father, de Blays would be a headless, disemboweled corpse. He hadn't known exactly what disemboweled meant but he knew it couldn't be good. Inside, he said prayers to the Blessed Virgin that death would come swiftly. He couldn't bear the thought of seeing the man he worshipped suffer.

The door flew open and the king entered with Despenser close on his heels. Landon curled up and pushed himself against the wall, willing them not to see him.

The royal chamberlain laughed heartily. "Where's the boy? I want to see the boy."

Reluctantly, Landon pushed himself to his feet and came forward. He bowed to the king and stood motionless, his eyes downcast.

"Lord Adelard is dead, little boy," Despenser said. "His head rests on a pike that the king had placed just outside the palace. That way everyone can see what happens to a traitor." He paused. "Are you a traitor, Landon de Blays?" Despenser asked in honeyed tones.

"Nay," he said, keeping his gaze focused on his feet.

"You look so like him," Despenser continued. "We must see that you never become like him. Isn't that right, your majesty?"

Landon dared to raise his eyes and saw the king studying him.

"He's no traitor," the king said, tilting his goblet up and drinking. "He's a boy."

"We have to make certain, though," Despenser said.

Landon saw the venomous look in the man's eyes.

"Our boots were muddied during the hunt. I think this . . . boy . . . should lick them clean."

Despenser had been malicious but this was the worst he had asked.

"What do you think, your highness? Shall the boy clean our boots?"

Edward waved his hand in a gesture that could have been interpreted in various ways. His companion took it as meaning the king was in agreement.

"Start with mine, boy. Once you have perfected your technique, you may clean the king's."

Landon closed the gap between him and the older man and dropped to his knees. The boots before him were layered in mud, with bits of grass mixed in. He also smelled horse shit. He shuddered but kept quiet. Kneeling, he braced himself with his hands placed on either side of Despenser's left boot.

And licked.

"The Prince of Wales has arrived, your highness," a servant said.

"Bring him to me," the king commanded.

"Why did you send for young Edward?" Despenser asked.

"I don't want to leave the country to perform homage to Charles of France regarding Aquitaine."

"The prince is only twelve years of age. Do you think him an adequate representative, your majesty?"

"It's time he takes on certain duties so he can become a man," Edward replied. He paused and then said, "I'd rather stay here and hunt with you, Hugh. The barons are restless. I don't think it wise for me to be in France and allow them time to plot against us."

Landon continued his distasteful task. He sensed the arrival of the royal heir as he swallowed and kept to his task.

"Your majesty," said the prince.

He recognized the younger Edward's voice from a previous visit he'd made two days earlier. Landon forced the bile down as his mouth filled with more mud and shit.

"I am making you not only Earl of Chester but Duke of Aquitaine, my son. In that role, you will journey to Paris and join your mother. She's there with my envoys, negotiating a peace with her brother, the King of France. You will perform homage to your uncle in regards to the Duchy of Aquitaine. I am informed the peace accord has been settled. You may sign on my behalf as the new duke. Afterward, you and your mother will return to England. Do you have any questions?"

"Nay, Father. Not about the French. I am eager to represent the crown in this matter and thank you for giving me such a great responsibility." The prince paused. "May I inquire why this boy cleans the royal chamberlain's muddy boots with his tongue?"

Despenser chuckled. "He's doing a fair job of it. More practice will make him an expert, though."

"Rise, de Blays," the king commanded.

Landon pushed himself to his feet, aware of the filth that now covered his face. He kept his lips pressed tightly together, not wanting the prince to be offended by the muck coating his teeth and tongue. Giving a bow, he stared just to the side of the prince's face, not daring to meet the older boy's eyes.

"This is a cousin of yours, Edward, Landon de Blays. His father thought to commit treason against England with a small band of noblemen. Who knows? If not himself, Adelard de Blays might have tried to put this boy on the throne in your stead. Cousin Adelard's head now rests on a pike. You may have seen it."

"Nay, Father, I haven't, but I, too, have boots that could use a thorough cleaning. This cousin of mine should do nicely."

Landon's eyes cut to the prince but he saw no malice on the older boy's face. Instead, he saw intrigue. Standing firm, he kept his jaw clamped.

"Would you give me this cousin, Father? After all, he is family and quite young. I am sure I can dispel any notions of grandeur that Lord Adelard might have given him. 'Tis best to keep an enemy close and turn him into an ally instead."

His heart began beating wildly. Something told Landon that this cousin of his would not mistreat him. Still, he stood stoically, not knowing whether the king would agree or not.

"An excellent idea," the monarch said. "The boy is only six. He should prove malleable enough. Take him to France with you then. I'm tired of him being underfoot."

Victory sparked in Prince Edward's eyes. "Thank you, Father. I will represent you well in Paris." He moved and kissed his father's hand and then looked to Landon.

"Come along, Cousin."

Without waiting, the young prince strode from the room. Landon quickly followed him. His only regret was that he couldn't stop to spit what sat in his mouth in Despenser's face. The king's rooms were vast and it took some minutes to reach the corridor. The prince sailed through the two lines of royal guards and Landon made sure he was close enough that he wouldn't be swallowed by the soldiers.

Turning to the left, the prince kept to a brisk pace before he stopped and threw open a window.

"Spit out as much as you can," he commanded.

Wide eyed, Landon stepped to the window and used his tongue to push out the excess muck in his mouth. He took his fingers and scraped his tongue and then wiped them on the borrowed clothes that were too large and now smelled like manure.

The prince nodded agreeably and closed the window. Landon followed him once more until they reached another wing of the palace. They entered a suite of rooms, where a horrified servant looked at Landon, his mouth gaping wide.

"Bring hot water. My cousin needs a bath," Edward said pleasantly. "And send for my tailor. He needs a new wardrobe and I, too, am in need of something elegant to wear to the French court."

When the servant stood rooted to the spot, the prince firmly said, "Now," and the man scurried away.

"Come this way, Landon."

He followed the royal to another room, where a lavish meal had been set out. His stomach gurgled noisily at the sight.

"I'm sure they haven't been feeding you well," the prince noted. "You can eat and drink in a moment. First, let's clean you up some."

Edward led him to a basin of water that would be used for washing hands before a meal. "Go ahead. Plunge your face into it."

Landon did as instructed and rubbed his face while it remained in the water. He raised his head, water dripping down the front of him, as the prince reached for a linen cloth set on the table.

"Use this to wipe away the dirt," he suggested.

Once more, Landon did as he was told, hardly believing his good luck.

"Come and sit. After you eat and drink, the water will have arrived for your bath."

"But . . . this is your food, your grace."

"I'm not that hungry. Go ahead."

Landon sat and though he tried to use good manners, he found himself shoving food into his mouth. Ashamed of his behavior, he stopped and dropped his hands to his lap.

Edward, who'd taken the seat opposite him, said, "You have nothing to be embarrassed about, Cousin. Despenser is the one who should feel contrite. He is a greedy, evil man. I am sorry he is so closely associated with my father. Has he mistreated you in other ways?"

"Aye, your grace." Landon thought it best not to elaborate.

"No more worrying about Hugh Despenser. You are in my care now. I will teach you what is important. The things a good man needs to know." A shadow crossed his face. "I met your father before. I am sorry that he got caught up in a plot against the crown."

Landon sensed his cheeks burning, shame filling him. "Father was always good to me and my sister." It was all he could say. He had no words to explain how the man he loved was the same one who'd done such terrible things.

The prince leaned closer. "You have a sister?"

"Aye. Katelyn is five."

"My father would not harm a child so young, especially a girl. She is safe, wherever she is. When the time is right, I will also take her under my wing. Would you like that, Landon?"

Relief flooded him. "I would."

Soon, the bath water arrived and the prince supervised two servants as they scrubbed Landon from head to toe. Clothes had been found for him. The tailor also arrived and measured him. The prince told the tailor they would be leaving for Paris in two days' time and he wanted several new changes of clothes for his young cousin, as well as something he could wear to meet King Charles.

"Mother says that my uncle pays close attention to details, so spare no expense," Edward instructed.

After the tailor left, Landon began yawning. He tried to cover it, only to hear Edward laugh.

"You've had a trying week, Cousin Landon. It's time for bed."

The prince led him to a room with an enormous bed.

"A dozen people could sleep in that!" he exclaimed.

"Well, only two of us tonight," the prince quipped.

"I'm . . . to sleep . . . with a prince?" Landon asked, overwhelmed.

Prince Edward placed his hands on Landon's shoulders. "A time is coming when I will need people loyal to *me*. The nobility throughout England rumbles in displeasure at the power both Despensers have at court and over the king. They have stolen lands and fortunes from too many to count. Their day of reckoning is coming. When it occurs, I will need to step forward and lead.

"Blood is blood, Cousin. Can I count on you to be by my side when I claim England's throne?"

Landon fell to his knees in order to show his gratitude. "I am your loyal servant. Always," he said vehemently.

"I will hold you to that vow, young Landon de Blays, both now and in our future."

Chapter Two

Briarwood Castle, Northumberland—June, 1340

CASSIANA CAMPION, DAUGHTER of the Earl of Briargate, finished her evening meal. Turning to her brother, Tobyn, she stared for a moment, wondering if she would lose him as she had all of her other siblings.

As the oldest Campion child, she had watched her mother give birth to a dozen children. Only Cassiana and five sons survived. Her mother, who'd grown weaker after each birth, had died moments after birthing a final daughter, who followed her mother to Heaven moments later. That meant, at twelve, Cassiana became mother to five little boys. She had bathed them. Played with them. Sewn their clothes. Taught them to ride and hunt and even read.

And then watched four of them die.

Two passed away from fevers in childhood. Another two came home from the border wars with Scotland with injuries too severe to survive. No matter how much she nursed them and implored the Virgin to intercede on their behalf, Cassiana had watched both slip away.

Now, only Tobyn survived. Her brother would leave in the morning with thirty of Briarwood's best men, marching to Berwick-upon-Tweed to join up with Sir Robert Morley. The nobleman had assembled fifty merchant ships that would join those of King Edward's. The king would lead this fleet across the North Sea to the English Channel, where they would unite with Morley's northern ships and then attack France.

Cassiana hoped her brother would live through any battle at sea and subsequent ones on land. It was important for the Campion heir to return home since he was their last hope for the line continuing at Briarwood.

"Tobyn, I will see to Father's meal now," she told her brother. "You can come say your goodbyes to him in half an hour."

He nodded, lost in thought. Cassiana knew Tobyn had to be thinking about previous battles in Scotland and his brothers' deaths, wondering if he would return to Northumberland.

She wondered the same.

Stopping in the kitchen, she retrieved a tray for her father, knowing he would eat little of the food on it. His appetite had never been strong since he'd become bedridden five years ago, suffering deep wounds in his back and leg in the same battle that had cost him two of his sons. Since that day, Cassiana had served as both Earl and Countess of Briargate, though she held neither title. When her mother passed on, Cassiana had not only become mother to five sons but she'd taken on all responsibilities held by her mother. She'd learned to rule the keep with a firm hand, wise beyond her years, doing a better job than those double her age.

Once her father took to his bed and it was obvious he would never leave it, she'd also taken up the mantle of earl and seen to his duties regarding their estate, both its tenants and soldiers. At first, her authority was questioned, due to her youth and status as a woman. Soon, though, the people of Briarwood found her more than competent. Under Cassiana's direction, the lands flourished and the soldiers became even more prepared than before. It wasn't unusual to find her in the training yard, demonstrating ways to better use weapons, since her father had insisted she learn to handle a sword and mace as her brothers did. As a woman, she had trained longer and harder than any man and her skills reflected the many hours of practice.

She'd also taken over supervising every aspect of the estate, from handling the harvests to bringing new tenants to Briarwood to purchasing additional horses. In effect, she served as both master and mistress of Briargate, holding it in trust for Tobyn since her father no longer could perform the tasks necessary to make his estate thrive.

In a way, she was slightly resentful of Tobyn, who'd been gone for many years, fostering in another Northumberland household some distance from home. He'd gone away at seven, returning for short visits over the years, while Cassiana never left the land except for short journeys to Berwick-upon-Tweed, where she bought supplies and sold livestock. She'd been the one her father turned to when he couldn't leave his bed and she'd seen that Briarwood was run efficiently. She was the one who knew the names of every person on the estate, from soldiers to servants to children of their tenants. When Tobyn returned a month ago having earned his knighthood at a score and one, he only remembered a few of those present, and he hadn't seemed interested in estate matters. In fact, he'd told her how he looked forward to leaving England to fight the French.

Cassiana supposed with the delicate nature of her father's health, Tobyn might return from battle to find himself the Earl of Briargate.

If he returned . . .

She shrugged off the thought. She loved her brother and would pray for his safe return day and night. Still, when Tobyn did come home for good, he would seek a wife and wish to run Briarwood as he saw fit. That left no place for Cassiana. The new countess would not want her sister-in-law hovering in the shadows, resentful of how the people would look to Cassiana for a decision and not their countess. Tobyn would want to put his own mark on the land, too, and not have his older sister instructing him in what to do.

But, where would that leave her?

She'd flirted briefly with Sir Tarquin Grosbeck, one of their many knights. A handsome man whose sword skills rivaled any she'd seen, Tarquin had stolen a few kisses from her when they'd met in the stables. Cassiana had hoped for more but his kiss left her empty. The knight had hinted at wanting to wed her once their men returned from France but she didn't think it wise. Even if Tobyn granted them a cottage of their own on the estate, she would still be underfoot and might be considered a hindrance. She would never want to undermine Tobyn and his wife as they built their own family and he settled in as the earl but Cassiana could see how torn their people might be if she remained.

The best thing would be for her to seek a marriage with a man far from Briarwood, with no ties to the area. She supposed she must ask Tobyn to arrange this upon his return from France.

Again, an unsettled feeling overwhelmed her. What if her brother succumbed to death as all of her other siblings had? The king would name a new earl to step in once her father passed. Cassiana hadn't worked tirelessly for so many years only to see the estate turned over to a stranger. Tobyn must return home. He must.

She entered the solar and then her father's bedchamber. Placing the tray on a nearby table, she helped him to sit up and plumped the pillows behind him. His pallor was gray. He gave her a feeble smile.

"How is my favorite daughter?" he asked.

"I'm your only daughter," she answered, not bothering to hide her smile.

"And always my favorite of all of my children," he said honestly. "I know what you have put into Briarwood, Cassiana. You have run every aspect of it. I only wish you could become the earl upon my death and not Tobyn."

She sat on the bed next to him and lifted the tray into his lap. "Hush, Father. That's foolish talk. England will never have a woman become an earl. Besides, Tobyn is a knight now. I've watched him in the training yard. His skills have come a long way, especially in the last few years. He may need to work on being interested in things beyond warfare, but he will defend the estate and its people."

He gave her a sad look. "What if your brother doesn't come back from the French campaign? Like the others? What will happen to Briarwood—and you?"

She squeezed his forearm. "I have sent so many prayers to the Virgin regarding Tobyn's well-being that she would be foolish to ignore me. Please, Father, don't worry. Not about me. Not about Tobyn. Especially not about our people."

They visited for a while as he attempted to eat, discussing her day and a new mare that had given birth that afternoon. Then Syndor entered the bedchamber. The servant had helped Cassiana care for her father—bathing and dressing him, bringing him his meals, and spending time with him so that he wouldn't grow lonesome. The earl never appeared downstairs anymore. Usually, it was only the two of them that were allowed to see him. Her father was embarrassed to be seen as he was now, old before his time and helpless. She even cleaned his chamber so that no other servants bothered him.

"My lord, your son wishes to visit you. May I bring him in?"

Though Cassiana knew her father had grown tired from her visit and trying to eat, she knew it was important for both men to have a final conversation before Tobyn went off to war in the morning.

She patted his arm. "I'll let you and Tobyn talk privately."

"Nay, Daughter. Stay," he begged.

"If you wish." She seated herself in a chair across the room so that Tobyn could sit in the one near the bed.

Syndor left and returned moments later with Tobyn. He'd only visited with his father twice since he'd returned to Briarwood. Her brother shuffled in, looking uncomfortable as he took a seat. Her father reached out and grasped his son's hand. It bothered Cassiana when Tobyn didn't bother to hide his look of disgust. Her brother had never tolerated being around anyone who was sick or frail. She supposed it went back to childhood and watching their two younger brothers cling to life. Tobyn had no patience for illness then. Nothing had changed since that time.

"You go to war with Morley," the earl said softly.

Tobyn sighed impatiently. "I do. The king is said to have more than three hundred vessels at his command. Most ships will be small, with a crew of five or so, but they will carry another fifteen archers and soldiers."

"I know you look forward to fighting our enemies. I am proud you do so, my son. I only ask that you be wary at all times."

Tobyn's brows shot up. "You think I am not alert in a fight?"

"Nay, I know you are. You have fought against the Scots for several years. This will be different, though."

"How?" Tobyn demanded.

"Because you are my last son. I need you to be cautious so you will return to Briarwood. I fear I won't last much longer. Our people need you, Tobyn."

"They have Cassiana," he snapped. "She runs everything effortlessly."

His words wounded her for she heard the sarcasm laced in his sharp tone.

"It sounds as if you are jealous of your sister."

Tobyn shook off his father's hand. "Nay. I am a knight of the realm—and your heir. She is but a weak woman."

Her father's face grew red with rage. He pushed up on his elbows and leaned toward his only son. "Cassiana has had to be all things to all people, Tobyn. She has never been weak. Do not disrespect her." The effort exhausted him and he fell back against the pillows.

Tobyn shot to his feet, dismay on his face. "I do not hold her in disdain. I know how capable she is. There isn't anything Cassiana cannot do. Farewell, Father," he said brusquely. "I will see you upon my return from France."

Her brother fled the bedchamber.

"Go after him," the earl urged. "Make peace with him if you can. He is resentful of you and all that you've accomplished. You've done more than ten men could have, my dear. Tobyn lashes out because he is unsure if he can live up to your high standards."

Cassiana crossed the bedchamber and kissed his wrinkled cheek, worried about his shortness of breath. At least the angry red that had flooded his face now faded.

"Goodnight, Father. I will see you in the morning."

She hurried from the solar and found Tobyn pacing the corridor. Immediately, her brother halted and looked contrite.

"I'm sorry, Cassiana," he began. "You know that I love you."

"But?"

He laughed. "You are so difficult to live up to. You still swing a sword better than I ever will. Our people love and respect you. I'll admit it. I'm envious of you and all you've done during my years away from home." Tobyn grew serious. "But Briarwood is *my* home. It's not large enough for the two of us. I realized that the moment I returned and saw how revered you are. How you've taken charge. Not only as a woman inside the keep but as a man would his entire castle and estate."

"Father's injury kept him from much that he longed to do," she said. "I merely stepped in to carry out his duties."

"And you've done them better than he—or I—ever could." Tobyn sighed. "I will never grow to become the man I need to be with you always looking over my shoulder."

She took his hand. "I realize that, Brother. I will keep Briarwood safe for you while you are away fighting our enemies. You can trust me to do so. I will also ask you to look for a husband for me. When you return, it will be time for me to leave and you to wed, as well.

Find a good man for me, Tobyn. One I can respect."

He grinned, his good humor returning. "I'll find you a rich one, Cassiana. One with a huge estate. He'll be smart and handsome and give you plenty of children. You'll have as many as Mother had. Nay, more!"

That gave her pause. Cassiana feared three things. One was bearing children. She assisted her mother many times as she gave birth and saw the agony involved. Between the physical pain and the knowledge that so many babes died, it made her wary of childbirth—and that meant the marital act that brought about those children, as well.

She also feared that if she wed, she would lose her independence. For too many years, she had proven capable at whatever she tried. If regulated to only a few domestic duties, she might go mad.

The last thing she feared was one she could never admit aloud.

Losing control of Briarwood.

It had taken her many years to create something special at her family's home, first in the keep itself, and then as she expanded her authority throughout the castle and beyond. Though she had admitted it no one, not even herself, she didn't want to leave. Instinct told her, though, that for Tobyn to succeed, she must be far away and not influence their people in any way.

Cassiana gave him a lukewarm smile. "I already raised five sons. I'm not sure I have it in me to raise a dozen more."

"Is that how many Mother had? It's hard to remember. So many of them were lost." Tobyn shook his head. "I was never good with numbers. No matter how many times you tried to teach me my sums, I couldn't remember from one moment to the next. If you choose not to wed, Sister, you could always become a steward and help run a vast estate somewhere," he teased.

If only she could . . .

"Get some sleep, Tobyn," she urged, hugging him briefly.

"I'm sorry I was so churlish to you and Father. I want to leave with things right between us. Are they?"

She gazed at him fondly. "They are. No need to worry. I bid you goodnight."

Tobyn kissed her cheek and then entered his bedchamber. Cassiana should do the same but knew her restlessness would cause her to toss and turn. Instead, she decided to visit Tressa. Nothing could ease her mind more than spending time with her horse, brushing the bay's coat and sharing her day. She stopped to collect an apple from the kitchen before heading to the stables.

The bailey was still, blanketed by silence on this cool June night. She arrived at the stables and went to Tressa's stall. Her horse nickered softly in greeting and Cassiana rewarded her with the apple. The horse nibbled daintily at the treat. Once she finished, Cassiana decided to brush the animal. As she reached to open the stall door, arms went around her waist from behind and she stiffened.

A voice in her ear said, "I was hoping you might come to see me off, my lady."

She turned and saw Tarquin smiling at her.

"Shouldn't you be abed?"

"Not when I can kiss you," he replied.

His lips brushed against hers. Once more, Cassiana felt nothing. She opened her mouth to tell him they had no future but he took it as a further invitation. Suddenly, his tongue thrust forcefully inside her mouth, causing her to gag.

Pushing him away, she demanded. "What was that?"

The knight gave her a lazy grin. "Just another way to kiss, Cassiana."

He had never called her by her name before. She definitely needed to put a stop to this.

"Sir Tarquin, I know—"

"I know how much I want you," he said, his hands spanning her waist, yanking her close.

"I must tell you that my father and brother plan to betroth me to a nobleman." She hoped that news would make him release her but his hands remained where they were.

"When?"

"As soon as Tobyn returns from France."

He chuckled. "What if your brother proves as unlucky as the rest of your siblings? What then?"

"Don't say such things. 'Tis bad luck," she warned.

Tarquin squeezed her waist. "Answer me. What if Sir Tobyn doesn't come back?"

Cassiana hesitated and then said, "The king would name a new earl for Briargate upon Father's death."

"Which is imminent," the knight pointed out casually. "You need to urge him now, while he's still alive and of sound mind, to petition the king to allow *you* to control Briarwood." He looked at her steadily. "And I will be your husband. Together, we can rule."

The gleam in his eyes finally told her what she'd missed before. Tarquin Grosbeck didn't find her attractive. His flattery had a purpose. He was enchanted not with her but in becoming the next liege lord of Briargate. The knight might have complimented her with pretty words but it was all to disarm her from his true purpose—wedding her and taking charge of the estate. He'd told her he was a fourth son and would never have land of his own.

Unless he wed a woman who possessed it.

Cassiana grabbed his wrists and forced them from her body. She didn't want his hands on her ever again.

"Tobyn will return and take over as earl once my father passes. I will wed another man. Not you, Tarquin." She crossed her arms protectively in front of her. "I wish you the best in France and in life but I cannot be your wedded wife."

With that, Cassiana stormed from the stables.

She had thought the knight cared for her but he merely wanted the estate. Not only would it be wise for her to leave Briarwood when

Tobyn returned from war, but she would be relieved never to see Tarquin Grosbeck again. Cassiana didn't know her heart could hurt but it did. Though she didn't have strong feelings for Tarquin, she had thought he did for her. Now that she knew he only used her, she felt foolish.

She swore she would never be used by a man again.

CHAPTER THREE

Berwick-upon-Tweed, Northumberland

L ANDON DE BLAYS came to an agreement for the price of his horse and collected the coin due him. He handed the reins to a young lad and left to head toward the harbor. He wished he could have arrived in Northumberland a few days earlier for he would have ridden to see his sister, Katelyn, the Countess of Northmere. He'd briefly stopped to visit her last summer while on a scouting trip for the king along the Scottish border. She'd been ready to deliver a child at any moment. It was hard to believe his sister was a married woman and now a mother. Hopefully, the French would quickly lose and allow for him to return to England. He wanted more than anything to meet his nephew.

Landon traveled a mile from the center of the city toward the mouth of the River Tweed, following his nose as the scent of salt and sea grew stronger. His cousin, King Edward, had sent Landon north to meet with Sir Robert Morley, who assembled a fleet of merchant ships in the north. Landon would share with Morley the point where the ships would join forces, as well as provide details of the attack.

Turning a corner, water came into sight, as did an array of ships. The harbor bustled with vast numbers of soldiers, including archers carrying their bows, quills attached to their backs. Others wore swords by their sides. Orders were being barked back and forth. Landon paused to take in the scene and see if he could spy Morley.

"Landon?" a familiar voice called.

He turned and saw Katelyn hurrying toward him, a dark-haired babe in her arms. Nicholas, Earl of Northmere and his sister's husband, strode behind her.

Katelyn reached him and threw an arm about his waist. "What on Earth are you doing this far north?"

"I'm on the king's business, as usual," he replied, his attention focused on her babe. "I'll wager this is my squirming nephew in your arms."

She laughed and handed the boy over. He solemnly studied Landon and then burst out into laughter as if he'd discovered some secret Landon possessed.

"What do you think of my son?" Nicholas asked as he offered Landon a hand and a smile.

"He is a handsome lad and seems good-natured. Thank goodness, he takes after my sister," he teased.

"According to Nicholas, Ruston is the most intelligent babe in all of Northumberland," Katelyn said, beaming with maternal pride.

"He is," Nicholas assured Landon. "'Tis no exaggeration. Look what he can do. Set him down on his feet." Nicholas dropped to his knees.

Landon eased the child down and released his hands. His nephew swayed a moment and then steadied himself.

"Come to me, Ruston," Nicholas urged. "Just like yesterday." He held his arms out and smiled at his son encouragingly.

Ruston thought about it for a moment and then took a step in his father's direction and paused.

"That's it. Come to me, Son."

The child took another tentative step and then followed with several in a row until he fell into his father's arms. Nicholas swept the boy up into the air and Katelyn went to stand beside them. The couple gazed adoringly at Ruston, who gurgled and kicked his feet.

In that moment, Landon knew a huge hole existed inside him. He looked from his sister and Nicholas to the child and back and saw the happiness radiating from the trio. Landon wished he could be part of a family. He had been, long ago, before his father betrayed the crown and his actions separated the de Blays siblings from each other and their parents. For the last fifteen years, Landon had done everything in his power to assert how loyal he was to his cousin, King Edward, and to England. He fought every day to restore the good name that Adelard de Blays had foolishly tossed away. Landon wanted Edward's trust—and he wanted a title and lands to call his own.

And a woman to love.

He'd missed being a part of a family. Seeing how Katelyn had found a new one gave him pause. Landon desired what his sister had. A loving mate. Children. A home of his own. The only way that might come to pass, though, was if he did something extraordinary in battle. Men earned knighthoods that way and Landon had done so, becoming the youngest knight in the land. The king could also award estates and titles to those who proved their valor in an exceptional manner. Landon had given every minute of his life for years to his king. It made him wonder if Edward would ever see him as he did other men or if Landon would always be in service as a royal guardsman, doomed to forever be alone.

Nicholas lowered his son and told Landon, "Ruston began walking just yesterday. I can't tell you how thrilled I am to have seen his first steps before leaving England."

Katelyn tucked her arm through her husband's. "Poor Ruston was worn out by last night. Nicholas had him walking all over Northmere. For the first time, my boy slept through the night and didn't require me nursing him once."

Her husband brushed his lips against her temple. "I had to see my son in action while I could. By the time I return, he'll probably be running."

Landon saw the pained look that crossed Katelyn's face. She quickly hid it. "You'll be home soon, Nicholas. I know it." Turning to Landon, she asked, "What does our cousin have you doing so far north?"

"I'm to find Sir Robert Morley and establish the number of vessels he's gained."

"Fifty," Nicholas said. "I spoke with Morley earlier when we first arrived. Do you know where we sail to?"

"Aye. Directly to Blankenberge on Flanders' coast. Additional vessels have been gathered by the Earls of Arundel and Huntingdon in the west and south. They planned to join the king's ships at Ipswich. Edward will lead the fleet to Blankenberge and meet up with the ships Morley has assembled. We'll attack first at sea and then after our success, continue on land."

"How many ships will sail in all?" asked Nicholas.

"Between three and four hundred."

"I'll come with you to speak to Morley," his brother-in-law offered. "I'll be back in a few minutes, my love," he said to his wife.

"Nay, say your goodbyes now, Nicholas," she said firmly.

He frowned. "You don't wish to wait and wave me off?"

"I want to remember you close to me, your arms around me," Katelyn said softly. "Not at such a distance that I can barely see your face."

Landon spoke up. "Give me my wriggling nephew so you can say a proper farewell to one another." He plucked Ruston from Nicholas and the child wrapped pudgy arms about Landon's neck, pressing slobbery kisses against his cheek.

Though he tried to focus on other things, Landon couldn't help but see the tenderness in the couple's eyes as they stared longingly at one another for a moment. Then they were in a fierce embrace, with a scorching kiss that ignored the world around them as they clung to one another.

"They're always like that," a voice at Landon's elbow said.

He turned and recognized Sir Albert, one of Northmere's knights.

"At least I know my sister is loved."

"Aye, that she is. By her husband and her people," Sir Albert agreed.

The pair finally broke the kiss. Nicholas cupped his wife's face.

"I love you, Kate," he said hoarsely.

"Come back to me. Come back to us." She lowered a hand to her belly and rubbed it.

Joy filled Nicholas' face. "Again?"

"I think so," she replied. "I will know for sure soon but I wanted to tell you before you left."

Her husband kissed her with enthusiasm. "I hope this time it will be a girl, Kate. A girl strong and beautiful, just as her mother is."

Katelyn's eyes welled with tears. "Go. Before I decide to chain you in the dungeon at Northmere to keep you from leaving me to fight the bloody French."

Nicholas gave her a swift kiss and then bent and kissed her belly. "I'll be back. I promise." He looked to Landon and swept Ruston into his arms, tossing the boy in the air and catching him. Ruston giggled. "And don't grow too much or too fast, my sweet boy." He kissed the top of his son's head. "I love you both. You are the little man of Northmere now. Take care of your mother."

He handed Ruston back to his wife without looking at her. Turning to Sir Albert, he said, "Get them home, Albert. Watch over them."

"Always, my lord," the knight replied.

"Come," Nicholas told Landon. "I see Morley." Without a backward glance, he strode off.

Landon went and brushed a kiss on his sister's cheek. "Take care, little sister."

"You, too," she said softly.

He caught up to Nicholas and soon found himself introduced to Robert Morley. Landon liked him immediately. He'd always found himself a good judge of character and knew Morley was an excellent choice to be in charge of the northern fleet. The nobleman appeared intelligent and confident and had organized the merchant ships he'd gathered into groups, assigning various families from Northumberland and their soldiers to each. They discussed the particulars of the rendezvous point as more men arrived and boarded the ships in the harbor.

Morley looked around. "We're ready to sail, Sir Landon."

Nicholas had already departed and seen his men aboard two nearby vessels. Morley offered for Landon to sail with his ship but Landon told the nobleman he would get to know the men aboard another one instead.

"I already have great faith in you, Morley. I wish to become familiar with others from the north who sail with us."

"A wise decision, my lord," Morley confirmed and wished him well before boarding the ship directly behind them. Immediately, the nobleman began calling for all in the harbor to climb aboard, as their departure was imminent.

Landon looked around and saw two ships over from where he stood was a vessel only about half full. A young man looked anxious as he listened to Morley's shouts. Landon decided this was the ship he would take across the Channel. He wanted to quiet the man's fears. He joined five other soldiers who swung onto the deck and went directly to the young nobleman to introduce himself.

"I am Sir Landon de Blays," he said, offering his hand. "A member of King Edward's royal guard."

The nobleman took it. He had a surprisingly firm grip. "Sir Tobyn Campion of Briarwood, my lord."

"Have you been a knight long, Sir Tobyn?" asked Landon.

The young man looked sheepish. "Does it show? I gained my knighthood less than two months ago. I have fought several years in the border wars with Scotland, though."

"So have I," confirmed Landon. "A nasty business at times."

"Aye. I lost two brothers in battle and my father's wounds from one of the skirmishes have never healed. He is bedridden."

"I am sorry to hear that. Do you have other brothers?" he asked.

"None living, my lord," Campion replied. "My sister, Cassiana, is in charge of Briarwood. She has taken on the responsibilities within the keep and on the estate itself, both during my father's illness and now in my absence. There's nothing she cannot do. Why, I think she would have it in her to rule England itself," he exclaimed. "If the king allowed Cassiana to lead this assault against the French, they would run all the way to Paris with their tails tucked beneath them."

"She sounds like a most capable woman," Landon said, though he realized this young man exaggerated. No woman of his acquaintance, not even Katelyn, was that exceptional.

Campion laughed. "The most capable woman in Europe, I'd wager. There's nothing Cassiana can't do." He studied Landon a moment. "You wouldn't happen to be wealthy, my lord, and possess a large estate? I am looking for a man my sister can wed. I want to make it home and relieve her of all the responsibilities that she has carried on her shoulders for far too long. As a member of the king's royal guard, I know you must be trustworthy."

Landon chuckled. "I have no title and no lands, Sir Tobyn. You'll have to find someone far better for your remarkable sister than me."

His companion shrugged. "It was a thought. I promised her I'd be on the lookout for a brave, intelligent, wealthy man."

"Were those her requirements?" he asked, his curiosity growing about this woman.

"Nay. The only thing Cassiana wishes for is a man she can respect. She wouldn't be impressed by material wealth. I, on the other hand, want nothing but the best for her. That means I require she marries a man with a large estate and an even larger treasury."

Though Landon was intrigued by this man's sister, he knew he did not fit Campion's lofty requirements.

"We could speak to my brother-in-law," he suggested. "Mayhap you know Lord Nicholas Mandeville of Northmere?"

"Lord Nicholas?" The knight's face grew flush. "He is the most powerful lord in all of Northumberland. Northmere is the largest estate of the north. Do you think he could help me as I search for a husband for Cassiana?"

"We can ask him," Landon said. "Let's tackle the French first— then we'll see if Nicholas can recommend a nobleman for your sister to wed."

CHAPTER FOUR

L ANDON ENJOYED THEIR short time on the seas, his first ever on a
ship in open water. He pitied the men on board who'd turned
green and puked over the sides. Most of those who'd been ill had
recovered quickly from their seasickness but two remained huddled on
deck, sweating and groaning.

Now, they approached Blankenberge. Within an hour, Landon
spotted a massive group of ships and knew the king had arrived before
them and dropped anchor. As they drew near, he recognized the cog,
Thomas, and knew this was the one his cousin had planned to sail on.
The Royal Standard that rippled from the masthead was a group of
lilies. Ever since Edward had assumed the title King of France six
months earlier, he'd taken to quartering his coat of arms with the lilies
of France. Landon believed his cousin had a strong claim to the French
throne, being the nearest male relative of Charles the Fair, who'd died
leaving only daughters behind. The French people thought otherwise.
Edward's cousin, the Count of Valois, had been chosen France's new
king instead, since Charles left the choice of his successor to his nobles.

That decision had led them to this day and England's recent alliance with the Flemish.

Landon wondered if Edward proved successful at invading France and dethroning King Philip, would he be able to hold the French throne for long? At heart, Edward was an Englishman. The monarch would long to return to his home. He'd been born at Windsor Castle and it was dear to him. The queen also loved living for a majority of the year at Windsor. Landon could not see Philippa uprooting her expanding family and moving them to Paris. Yet, if Edward didn't remain in France after his victory, how could he rule from across the Channel?

Finding Tobyn Campion, the ranking nobleman aboard, Landon told him, "I need to meet with the king once his ship comes near. Would you care to accompany me?"

The knight nodded eagerly. "I would be honored to meet the king, Sir Landon."

No rowboats had been placed aboard in order to get as many soldiers on each ship as possible, so Landon waited until they came within shouting distance of the *Thomas*. He made known his intention and their small merchant vessel drew as close to the ship as it could. Landon signaled to Tobyn and the two men climbed to the edge of their ship and leaped across to the king's.

A member of the royal guard greeted him. "The king wishes to speak to you immediately, Sir Landon, regarding the situation. He said no one but his cousin would do."

Landon nodded and motioned for Tobyn to accompany him as the guardsman led them to Edward.

"I had no idea you were the king's cousin," the young knight said and then grinned. "Had I but known it, I would have asked that your cousin help find a husband for Cassiana."

"Enough about your sister," he said good-naturedly as the guardsman slowed and then stepped aside, revealing England's monarch.

"Cousin!" the king exclaimed, a wide smile on his face.

The two men bowed and Landon said, "Your majesty, may I present Sir Tobyn Campion of Briarwood, son of the Earl of Briargate."

"Greetings, Sir Tobyn," the king said. "I have a great deal of respect for your father. He has helped keep my northern lands safe for many years. How does he fare?"

"He is confined to his bed these days, your majesty, thanks to wounds he suffered fighting the Scots."

"I am sorry to hear that." Edward frowned a moment and then addressed Landon. "Give me news of these northern ships, Cousin."

"Sir Robert assembled a good fifty ships, sire, and we bring close to eight hundred men on them. Half are archers and the other half men-at-arms."

"Your majesty? The scouts have arrived," a guardsman said.

"Bring them to me at once," the king commanded. Looking to Landon, he said, "After we dropped anchor last night, I sent three men ashore to reconnoiter the French fleet. I have been awaiting their report."

The trio appeared before the king. Landon recognized Sir Reginald Cobham and Sir John Chandos but did not know the third man. It was this nobleman who spoke first.

"The enemy vessels are anchored at the entrance of the Zwin, sire," the unknown man said. "So tightly packed that they cannot move, thinking to block our path."

"We spotted our captured cog, as well," Chandos added. "The *Christopher* is intact, waiting for us to reclaim it, as are several other English ships the French seized in recent months."

"How many lines are the ships arranged in?" Edward asked. "And who is in command?"

"Quiéret and Béhuchet are leading the French. Admiral Babavera commands their Genovese allies," Chandos revealed. "From what we gathered, the French are ignoring Babavera's advice regarding the lines. Babavera insists the French should put out to sea so they are able to maneuver freely."

"The French ships are in three, and sometimes, four lines all within the harbor, your majesty," Cobham added. "They're lashed together with boarding lines."

Landon knew ships often did this at sea in order for soldiers to move easily from ship to ship. In a narrow harbor, though, they would be at a disadvantage for they would have no freedom of movement. Without being able to maneuver, England would have the advantage as they entered the harbor.

A slow smile spread across the king's face. "Summon my commanders. With this information, I'm ready to finalize our plan of attack."

Landon signaled Tobyn and the two men retreated and found Sir Robert. "The king is ready to talk strategy, my lord."

The nobleman nodded curtly to Landon. "Take me to him."

He suggested that Tobyn remain behind and the knight quickly agreed, thanking Landon for his brief introduction to the king.

An hour later, the battle plan had been drawn up.

LANDON BID TOBYN Campion farewell, again promising to speak to Nicholas about the availability of a prospective bridegroom for Tobyn's sister. He'd spent several hours in conversation with the young man and liked him quite a bit so he was happy to ask his brother-in-law for a small favor on behalf of the young knight. Landon found Sir Robert, whose task was to recapture the missing English vessels that lay on the left side of the harbor. Morley would attack the left flank of France's fleet, first having his archers shoot down any visible French crewman and then having each vessel's men-at-arms board and clear the seized English ones in hand-to-hand combat.

"I'm returning to the king's side, Sir Robert. I know the northern fleet is in good hands."

"'Tis been a pleasure meeting you, Sir Landon. When this is over, we will find a quiet corner and a good glass of wine and talk of things other than war."

"I'll hold you to it," Landon said.

He reboarded the *Thomas*, wanting to remain in close proximity to the king during the battle. His cousin was not a man to sit back and let others do his fighting for him. Edward would be in the thick of battle from the moment it started. Landon intended to protect the monarch from danger at all cost.

The signal came and the English fleet set sail. Edward planned to navigate up the Zwin estuary to Bruges and land his army. Bruges would then become the base that would support his plans for invading France. Landon knew why the French ignored Babavera's advice. They hoped to bar Edward's way inland.

But at what cost?

He found the king, sword and shield in hand, his face heightened with color. Landon quickly gathered four of his fellow royal guardsmen nearby.

"Don't prevent the king from fighting but keep your eyes on him at all times," he instructed. "He's prone to taking risks in battle. Our task is to make sure he comes out of this battle not only alive—but without a mark upon him."

The men all nodded and readied their own weapons.

Landon glanced at the northern portion of their fleet and saw Morley's ships breaking to the left as the rest of the English fleet forged ahead. Then, as planned, the ships began splitting off in groups of threes. The first two ships in each trio were filled to the brim with archers, while the last contained nothing but soldiers. He watched the first group of ships rain arrows upon the enemy decks in quick succession. Screams of the wounded began to fill the air. Thanks to the longbow, an English archer fired twenty arrows each minute. The

French and Genoese crossbowmen could only return two in the same amount of time.

The signal came for him and his fellow swordsmen to spring into action. Ever watchful of where the king was, Landon remained near the monarch's left as they boarded their first French vessel. Swords unsheathed, the English soldiers charged onto the deck with shouts.

The conflict started brutally and never let up. In essence, it was the same as fighting a land battle, except they were at sea. Soldiers fought against soldiers exactly as they would on a battlefield. Soon, the decks grew slippery from the spilled blood as scattered bodies fell to the planks. The archers continued to wage a war of arrows as men-at-arms quickly followed up in individual combat, taking ship after ship. Landon's arms began to tire from swinging and thrusting his sword so many times. He had no idea how many men's lives he had taken in the hours they'd fought. The sun dipped low on the horizon. Darkness would soon fall.

Landon spotted Tobyn Campion on the deck of the next ship, mere feet from where he himself fought. The young knight's face was covered in blood and dirt but his body spoke of his determination. Campion struck down two Frenchmen and turned to face a third. Then Landon spied a swordsman racing toward the English knight. Landon cried out a warning, hoping the soldier to Campion's left would move swiftly to aid the young man. The soldier turned and looked—and remained rooted to the spot, his sword hanging by his side.

A smile on his face.

Landon jumped onto the ship as the French swordsman reached Campion. Suddenly, the enemy's sword protruded from the knight's throat, having been shoved through the back of his neck. Young Tobyn's eyes widened in pain. The French bastard kicked the knight in his back. Campion fell face down on the deck.

With a roar that echoed above the din of the fight, Landon arced his sword and slammed the weapon deep into his enemy's skull. A look of surprise flickered on the man's face and then Landon's booted foot knocked the man to the deck. He quickly turned, wanting to find the soldier who had deliberately ignored the threat to Tobyn Campion, but the deck was full of men with clanging swords. Landon would never find—much less punish—the Englishman who failed to intervene and possibly save Tobyn Campion's life.

At that moment, he saw the king leaping onto a neighboring ship. Landon quickly jumped back to where the king had stood and then he and the band of men guarding the monarch followed suit to the new deck. As the group boarded, an arrow pierced Edward's upper arm. A loud curse erupted from the king.

Rushing to his cousin's side, Landon pulled him away and ordered, "Come with me, your majesty."

The other royal guardsmen kept the enemy away so that Landon could get their king to safety. He spied the *Thomas* and headed in its direction. It took moving across seven other ships before they reached the king's vessel. Gripping his cousin's elbow, they made the final leap and arrived to safety.

"Find the healer!" Landon shouted. "The king has been injured."

Quickly, he brought Edward to the center of the ship and found the four guardsmen had all followed.

Pushing his cousin to the deck, he commanded, "Surround the king. Lift your shields. Make sure nothing gets through."

The men moved as one and encircled their monarch. Landon knelt beside him.

"You take far too many chances with your life, sire," he chided.

Edward shrugged. "I cannot attempt to claim another crown if I don't lead my own men, Landon." He looked down at the arrow sticking out from his arm. "Besides, this is nothing. It will leave a scar but that will be a reminder to me of this day's great victory." Grinning, he added, "And Philippa will fuss over me. I rather enjoy the attention

I get from my queen."

After having spent years in service to Edward, he knew the king and queen were a love match. Though their marriage had been an arranged one, the couple had grown to love each other completely.

The healer arrived and was allowed through the barrier that guarded the king from any more harm. He agreed with the king's assessment that the wound wouldn't cause any problems. It was cleaned and dressed. By the time that occurred, the fighting had trickled to a halt.

Edward rose and gazed across the harbor, a jubilant smile touching his lips.

"What do you think of our day's work, Cousin?"

Landon replied, "'Tis some of the fiercest fighting I've seen, your majesty. French ships were seized and then retaken by our enemy before we English captured them again. Good men died today for the glory of England. The water runs red from the blood of many corpses, most of them those of our enemies."

Various commanders began reporting in as darkness swept across the harbor and the port of Sluys itself.

"The French fleet is decimated, sire. Only two English ships were captured," Arundel shared.

Morley added, "We reclaimed the cogs, your majesty. The few Frenchmen who made it to shore were met by the Flemish and clubbed to death. It is an overwhelming victory."

A string of loud curses filled the air as two knights dragged a man along the deck and flung him at Edward's feet. He glared up at the king.

"This is?" Edward asked.

"Hugues Quiéret was killed in battle," Chandos said. "This is Nicolas Béhuchet, the French commander who lives."

"It seems your tactics proved unfortunate today," the king told the prisoner. "You have cost your country your entire fleet." Edward smiled. "And most likely, you've put me on the throne of France."

Béhuchet spit on the king's boots.

Landon kicked the French bastard in the face, knocking him on his back.

"Hang him, Sir Landon," Edward's voice rang out. "From the mast of his own ship."

Landon latched on to the Frenchman and yanked him to his feet. "With pleasure, your majesty."

CHAPTER FIVE

C ASSIANA TOLD THE new mother goodbye and left the cottage. She had delivered the woman's babe three days earlier and always liked to return to see how mother and child fared. In this case, the mother was already up and about, her son being her fourth child. The babe had a lusty cry and already thrived. Satisfied that all was well, Cassiana mounted Tressa and decided to make her way back to the castle since afternoon would soon turn into evening.

She tried to devote at least one day a week to riding the property and spending time with their tenants. That was how she knew so much about their people—who ailed, who was with child, who had a disagreement with his neighbor. Her mother had impressed upon Cassiana at a young age the importance of allowing adequate time for visiting with their tenants and others on the estate. It let the people know the Campions cared for them and kept her abreast of all news, good or bad. By being so involved and a part of the fabric of daily life, she had stopped several problems in the making before they raged out of control and needed a verdict rendered on a judgment day.

It also gave her time alone, riding between cottages and then across the property itself, checking on livestock and fences. Though she enjoyed being in the presence of others, sometimes all of the many responsibilities weighed her down and she craved solitude. Time riding Tressa soothed her. Truth be told, the horse was her closest friend.

Cassiana had learned that she really couldn't have friends, being in charge of everything. She learned that lesson early as she mothered her four younger brothers. She found if they believed she favored one over the other or she appeared closer to one and not another, it caused squabbling among them. Learning the fine balance of being friendly yet firm and without revealing too much of herself to the boys was something she carried over as she ran Briarwood. Her demeanor remained steadfast no matter what her activity—deciding menus for the keep's meals with Cook, training in the yard with their soldiers, or selling livestock and buying supplies in Berwick-upon-Tweed.

Everyone thought her strong and capable. She was—but a part of her longed to be able to relax. To simply be herself. To share the many burdens of running a large estate. At least she'd learned many things over the years that would make her an excellent choice for a wife when that day arrived, even though she was a little old. At a score and three, most females her age had long wed. Her family had needed her too much, though. Cassiana hadn't minded doing her part and stepping up when called upon.

Sometimes, though, she seemed weary beyond her years.

Allowing Tressa her head, the big bay raced across Briargate lands. Cassiana breathed in the air, already cooling in the late afternoon. Northumberland was never truly hot. Summers here were probably much different from those in the south of England. She caught a whiff of the sea, only a couple of miles from Briarwood, and longed for the days when she took her brothers fishing. Tobyn, in particular, had enjoyed the activity the most and took pride in bringing home something for the evening meal that he'd caught from the sea.

It made her wonder what Tobyn was doing now. Where he was. If he'd been frightened going into battle or if his confidence had grown. By now, King Edward's fleet would have united with the northern one Morley had assembled. She wondered how the English navy had fared against their enemy and if France had now been invaded by men such as her brother.

Cassiana rode through the gates, waving jauntily at their gatekeeper, and steered Tressa toward the stables. As she neared the structure, she saw Justin Cecil pacing in front of it. The squire had not been allowed to accompany Tobyn to Flanders since the ships were small and only fighting men had been allowed on board. At two and ten, Justin was too young to participate in the campaign directly. She had tried to keep the boy busy while Tobyn was away.

Justin caught sight of her and rushed over. "My lady, you need to come at once. It's the earl."

The squire's urgent tone and anxious manner let Cassiana know that her father had taken a turn for the worse. His health had begun declining in the spring. With Tobyn's departure, it had accelerated further. She'd been afraid these past few days that she might lose him soon and had spent hours with him, urging him to eat his evening meal while she told him about her day and all that occurred throughout Briarwood.

Tossing Justin the reins, she said, "See to my horse," and hurried across the bailey.

The training yard still saw activity. With some of their best troops provided to the king as he pursued his claim in France, Cassiana made sure that those who'd remained at Briarwood continued their normal routine. It wouldn't surprise her if the Scots, usually allied with the French, took advantage of the absence of so many soldiers from Northumberland and tried to cause more mischief than usual.

Entering the keep, she went directly to the solar, only to find Malkyn leaving. The healer's eyes met Cassiana's.

"The earl is gravely ill," the older woman said. "I'm off to locate

Father Peter."

A tightness gripped her heart. "The end has come?" she asked, knowing what Malkyn's reply would be.

"I believe so, my lady." Malkyn's hands framed Cassiana's face. "You have been strong for so long. Keep on for a bit longer. Your father needs to be at peace and know he leaves Briarwood in good hands."

"Of course."

She drew away from the healer and stepped inside the solar. The family room was empty. Crossing to the chamber where her father lay, she opened the door. The bedchamber smelled different than it had on her previous visit. This time, death blanketed the room.

Syndor wiped the drool that hung in the corner of the earl's mouth and then set the rag aside. Joining her, he said, "I've sent for Father Peter. I will leave so that you may have some privacy."

Cassiana saw the tears welling in the servant's eyes. She gripped his hand, trying to reassure him, and then Syndor exited the chamber. Moving to the bed, she saw her father's face had lost even the grayish tint it had held for the past week. Now, he was as pale as moonlight. She sat on the bed and wrapped her hands around his, finding them freezing.

He opened his eyes. "Daughter," he gasped.

"Don't try to speak, Father. Save your strength."

He shook his head. "My time is over. I will soon be with your mother. I'm only sorry to leave you with so much to do."

Cassiana smiled gently at him. "You know I am capable of doing whatever must be done, Father. You have taught me well over the years."

Sighing, he said, "You should have been a man. You have all the qualities that make an honorable one. And courage. I never saw you back down from any challenge that came your way."

"You wouldn't have let me," she teased. "Besides, I couldn't look weak in front of all my younger brothers."

He gazed at her with tenderness. "You are the best of me and your mother, Cassiana. I only hope you will find a man to love as much as I did her."

A fit of coughing seized him. Once it ended, he lay spent. She let the silence grow between them, willing him to draw on strength from her, yet knowing it was too late.

The air in the room altered slightly. She glanced over and saw Father Peter had arrived. The priest had only been with them two years. He was around a score and ten, with the most compassionate brown eyes ever placed in a man.

Cassiana started to rise but the priest said, "You may continue to sit with him, my lady, as I hear his last confession and help him into the next world. The Living Christ's world. Hold fast to your father's hands. Let your love flow from you to him and bring him comfort in these last moments."

She nodded, grateful to be able to remain. Closing herself off from the Latin prayers that Father Peter began to speak, Cassiana shut her eyes and remembered all the good times with her father. What he'd taught her about the estate and horses. How he'd shown her the correct way to hold a dagger and then a sword and the best ways to use them. The times he sang to her. When he sat at her bedside as she tried to fall asleep at night. So many treasured memories.

She'd been so lost in thought that when she became aware of her surroundings again, she realized Father Peter had ceased to speak. Opening her eyes, she looked at her father and saw how peaceful he seemed.

"He is gone, my lady," the priest said softly as he laid a hand on her shoulder. "You gave him the comfort and love that he needed."

Looking down at their joined hands, she brought them to her lips and brushed a kiss upon his knuckles a final time. Then she released his callused hands and settled them to where one lay atop the other on his chest.

"Thank you, Father."

"If you have need and wish to speak to me—about anything—feel free, my lady. I will say the funeral mass tomorrow morning."

Cassiana nodded and excused herself, going downstairs to the records room. She retrieved a fresh parchment and gathered quill and ink. Steeling herself, she began a missive to inform King Edward III of the passing of the Earl of Briargate.

And hoped beyond hope that Tobyn would come back safely.

LANDON STOOD GUARD in front of the royal tent, admitting various commanders that had been summoned to meet with the king regarding the current siege of Tournai. He wasn't surprised when Nicholas Mandeville appeared. They greeted one another, clasping elbows.

"I haven't seen you since our forces arrived in Ghent after the king's victory at Sluys," his brother-in-law said.

"Don't forget that my cousin first went on a pilgrimage to Our Lady of Ardembourg to give thanks for his great victory. The king has been mindful about giving God the glory for such a victory."

"At least the citizens of Ghent committed to Edward and renounced Philip, unlike the poor city of Tournai. The place has remained true to Philip throughout this siege."

"We intercepted a messenger only yesterday and learned they are running out of food," noted Landon. "Three months is a long time to hold out. The king gathers his commanders to discuss where we will go next once the city has fallen."

Suddenly, a commotion appeared to his right. Landon focused on a small group of soldiers who marched with a white flag. In the center stood a nun of regal bearing. Immediately, he knew who had come to call and stepped forward to acknowledge her.

"My lady." Landon bowed deeply.

"Rise," the woman commanded, looking at him thoughtfully. "You seem to know who I am."

"Aye, my lady. You are Lady Joan, sister to Philip of Valois and mother-in-law to my king."

She eyed him with appreciation. "And who might you be, good sir?"

"I am Sir Landon de Blays, cousin to King Edward and a member of his royal guard."

"I see. Well, Sir Landon, please inform my son-in-law that I am here and have an urgent need to speak with him."

"Of course, my lady."

Landon stepped inside the tent and hurried to the king's side. He whispered in Edward's ear.

"By the Christ! Bring her in, Landon. At once."

He saw Nicholas had slipped inside the royal tent and stood near the rear. Landon ventured outside and said to the nun, "The king is most happy to receive you, my lady. Please, come."

Lady Joan stepped inside. As Landon escorted her to the king, he saw all the English noblemen within had melted away, hovering in the shadows at the edge of the tent so as to give the former countess room to meet with her son-in-law. Landon stayed several paces away from the couple, yet remained close enough to hear their conversation clearly.

Edward took her hand and kissed it and then kissed her cheek, as well.

"I am delighted by this surprise visit, my lady. Philippa will be sorry she missed seeing her mother. I hope you are well. Please, have a seat."

Lady Joan perched on the edge of a chair. "My health is good but I am not here to speak about that. Pope Benedict has asked me to mediate this . . . situation."

"I see," Edward said, seating himself opposite and studying her.

"You should know that I have already met with my brother and have begged him to cease fighting against the English." She gazed steadily at the royal before her. "Now, I do the same with you, Edward. I am asking you to sign a truce at the pope's behest. No one will lose face because it is the Holy Father who asks for this peace. Will you do it, my son? For your wife? For your family? For the people of England?"

Landon held his breath, wondering if the king would waver in his pursuit. Already, dispatches had arrived from London, pleading for the monarch to halt any further invasion and return home. The royal treasury had almost been emptied. With no funds coming from Parliament, Edward would be hard pressed to continue moving inland toward France. From what their spies had ascertained, Philip was in a similar situation.

The king expelled a long breath. "I will sign a truce because the pope wishes it."

Joan smiled graciously. "Then it is to be arranged for three days from now. The terms will state that England cannot attack France for five years and that your army must return home. Will that be agreeable, my son?"

Edward sat silent for so long that Landon was afraid Lady Joan's intervention had been for naught.

Then he said, "I will consent to these terms."

The nun rose, as did the king. "A wise choice, Edward." This time she kissed his cheek. "Give my love to my daughter and all of my grandchildren."

"I will, my lady. Thank you for stepping in," he said, so softly that Landon doubted if any of the noblemen in the tent heard his words.

Lady Joan turned. "Sir Landon." She nodded brusquely and then exited the tent.

A dozen conversations broke out at once.

"Silence!" the king commanded. Every voice died away.

"We will sign this peace the pope desires and return home in three days' time. You are dismissed, commanders and guardsmen."

Slowly, those in the tent filed out as Edward added, "Lord Nicholas. Please come forth. Sir Landon, stay, as well."

Landon was curious as to what his cousin wanted with Nicholas and him, especially now that the war had come to a halt.

For now.

Once the space had been emptied, the king invited them to sit and said, "I have been doing nothing but reading dispatches from London over the last several days. It seems everyone in Parliament and half the country felt the need to send me missives in the four months I've been gone from England."

The king indicated stacks of parchment on a nearby desk, with many more scrolls left unopened.

Looking to Nicholas, the king said, "Defending the north is still of utmost importance to me, my lord. A strong border between us and the Scots is crucial."

"The north will not let you down, sire," Nicholas assured the monarch. "And the Scots know how you have reinforced numerous estates with additional troops, as well as giving your cousin in marriage to me." He smiled. "I am most grateful for that, your majesty."

"You're treating Cousin Katelyn well? She is happy?"

"Aye, sire. Kate and I are most happy together."

Abruptly, Edward stood and went to the desk, rummaging about until he found a certain parchment. He brought it back to them.

"I received word from Briarwood Castle. From a Lady Cassiana Campion, daughter to the Earl of Briargate."

"I know the earl well," Nicholas said. "He's been a staunch defender of England for many years, though recently he has fallen into ill health."

Landon spoke up. "Although I do not know the lady, sire, I met her brother when we traveled from Berwick-upon-Tweed to Flanders. Sir Tobyn spoke generously of his sister and held her in high esteem. Unfortunately, I saw him fall during the fighting at Sluys." He paused. "I had hoped to give Lady Cassiana this news in person, especially since I'd grown fond of her brother in such a short time."

Edward steepled his fingers and became lost in thought. Landon and Nicholas sat silently, waiting for the monarch to speak.

Finally, the king said, "Lady Cassiana wrote to notify me of her father's passing. Now, hearing that the heir to the earldom fell in battle, it is most important that I send someone I can trust to not only be the keeper of Briargate but a man who can help keep the Scots at bay."

Edward looked at Landon. "Philippa has reminded me many times of your constant good faith and loyal service to me and the crown, Cousin. Although I hate to lose your steady presence and sage advice, the time is at hand for you to hold your own title and estate.

"I am making you Earl of Briargate, Landon. You will work with your brother-in-law to see that the Scots never invade England. And since Lady Cassiana is familiar with the estate and it would make for a smooth transition, I command you to wed the lady upon our return home."

CHAPTER SIX

L ANDON WAS STUNNED by the king's words.

"Your majesty, I cannot thank you enough."

"No thanks are needed, Landon. I meant to give you your own estate and title all along. I only wished for the right opportunity. With the Earl of Briargate's death and no heir apparent, who better to send to protect the north from those miserable Scots than my most trusted knight?"

Pride swelled within Landon at hearing the rare compliment from the king. "Sire, I have striven to serve you every day of my life. From the moment you first rescued me from that blackguard Hugh Despenser, I wanted to prove to you my loyalty and win back my good name that my father tossed away so carelessly."

The king game him a long look. "There was never anything to win back, Landon. You are not your father and neither am I mine. History will look upon both of our sires with disdain. It is up to us to become better men than they ever thought to be and rise to our full potential. I never judged you based upon the traitorous actions of Lord Adelard, just as I hope you never found me to be anything like my weak, arrogant one.

"We are family Landon. We will always be family. As an only child, I find you are the brother I never had, and I look upon you with love. Believe it or not, it's hard for me to let you go even now, knowing how much I value not only your counsel but your friendship. Know that I place great trust in you and that you—as well as your sister, Katelyn—will be my representatives in the north. The Scottish threat may be greater than ever before, despite the fact that we've declared a truce both with both the French and Scots. Tensions will always simmer between us. I need you in the north, with your brother-in-law, to be my strongest lords that hold the line of defense between England and Scotland."

Landon fell to his knees and took Edward's hand in his, kissing it fervently. "Thank you for your faith in me, Cousin. I promise I will never, ever let you down."

The king urged him to his feet and Landon stood, a different man than he was moments earlier. Nicholas flashed him a brilliant smile and gave him an approving nod.

His cousin said, "I will make sure my scribes draw up the necessary papers that will award you the earldom of Briargate so that you may carry the news by official royal seal to your new estate. I will also write to Lady Cassiana to let her know you are my trusted friend and brother and it is my desire that you wed."

Edward rose. "I have every confidence in you, Landon. I only wish there had been more de Blays men cut from the same cloth as you. I could rule all of Europe if there had been."

Guilt washed over him. Landon recalled his father's final words to him, urging him never to mention Quill to anyone. In all these years, Landon had thought often of his half-brother, the bastard son of Adelard, but he had never revealed Quill's existence to anyone.

Not even to the king.

Though he trusted his cousin beyond words, this wasn't the appropriate time for Landon to disclose that he had a half-brother. It had been hard enough to track down Katelyn after so many years. Finding Quill might prove impossible. For now, he would continue to hold close the secret his father had begged him to keep. Yet, Landon now realized he would have vast resources at his fingertips.

When the right time came, he would move Heaven and Earth— and locate Quill Cardon.

"Thank you again, your highness. Please give my best to the queen and your children." Landon exited the royal tent, Nicholas close behind him.

His brother-in-law stepped to him, clapping him on the back. "I am thrilled for you, Landon. This is long overdue. And to think, we will be within a day's ride of each other. Kate will be so pleased. She has missed you dreadfully."

"It's still hard to believe, Nicholas, as if I'm emerging from a dense fog. I will have my own land. My own people," Landon said in wonder.

"And your own wife," Nicholas added, humor laced in his voice.

"Do you know the Lady Cassiana?" Landon asked, hoping to learn more about the woman before he set eyes upon her.

"I have met her on several occasions and can assure you that many sing her praises," Nicholas revealed. "Her mother died when she was quite young and Lady Cassiana raised all five of her brothers."

"I liked Tobyn Campion," Landon said. "My intention, once we returned from the Continent, had been to ride to Briarwood and tell her in person what happened to her brother. How bravely he fought, until his last breath." He paused and then asked, "What do you know of Briarwood?"

Nicholas thought a moment. "The estate lies near the coast, no more than a mile or two away. 'Tis south of Berwick-upon-Tweed, mayhap ten and five miles. The earl was a fierce fighter in his day and very protective of his people. He was injured four, mayhap five, years ago, while fighting the Scots. From what I gather, his daughter has controlled all aspects of running the estate ever since the earl took to his bed."

"Tobyn Campion mentioned how impressive his sister was." Landon chuckled. "He seemed to believe that she would find more success leading the men from Briargate in battle against the French than any man could."

"It would not surprise me," Nicholas said. "Lady Cassiana is the most like her father, which makes her outstanding in every way. You might also want to know that she is acknowledged as one of the great beauties in the area, as is your sister."

Landon shrugged. "Looks matter nothing to me. As long as the lady can give me sons, I will be happy."

Nicholas shook his head. "You will want more than sons, Landon. You will want daughters. I speak from experience. And more than that? You'll long for love."

Landon snorted. "Love? *Love?* True, I have seen it between the king and his queen but even then, they came to their arranged marriage as we all do. Look at you, Nicholas. You didn't even attend your own wedding."

Nicholas' eyes gleamed. "But I have been there for the nights that followed it. I cannot begin to tell you how much I love Kate. Your sister is my life. Every breath I take gives me purpose because Kate lives in my heart. I hope you will find the same with Lady Cassiana, Landon. I pray you do."

The men parted, with Landon promising to send news to Northmere when his wedding would occur. Nicholas told him that his sister would have both of their heads if she wasn't present when Landon spoke his vows. As he walked away, Landon scoffed at the idea of love between him and a woman he'd never met. Beyond seeing the devotion between the king and queen, he was too used to the machinations of the royal court. Love had nothing to do with marriages. Unions were built upon property and power and what a man and woman could bring to their alliance. Landon, relieved that his good name had finally been restored after so many years of heartache, would only bring himself and his fighting skills to Briarwood—but he would pledge to this new wife and his people that he would give everything he had to them. He would make Briarwood the premier estate in the north, Northmere notwithstanding.

Three days later, Landon stood near the king's side as he and his fellow royal guardsmen and an assortment of advisers and commanders watched as Edward and Philip sign their armistice. With both countries teetering on the edge of bankruptcy, the truce the pope had demanded through Lady Joan's intervention would be best for both nations. Much could happen in five years. This would give each country time to lick its wounds and allow the scars to heal from what fighting had already occurred.

Standing there, Landon was aware of the two documents signed by the king resting next to his heart. The first transferred the earldom of Briargate to Landon de Blays and his subsequent heirs. The second was a missive addressed to Lady Cassiana Campion, informing her of the king's decision to have her wed the new Earl of Briargate and remain on the property as his wife. Landon thought it a wise move on his cousin's part. Lady Cassiana would be familiar with all the workings of Briarwood. It would ease his transition as its new earl. He looked forward to meeting everyone involved in the estate.

His estate.

A glow filled Landon, knowing his years of hard work had finally been rewarded. He'd never realized the king did not hold him responsible for Adelard de Blays' treasonous actions but it made sense why he refused to do so. Edward's father, the previous king, had been a terrible monarch. He had alienated his people and made many unwise decisions. The former king's friendship with the Despensers, both father and son, almost toppled England into civil war.

Now, Landon would look ahead, a nobleman in his own right,

nothing handed to him by his father. He had earned his status and would continue to prove his fealty to the crown.

He knew war, having fought for Edward for so many years. He would not let his cousin down, especially regarding the Scots. It helped that Landon already placed great trust in Nicholas, his brother-in-law and good friend. Together, along with other nobles of the north, they would defend England from any threat of Scottish invasion.

Scribes distributed the various copies they'd made of the truce and the kings of England and France signed all of them. The French contingency vacated the premises with much fanfare and then the king began saying his farewells to the various commanders. He motioned to Landon and Landon responded quickly. Edward drew him into a far corner of the tent so no one was privy to their conversation.

The king placed his hands on Landon's shoulders and gazed at him steadily. "This is goodbye for now, my friend. My brother-in-arms—and in life."

"Thank you for everything you've done for me, your majesty."

"It was all well deserved. I have requested the men from Briarwood meet with you before they board the ships to sail home." The king gave him a smile. "You'll need to bring your bride to court someday so Philippa and I can meet her."

"I will do so, sire. Or better yet, bring the queen and your children to the north in a time of peace. You've only been there when conflict has prevailed."

A gleam sparked in Edward's eyes. "'Tis a sound plan, Cousin. Mayhap a future summer progress will see me at Briarwood. Until we meet again."

Landon gave a final bow and exited the royal tent. He said his goodbyes to several fellow guardsmen, all who knew where he ventured, then made his way toward the harbor where the English merchant ships would ferry the soldiers home for good. He found the Briarwood soldiers and called them to his side. About thirty men surrounded him. He could see by their faces that they were curious as to why they had been asked to meet with him.

He looked across the group assembled, knowing these men were now his men. His knights. His soldiers. He took great pride as he addressed them for the first time.

"Men of Briarwood, I am Landon de Blays, your new liege lord. As you know, Sir Tobyn Campion fell in Flanders, fighting bravely until the end. King Edward has recently received word from your own Lady Cassiana that her father, the earl, has passed. With no heirs, the king decided to grant me the earldom of Briargate and has given me Lady Cassiana's hand in marriage."

The men did not react. Landon didn't know what he'd expected, but the silence seemed eerie. Then a cheer broke out, loud and resounding. Relief swept through him. A dark-haired man with an air of authority stepped forward.

"Lord Landon, I am Sir Baldwin Gifford and have been in charge of the Briarwood soldiers since Sir Tobyn's untimely death. I would like to say on behalf of all of those present how happy we are to welcome you as our liege lord. Many of us have seen you in action and know your fighting skills are second to none. The threat of Scottish invasion is always upon us in the north. We will look to your leadership while we keep the Campion lands safe for all who dwell on them."

Landon accepted the knight's extended hand. "Thank you, Sir Baldwin. I look forward to speaking with you and each man present as we journey home to England."

The men began boarding the three vessels designated to take them back to Berwick-upon-Tweed. He stood with Sir Baldwin as they did so, asking the name of each soldier and committing as many to memory as he could.

"These are some of Briarwood's finest men-at-arms," his companion told him, "though many more skilled ones remained in Northumberland to protect the estate. Lady Cassiana was concerned that with so many soldiers vacating the north that the Scots might get it into their heads to cross the border and test the waters, so to speak."

"Are you Briarwood's captain of the guard, my lord?"

"Nay," Sir Baldwin said. "That honor falls to Sir Adam Crane. 'Tis custom to leave the captain behind anytime the king requests men to join his armies. I am Sir Adam's second-in-command and take over his duties in the training yard when he is out on patrol."

"Do these patrols occur often?" Landon inquired.

"Aye. Briarwood backs up almost to the sea. Lady Cassiana schedules regular patrols to guard not only the road that runs along the coast and the one to the north of Briarwood but she also sets men at staggered points to watch the seas in case the Scots—or even the French—try to land."

He thought it odd a woman would set the patrols. "Sir Tobyn did not plan the patrols?"

"Nay, my lord. Sir Tobyn only returned home a couple of months before we answered the king's call to sail to Flanders. He had been fostering elsewhere in west Northumberland and only recently achieved his knighthood. With the earl ailing for so many years, 'tis Lady Cassiana who determines everything that occurs at Briargate. And a fine job she does of it all. No one can hold a candle to our lady," Sir Baldwin said with evident pride.

Landon knew when noblemen were called away from their estates, whether in battle or at court, they oftentimes left their wives in charge. Still, he couldn't imagine one young, unwed woman doing the job half as well as a man could. He only hoped this new wife-to-be would gracefully accept that new leadership had arrived with him and that he would remain in charge of everything regarding Briarwood in the future. Landon longed to place his mark on his land and its people.

And be a better man than Adelard de Blays ever had been.

CHAPTER SEVEN

C ASSIANA ADDED A column of numbers, checking Hobart's sums. The steward's neat hand was always a pleasure to read. None of her brothers had had a head for figures. When she'd tried to teach them about adding and subtracting, their columns had been crooked and their numbers sloppy, making it impossible for them to know what to do and even harder for her to correct their errors.

"As usual, I can't find a single mistake. What would Briarwood do without you, Hobart?"

The steward pinkened slightly, his bald head glowing. "Thank you, my lady. I hope you are pleased with the number of sheaves collected so far. The autumn harvest has been especially abundant this year."

"Our workers have labored from dawn until dusk," she replied. "Because of that, it should be completed on time. I'm glad I decided to go forward with the tying, though, especially since we've produced so much wheat this year."

Running footsteps distracted her from their conversation. Cassiana raised her eyes and moments later, Justin arrived, out of breath.

"My lady." The squire bent and drew in a long breath before righting himself. "I thought you'd be pleased to know that our men have been spotted from the wall walk."

Cassiana sprang to her feet. "Already?"

Just over three months had passed since the group of soldiers from Briarwood had walked to Berwick-upon-Tweed and left for Flanders. They'd had to leave their horses behind since the motley group of assembled merchant ships had no room for their steeds. She'd had to create a schedule that allowed rotating the many horses left behind to ensure they received enough exercise. That had cut down on some of the training time with the men left behind.

She told Justin, "Notify Cook at once. They will be hungry and thirsty when they arrive." To Hobart, she said, "Will you excuse me? We'll continue this tomorrow. With Sir Tobyn."

Now that her brother returned, she needed to see that he became more involved in the management of the estate. It would be important to include him as they completed the harvest, which included the tying, winnowing, and milling of the wheat gathered.

Especially if Tobyn brought news of a bridegroom for her.

Cassiana made her way outside the keep. She couldn't help but wonder why the men returned so soon. She had prepared herself for them to be away for at least a year and possibly much longer. Even if the king's impromptu navy had been successful in Flanders, she couldn't see how English troops had moved inland so fast and far and dominated France so well that Philip would have yielded to his sworn enemy this quickly.

Unless the French king had been captured. A common tactic in war was to seize an important figure, such as a king or one of his princes, from the battlefield and then call a cease-fire. The prisoner would be transported and held in captivity until a hefty ransom had been paid. If this was the case, King Edward would order his troops home while France gathered the monies necessary to free the man they called their king. There'd be no sense for the English army to remain in France for what could be months while the ransom was assembled and then delivered.

Her heart beat fast as she climbed the ladder that led to the wall walk. From this height, she could see their many workers in the fields, scythes in hand, as they bent low to cut through the wheat, as well as two carts ferrying the sheaves away to the drying shed. Then her eyes landed on the dust being kicked up in the road as the men marched toward Briarwood.

That surprised her. Tobyn had never been one strong on discipline. She would have expected with him in charge that the returning soldiers would be walking in small groups. Instead, they came in rows and marched in time to a beat. That made it easy for her to complete a quick count. Her heart grew heavy as she discovered six missing from the total which had left back in June. Those six men from Briarwood would have been buried on the Continent instead of being brought back to Northumberland. It pained her that good Englishmen had to be left behind in graves on foreign soil.

Eagerly, she skimmed the mass of men, looking for her brother, but finding it impossible since each soldier wore his sugarloaf great helm. Though their face masks were lifted, she couldn't identify Tobyn from this distance without seeing his hair, which had appeared brown unless in sunlight. Only then did the deep shade of red stand out.

Frustrated that she couldn't spot him, Cassiana returned to the ground and ran to the gates. They now stood open, ready to receive the men. She hurried through them and saw work stopping in the fields as the people greeted the returning soldiers. Behind her, she heard others joining her, from soldiers in the yard to servants from the keep. All were ready to welcome their men home.

She lifted her skirts and trotted down the road, ready to throw her arms around Tobyn. She hadn't realized until now just how much she'd missed her only sibling. It would be difficult to tell him about Father's death during his absence. Mayhap being at war against France had hardened Tobyn some to the reality of death and he would be able to accept their parent's passing better than he might have before.

Reaching the block of men, she saw it no longer marched in straight rows. Soldiers had fallen out, yanking their helms from the heads, greeting others. Cassiana skimmed the group anxiously, searching for Tobyn. A sudden uneasiness enveloped her.

What if he hadn't returned? What if her brother had been killed by the French?

The thought brought her to a halt. Again, her eyes danced from soldier to soldier, seeking Tobyn.

Then a man approached her, carrying his helm under his arm. Someone she'd never seen before. He was tall, causing her to throw back her head to look up at him. Thick, dark hair, black as a raven's, contrasted sharply with brilliant, green eyes. Sharp cheekbones and sensual lips made him very appealing.

In truth, the knight was the most devastatingly handsome man that she'd ever seen.

"Lady Cassiana?" he asked, his voice low and rich, filled with hidden secrets.

"I am Cassiana Campion. Who might you be?" she asked boldly, locking her knees to steady herself and stay on her feet. The man loomed over her and seemed to sap the very energy from her.

"Lord Landon de Blays. Is there somewhere we might speak privately?"

"I have no idea why you've come to Briarwood, my lord. Let me first speak to my brother and then we can discuss any business—"

Sympathy filled his eyes. "'Tis your brother I wish to discuss," he said softly.

Cassiana's hands pressed against her belly. A wave of nausea filled her. "Nay," she said abruptly. "Nay. I don't wish to hear what you have to say."

She wheeled and walked away briskly. She refused to listen to whatever this nobleman had to say. Instead, she would return to the records room and finish tallying the numbers from yesterday's sheaves. Then she would go to the training yard and spar with a few of their squires. Or take Tressa for a long ride.

A hand clasped her elbow, forcing her to stop. Angrily, she looked up into Landon de Blays' eyes.

"Don't tell me," she hissed. "If you don't say the words, I can pretend for a while longer. That Tobyn is still alive. That he's in the group of soldiers who just came home. That he and I will dine side-by-side tonight and he'll tell me stories of French cowards and English victories. If you stay silent, my lord, then I don't have to think about being alone. The last Campion standing. About having to leave the only home I've ever known when the next Earl of Briargate comes to claim everything that I have worked so hard on for so many years."

Cassiana glared up at him and tore herself from his grasp. Then understanding dawned within her.

"You!" she accused. "*You* are the new earl." She took a step back, her body trembling.

"I am," the nobleman confirmed. He withdrew something from his sleeve and handed it to her. "This is a declaration from the king, naming me as the new Earl of Briargate since your father passed on without any heirs."

Furiously, she yanked open the small scroll and scanned the page, tears welling in her eyes. Cassiana blinked several times, not daring to allow this usurper to see them fall. She handed it back to him and said, "If you would like, I can take you around the estate in the morning. There are things you should be made aware of before I leave. Did the king give you instructions on where I am to go?"

She hated having no male family member in her life now. It would cause her to be at the king's mercy. Who knew what whim might strike Edward Plantagenet, known for his sudden mood swings, and where he might send her.

Lord Landon removed a second, smaller parchment. "This is a

missive from the king. 'Tis addressed to you. It will clarify the situation."

"Clarify the situation?" she asked angrily. "What's to be explained? Oh, I understand all too well, my lord. I've lost my beloved father. My last brother. And now I will lose the only home I have known. The place I love."

Savagely, she ripped at the seal and read the few lines penned. Then read them again. Looking up, she saw no emotion on the new earl's face.

"You . . . are to be . . . my husband?"

"Aye, my lady. The king is aware of the work you have done at Briarwood. How the land thrives under your leadership and of the good decisions you have made in your father's stead. My friend, Nicholas Mandeville, has sung your praises and explained to me his admiration for you and all you've accomplished."

Lord Landon smiled at her. "You will remain at your home, my lady. Only you will be a Campion no longer. You will soon be a de Blays."

LANDON ADMITTED TO himself that he had been a fool when he told Nicholas he didn't care what his bride looked like.

Cassiana Campion was the most stunningly beautiful woman he'd beheld—and he'd certainly seen his fair share of beauties at both the English and French royal courts. He'd coupled with many a willing woman over the years but none had ever affected him as much as the furious noblewoman standing in front of him.

Her hair was a mixture of reds and golds, as if sunrise and sunset had collided. He longed to run his fingers through the silky waves. She was of average height but the snug cotehardie of deep brown hugged her every curve.

Landon couldn't decide the true color of her eyes. They were a warm brown when he'd first approached her. As her anger grew, the amber that ringed them spread like a wildfire and they blazed at him now, more gold than brown. Even more tempting than the long tresses restrained in a single braid that fell past her waist was her mouth. His lips burned to touch hers.

And they would—once he made her his.

"We will need to wed at once," he announced.

Lady Cassiana gave him a long look. "I think not, my lord."

Anger sizzled through him. "You question my authority?"

She had the audacity to roll her eyes at him. "I question your upbringing," she said succinctly.

"What mean you?" he demanded.

She gave him a disdainful look. "Obviously, you had no other title and estate before the king granted you this one, Lord Landon. True, you're now one of the most powerful noblemen in all of Northumberland, with an estate whose only rival is Northmere, at the border."

Lady Cassiana paused, her lips twitching in disapproval. "Because of that, certain customs must be upheld. The new Earl of Briargate cannot simply wed. His marriage must be an event of some importance, with all his neighbors invited, as well as other important nobles throughout the north."

She shook her head. "That requires planning, which means time devoted to that planning. A feast unlike any you've known must be decided upon before being prepared and served. My wedding attire should rival that of what Queen Philippa wore to her own wedding with the king. You yourself must be outfitted in splendor to acknowledge your title and position."

The noblewoman sniffed. "That all takes weeks, my lord. At least a month. Mayhap longer."

Landon remembered how different Katelyn's wedding had been to the Earl of Northmere. The old earl had ordered it to take place soon after they'd arrived from their long trek from Windsor Castle. Landon supposed the earl had been able to do so since it was a second marriage and he already had two sons to serve as heirs and no one left to impress. Katelyn's second wedding, a day later, had been by proxy, taking place in the Northmere solar.

His own wedding would be a much different affair. Still, he understood the reason for the display of grandeur, though his bride-to-be's words had wounded him.

"You are correct, my lady. I enter this marriage with no previous title and bring no land or monies, only my skills in the art of war." He gave her a wicked grin. "However, I'm no heathen, as you make me out to be. I was raised at court and know how important appearances can be."

"Then you'll give me a month to see to all of the arrangements?" she asked haughtily.

"A week," he said firmly.

Her eyes narrowed. "Two weeks," she countered.

"Done," he agreed, secretly thinking he'd come out ahead in their compromise.

They both eyed one another warily and Landon knew she wasn't sure which of them had just won their first battle.

"See me into my castle," Landon ordered, not willing to lose the upper hand he'd gained. Already, the noblewoman had proved to be intelligent and quick. He would have to stay on his toes around this one and never let down his guard or she would take advantage of him in ways small and large.

"Of course, my lord."

Lady Cassiana turned quickly and left him standing alone. Quickly, he closed the gap between them and grasped her elbow to bring her to a halt. Rage simmered in her eyes as he tucked her hand through the crook of his elbow.

"Now, you may lead the way for us," he said. "Together."

She emitted a low growl of frustration as they started through the gate, causing him to suppress a smile.

"Are you always so stubborn?" she asked.

"Only when crossed," he said good-naturedly.

Cassiana Campion looked up at him.

And laughed.

A frisson of pleasure shot through him at the low, throaty sound. By the Christ, if she affected him so with a mere laugh, what would it be like to bed her?

At that moment, Landon swore to encase his heart in steel. He'd never been swayed by a woman before. Other than his sister and the queen, he'd never really liked or even respected another female, especially after seeing the duplicity in so many of the women at court. He couldn't let this future wife get under his skin. He would wed her. Bed her. Get sons off her. But he would never let her call the tune. Ever. His mother had done that, ruling Blackstone like a queen, ordering everyone about as if his father hadn't existed.

"Come," he ordered, moving through the gates with her. As they entered the outer bailey, pride swelled within Landon.

All this . . . was his . . .

To spend so many years feeling worthless. Having few possessions. Knowing there were those who still looked at him and whispered the old tales of his father's treachery. And now, to have this magnificent place belong to him. It was unimaginable.

He took in everything with new eyes. A blacksmith shed wasn't a mere structure. It was here his soldiers' horses would be shod. They passed the tannery where leather would be prepared for saddles. Looking across the wide area, he supposed dozens worked for the estate.

His estate. Briarwood.

"Wait a moment," Landon said as they approached the training yard.

His eyes swept over the place where he would spend a majority of his time. He caught sight of a raised platform, the spot where he would stand and observe his soldiers at work. He would move among them, testing and teaching them, learning their strength and weaknesses. To the far left stood the butts. He wondered idly how many archers Briarwood had and which ones had been sent to Flanders because of their talent with a bow.

Suddenly, a knight stood before them, one who possessed a confident air. The long scar along his cheek attested to the fact that he'd been in battle and survived. His eyes skimmed Landon with curiosity but he addressed Lady Cassiana.

"My lady, I decided to dismiss the soldiers from their training for the day. It was only an hour away until we normally break and the men were eager to visit with those comrades who've returned from France."

"A wise decision, Sir Adam," she said. Turning to Landon, she told him, "My lord, I would introduce you to Sir Adam Crane, Briarwood's captain of the guard. Sir Adam, this is Lord Landon de Blays. The new Earl of Briargate."

The soldier's eyes widened and then he schooled his features. "Welcome, Lord Landon. You will find your men to be an exceptional group of soldiers. We've had to be with the threat of Scottish attack always a possibility."

Landon offered the knight his hand. "I'm glad to make your acquaintance, Sir Adam. We will need to meet privately and discuss the men and their training schedule. I'd also like to become familiar with the various patrols in the area and how often they occur."

"I'd be happy to, my lord, but Lady Cassiana can tell you anything you wish to know about the castle's defense. She's quite familiar with our training schedule and soldiers."

"Still, I will meet with you soon, Sir Adam," Landon said firmly.

He doubted Cassiana Campion could answer all of his many questions. She might know the names of Briarwood's soldiers but, as a woman, she would have no idea of the level of their fighting skills. It took hundreds of hours of observation in the yard and even direct contact, engaging a man in a fight, to know all Landon wished to learn.

Sir Adam bowed. "Again, 'tis good to have you here, Lord Landon." The captain looked to Lady Cassiana. "My lady, may I say that it's been a pleasure serving you and your family over the years. I wish you the best, no matter where you go."

"The lady will remain at Briarwood—as my wife," Landon informed Sir Adam. "I will share this news at the evening meal."

The knight broke out in a huge grin. "To have you remain at Briarwood is the best of news, my lady." He took her hand and pressed a kiss to it.

For some reason, jealousy stirred within Landon, an unfamiliar feeling. He shook it off.

"Good day," Landon said curtly, drawing his future wife away.

After they'd left the yard, she said, "You realize by the time we sit for the evening meal in an hour, most everyone will already know we are to be wed."

"Why do you say that?"

She laughed again, a sound he already coveted hearing.

Astonishment filled her face. "Have you lived under a rock all of your life, my lord?"

He stiffened, offended again by her words. "I told you that I grew up at court. I've served as a member of King Edward's royal guard," he said with pride.

She chuckled. "Surely, you realize how quickly gossip spreads. I would think it would move even more rapidly at court. The same is true at any estate. Sir Adam will tell a few men what he has learned. They will be all too eager to share what they know with others."

"I've never cared for gossip," Landon said dismissively.

"Probably because it was never about you," she retorted.

"True," he admitted. "I've made it a point to serve the king my entire life. What others speculated about never concerned me," though he knew how much he'd hated the gossip about him and his family.

"Your first lesson to learn as a newly titled earl, my lord, is to discover that within gossip can be a glimmer of truth. Information is a valuable commodity. It would be best not to ignore gossip. Instead, separate the truth from the fiction—and be better prepared for what you've learned."

Landon looked at her steadily. "I see you have much to teach me, Lady Cassiana."

And he would teach her, in return.

CHAPTER EIGHT

C ASSIANA FINALLY LED the new earl inside the keep, hoping he would release her once they arrived. The entire time they'd toured the outer and inner baileys, Lord Landon de Blays had kept her hand snug within the bend of his arm, covering it with his own hand to make sure she didn't wriggle from his grasp.

His touch had left her breathless.

Other than the few kisses she'd shared with Tarquin Grosbeck, no man ever touched her. Especially one as imposing and attractive as the nobleman who'd come to claim not only his land and title—but her.

Lord Landon's arrival had upset her because he brought news of Tobyn's death. She had reacted angrily and immaturely and found herself ashamed of her behavior toward him. He hadn't killed her brother. The French had. The gracious thing to do would be to apologize.

As long as she didn't have to gaze too long into those mesmerizing green eyes.

She'd never seen eyes so green. Never been affected by a man near her. His hand atop hers radiated heat, as did his body brushing against hers when they walked. It confused her. It upset her. Most of all, it made her fearful. Cassiana wasn't used to the idea of fear, thanks to the fact that she'd been in control of her destiny for so long. Now, with a simple directive from the king, she would be allowed to stay at Briarwood.

And submit to marriage with a stranger.

Obviously, he was a magnificent warrior. His build and graceful movements alone would have told her as much but when he revealed he was a member of King Edward's royal guard, that told Cassiana just how skilled Landon de Blays actually was. All of England knew that the king, a master soldier in his own right, surrounded himself with the best knights in the land. Not only had the monarch put his trust in this man next to her to guard him and his family, but somehow de Blays had accomplished something extraordinary for the king to gift him with a prized estate such as Briarwood.

Servants bustled inside the keep. Cassiana waved Messina over with her free hand since de Blays hadn't released his hold on her yet and introduced the faithful servant to Lord Landon and his new status as their liege lord.

"Stop whatever you are doing and see that the solar is prepared at once for the earl."

"Of course, my lady. I will have new bedclothes put on and see that firewood is laid in the grate." The woman looked to de Blays. "Would you like a bath before you dine, my lord? Cook is providing the returning men with something to tide them over. You would have time for a bath before the evening meal if you wish. I'm sure you'd like to wash the grime from you after fighting in France."

"Thank you, Messina. I appreciate your thoughtfulness."

The servant blushed and hurried away. Did the man affect all women? Cassiana tugged on her hand, wanting it returned to her so she could get hold of her confusing feelings.

"In good time, my lady." He patted her hand and then kept it in place.

He led her to the great hall, where the trestle tables had been pulled from the walls and benches placed beside them. She saw bread and ale had been provided to the returning men and those who'd been dismissed early from the training yard. Conversation flourished.

"Would you care to see the records room now? You can meet our steward. That will give time for your bath water to be heated."

"Lead the way."

Cassiana took the nobleman to what she thought of as her favorite room in the keep. She loved how orderly and neat Hobart kept everything, lining up ledgers by the year on the shelves that lined one wall of the room.

Hobart lingered at the desk, an open book in front of him as he scribbled away. He glanced up and started at the sight of the stranger.

"Hobart, I have brought the new Earl of Briargate to meet you."

The steward rose, casting a sympathetic look her way. From her introduction, Hobart would know that Tobyn wasn't coming home. "My lord." The steward inclined his head.

"You are Briarwood's steward, I take it?"

"Aye, my lord. I have been for nigh on ten and five years. My father served the Campion family before me."

"I am Landon de Blays. I will certainly be counting on you to help me as I transition into my new position. I have much to learn regarding the management of an estate, especially one as large and productive as Briarwood. You will be the perfect man to teach me all I need to know."

Relief swept across Hobart's face, knowing that he would be kept on in his current position. "I can go over any of our ledgers with you, my lord. Lady Cassiana would also be quite helpful in this matter. She knows as much about—"

"We'll set a time to discuss matters," Lord Landon said. "I look forward to hearing about the estate from you."

He led her from the records room. This time she yanked her hand from his possessive hold and stomped a foot. "I'm no halfwit, you know. I can be quite helpful to you if you'll let me." Her eyes narrowed. "Or do you think you already know so much that you have no need of my advice?"

De Blays shrugged. "Frankly, I prefer the advice of men. Your captain of the guard and steward are being generous when they flatter you, my lady. Although I know you have lived your entire life at Briarwood and have helped out somewhat since your father was incapacitated, I insist upon seeing the expertise of those in charge regarding—"

"Are you joking?" she interrupted. "Do you think I have played at running Briarwood? You told me your friend, Nicholas Mandeville, held me in high regard. That the king was pleased at how I managed to make Briarwood thrive." Cassiana crossed her arms. "This didn't happen by itself, Lord Landon. I have been actively involved in every aspect of the estate. For years. My brothers were gone. Or dead. My father remained bedridden and chose to see no one other than Syndor, one of our servants who helped me care for him in his last years."

It infuriated her when he gave her a sympathetic look. "That's all well and good, my lady. Now, though, you'll have time to concentrate on domestic matters inside the keep. As a woman should."

"While you dabble at being the earl?" Her breasts heaved in anger. "You know nothing of how to run Briarwood, my lord. You are merely a soldier. A very good one, I'm sure, but you yourself told me you've always lived at court. Do you know when ploughing and sowing occur? What about butchering and smoking? Or shearing? Have you any idea what is happening right now on your land?"

The nobleman flushed a dull red. "Nay, but I will learn."

"I'll tell you what your people are involved with. They've spent all of last month and this harvesting the wheat crop. This is the most difficult time of year. They cut and carry bundles called sheaves and every man, woman, and child on the land has worked long hours during the autumn harvest. If they don't get it done in time, the wheat can be destroyed by the cold and rain. Our people and that of nearby villages might starve. Bread doesn't simply appear upon a table, Lord Landon."

When he stared at her, speechless, she continued. "The tying has begun, where we tie the sheaves and move them to a huge shed to dry. Then the winnowing must occur. Do you even know what that is? Workers thresh the wheat to separate the grain from the stalk and then separate that from the chaff. And I won't even go into the milling."

His lips twitched in amusement. Her rage almost boiled over but she contained it and fell silent.

"Are you finished?" he asked calmly.

"Aye. For now," she said grudgingly.

Lord Landon placed his hands on her shoulders. Cassiana could feel each finger as it burned through her cotehardie and smock, almost singeing her flesh.

"I, too, am no halfwit. I've always been a quick learner because I've had to be. Mayhap I misspoke and judged you too quickly, my lady." A shadow crossed his face. "My sister and our queen are the only women I have ever felt any respect for. The ladies of the royal court are nothing but deceitful and hypocritical. They play every man false and are not to be trusted. I'm used to only hearing them gossip about one another and fashion. Not a one of them would have cared one whit about what you speak of."

His hands fell from her shoulders. "Forgive me. You are to be my wife. I hope we will learn to understand—even come to eventually trust—one another." He paused. "Your brother told me that he sought a husband for you and that all you wanted from a man was respect. I find respect is something to be earned." He gave her a tight smile. "You have shown me a small slice of how knowledgeable you are about Briarwood. My regard for you has certainly risen."

She ignored his apology. "You . . . spoke to Tobyn?" Her heart grew heavy as she began to truly feel her brother's loss.

"Aye. We traveled from Northumberland to Flanders on the same ship and shared much of ourselves with one another." His eyes shone at her. "Your brother loved you, Lady Cassiana. Very much. In our very first conversation, he did nothing but sing your praises. He even thought if you were chosen to lead the English into battle, the French would have never stood a chance."

She smiled. "I can hear him saying that."

Lord Landon added, "You would have been proud of Sir Tobyn in action. I fought near him at Sluys. He was a brave knight and took out many of our enemy before he fell."

Emotion overcame her and her voice broke as Cassiana asked, "How was he killed? Where is his body?"

The new earl gazed at her wordlessly, his anguish obvious, and then murmured, "Not now," as he drew her to him and gently stroked her hair.

Tears blinded her as great sobs escaped. Not even her beloved father's death had affected her so. She found herself grateful to be engulfed in Lord Landon's arms as she wept against him for some minutes, trying to come to terms with the death of her last sibling.

Finally, her tears subsided. She would be strong, as a Campion should. As Tobyn would have expected. This man had obviously befriended her brother and she must treat Lord Landon with more respect.

"I'm sorry. I have taken out my anger at Tobyn's death on you. You had nothing to do with it or being named the new earl."

His thumbs brushed against her cheeks, wiping the tears away. "Losing someone you love is difficult."

"Have you ever lost someone?"

His jaw tightened. "That is something we might discuss at a later time," he said dismissively and released her. "Might you accompany me to the solar and help me from my armor?"

Cassiana threw back her shoulders, once more in charge of her feelings. She didn't plan to show weakness to this man in the future. "Of course, my lord. Follow me."

He smiled at her then, a smile that caused her heart to stop and then leap within her chest. "Since we are to be married, mayhap you might call me Landon. At least in private."

The radiance of his smile melted any simmering anger away. "All right. Landon. Follow me."

Leading him to the solar, she noticed his eyes sweeping over everything they passed and put herself in his position. A man who had never possessed a title or home, arriving at what had been named his, seeing it for the first time, carefully taking in his surroundings. She might not know much about Landon de Blays, but this knight was to be her husband. They would share in caring for Briarwood and its people and act as stewards until the time their oldest son would step in.

A chill passed through her.

She would have to lay with this man. Many times over the years. He would get her with child. Or children. Babes that she would give birth to. Dread filled Cassiana as she thought of all the times she'd watched her mother in agony. Of the little ones she'd lost and how Cassiana had watched the light fade from her mother's eyes that final time. How she wrapped the newest, tiniest Campion to keep her warm and held her close, praying the girl wouldn't die. She pushed the painful thoughts aside. She wasn't wed to Lord Landon yet. There would be time enough to worry. Other matters must be addressed now.

They arrived at the solar as Messina shooed away the servants who'd brought up the buckets of water, their eyes turning to study the stranger.

"Your bath is ready, my lord."

"Much thanks, Messina."

The servant exited the solar and Lord Landon looked to Cassiana. "I have no squire. Might you serve as one temporarily and help me from my armor?"

"Aye, my lord."

"Landon," he reminded her.

He set down his helm and Cassiana began the process of helping him to remove his armor. It was superior in quality, the best she'd ever seen, and she guessed the king must have provided it for his royal guard.

"I would recommend a squire to you since you have none," she began. "Justin Cecil has fostered at Briarwood the past five years. He was acting as Tobyn's squire and had to remain behind since no horses or squires were allowed to set sail. He is a bright lad. Eager to please and well-mannered."

He placed his cuirass on the nearby table. "If you believe the boy to be the best choice, then I will accept him into my service. I'll speak with him after we dine this evening."

She'd forgotten how long it took to remove the gear since she hadn't done so for her brothers in several years. Finally, Lord Landon stood in his clothes.

Which were beyond filthy.

"I'll see that your clothing is washed." Cassiana frowned. "You don't have anything else to wear?"

Chuckling, he said, "An army on the move is not one which packs extra apparel for its soldiers to wear. I do have another change of clothing at Windsor."

His words surprised—and saddened—her. "You have no other possessions?"

"Nay. I've lived a most simple life up until now. I've never needed or even wanted much beyond a sharp sword and a swift horse."

"The Briarwood stables are large. You will have many mounts to choose from. Oh, dear," she fretted. "I don't have time to wash and dry your clothing before the evening meal where you address the people for the first time. I hate for you to bathe and put them on again once you're clean." Then a thought occurred to her.

Cassiana hurried into the bedchamber and opened a trunk. Kneeling, she began going through it. Lord Landon came to stand next to her.

"Though Tobyn was several inches shy of your height, you and my father are of a similar size. The last few years of his life he didn't dress in everyday wear." She removed a gypon of rust and held it up for his approval. "This should do. I can quickly make any adjustments that are needed for I am good with my needle. Still, we'll need to have several new items made up for you, including something special for the wedding."

"Our wedding," he murmured.

She looked up at him and sensed the heat rising in her cheeks. "Aye. Our wedding. Until then, we can make do with what my father left behind." She paused. "Justin is almost as tall as Tobyn was. I will see that he receives my brother's clothes. That will be good use of them."

Locating pants to accompany the gypon, Cassiana returned to the solar and placed them on the table. Then it hit her. As the ranking noblewoman of the keep, she would need to assist him in his bath.

Already, her future husband was casually stripping away his clothing, tossing it to the ground until he stood naked. His bare, muscled back and tight buttocks looking as if hard stone had come to life as flesh. Quickly, he eased into the large wooden tub and sighed.

"Let me assist you. Landon." His name felt odd on her tongue. Other than her family members, she was used to addressing members of the nobility with their title. Yet, this was the man she would wed. She must become accustomed to calling him by his Christian name.

Retrieving a low stool, where a cake of soap, a wash cloth, and bath sheet rested, she draped the sheet over the back of a chair and placed the stool next to the tub. Landon already splashed water over his arms and chest.

"I can do most of it," he told her, taking the soap and cloth from her.

Not knowing where else to go, Cassiana sat upon the stool, averting her eyes and yet totally aware of every move he made.

Landon soaped his face and scrubbed it thoroughly with the cloth before rinsing it. He lathered his arms and chest. She had seen soldiers bared to the waist in the training yard but none had the sleek physique of this royal warrior. Her mouth became so dry that swallowing seemed impossible. Landon continued to move quickly and efficiently, lathering and scrubbing. He bent his knees and then lifted a long leg, dark with fine hair, resting it on the edge of the tub. Cassiana studied it from the corner of her eye. His calves were a thing of beauty. She longed to run a hand along them.

What was she thinking?

"You'll have to help me with my back," he said, bringing her from her reverie. "I can't reach it as well as I'd like."

She took the wet cloth and cake from him, drizzling water over his shoulders and down his back. Lathering the cloth well, she moved it across his shoulders and up and down his back, growing warm as she did so. His muscles rippled as she ran the cloth along them. She wished to touch him with her bare hands and tried to expel those wicked thoughts.

Suddenly, he stood and took the cloth from her and slid it along his firm buttocks. Her eyes fell to his manhood. Before he could see her gaping at him, she turned away and busied herself, placing another log on the fire. By the time she completed the task he'd once more sat.

"Would you like me to wash your hair?" she asked tentatively as she returned to the tub.

"Aye. 'Twould be a luxury."

Cassiana lifted one of the two remaining buckets that sat beside the tub. "Slide toward your feet," she told him.

Landon raised his knees and moved toward his feet before tilting his head back. She stood behind him and poured warm water over his hair and then worked the scented soap into it, kneading his scalp as she dragged her fingers through the mass of dark, unruly hair. A sudden tightening between her legs startled her, as her womanly core seemed to pulsate with life. The longer her fingers ran through his locks, the more it tightened and tingled.

"Ah, you've a pleasant touch, Cassiana. I feel as spoiled as the king himself."

It was the first time he had used her Christian name. She hadn't given him permission to do so but it only seemed fitting since he had requested her to use his when they were alone. Somehow, hearing her name come from his lips was as if she heard it for the very first time.

"A nobleman should feel as a king inside his own castle," she responded, surprised she could even voice words, much less in an order that made sense. This man was having a strange effect on her, scrambling her thoughts and arousing new feelings within her. She seemed to be floating outside her body, watching another massage his scalp.

"I'd like to shave," he said. "Does your father have a razor I might use?"

"Aye." Pushing herself to her feet, she located the razor and brought it to him. "Lather your face. I shaved my father when he no longer could."

Landon did as she requested and Cassiana took his chin in hand, saying a quick prayer of thanks to the Virgin when the knight closed his eyes. She didn't know how steady her hand might have been under his penetrating stare. Slowly, she drew the blade over his cheeks and chin, dipping it into the water several times to clean it. He tossed his head back, exposing his throat to her as the blade glided along.

When she finished, she barely got out, "I'm through." Landon cupped his hands and splashed water against his face and throat. Cassiana had thought him handsome before with his days' old stubble but now that he was clean-shaven, she could hardly think. All she wanted was to touch him again. An idea came to her.

"Lean your head back. I need to rinse the suds from your hair."

Landon did as she requested and Cassiana slowly poured fresh water through his locks as she washed away all traces of the soap.

"I can do the rest," he said matter-of-factly. Without warning, he stood in the tub and lifted the last bucket of heated water.

Once again, she found herself struggling to breathe. She'd never seen a body as sculpted as his. As the water sluiced down it and the muscles glistened, she forced herself to remain in place and keep her hands to herself. The urge to reach out and touch him proved almost uncontrollable.

And it frightened her more than any fear she'd ever known.

Cassiana moved away to fetch the large bath sheet that Messina had left. She opened the folded material and raised it in her arms so that it wouldn't scrap the floor. Walking it to him, she waited for him to take it, hiding behind it so her gaze wouldn't fall places it shouldn't be looking.

"Thank you," Landon said and claimed it from her.

She turned and took her time retrieving the clothes she'd found in her father's trunk in order to bring them to him. Turning, she saw he'd stepped from the tub, the sheet now wrapped about his waist, leaving his upper torso and legs bare. Dark, fine hair covered his chest. She had the outrageous desire to stroke it. Run her hands over it. Lick it.

In that moment, Cassiana decided she had gone mad. Grief from her brother's death had driven her into some abyss where she'd lost the ability to reason. Thoughts she'd never dare put into words peppered her mind.

"Might I have the clothes?"

The question startled her. "Oh . . . aye." She hurried to him. "I did not mean to keep you waiting."

Her gaze met his, his green eyes shining like wildfire. "I think I would wait a great length of time for you, Cassiana," he said softly, danger lurking in his tone.

She licked her lips nervously and saw the fire spark into life. Before she could hand him his clothes, his hands gripped her upper arms and pulled her toward him. His lips slowly descended toward hers. It seemed as if they took a lifetime to arrive.

Then his mouth was on hers.

Chapter Nine

C ASSIANA'S FINGERS RELEASED the clothing she held. Her palms landed against his damp chest. But the idea of stroking him fled as his mouth moved on hers, dominating her every thought.

Her kisses from Tarquin had been soft and chaste. Landon's was the opposite in every way. His lips moved against hers, firm and commanding from the start. His tongue began to trace the outline of her lips, a hot, fiery swish that branded her as it swirled. Then he ran his tongue along the seam of her mouth, urging her to open to him.

She did.

Landon's kiss became more heated. More possessive. He drew her close, so that her breasts pushed against the hard wall of his bare chest. His hands slid down her back to her waist and stayed there, flattened so that she couldn't escape. His tongue swept along hers, teasing it as if he asked it to come out to play. Cassiana had no idea what she was to do but, suddenly, instinct took over. She slid her own tongue against his and heard the low growl he emitted. She did it again, playfully teasing him, enjoying the sounds she drew from him.

But this was no man to tease. Soon, he took command again, his mouth dominating hers as he greedily took. Her heart raced so rapidly that she knew he felt it pounding against him. Her insides began to melt and she might have become a puddle if not for him holding her close. Deep in her belly, no lower, something began to stir. Something strange and foreign and with a beat all its own. Cassiana longed for him to touch her there.

His lips finally parted from hers, sliding along her cheek and to her ear. She'd never realized what a man's tongue could do to a woman's ear until Landon thoroughly explored it. Shivers of delight rippled through her. Then he pressed his mouth to the tender spot directly below her ear and she gasped. His tongue swirled in small circles and then traveled along her neck and back up to her mouth. Another wave of kisses came, one blending into another, as Landon de Blays marked her as his. His alone. Cassiana understood this—and accepted it.

With joy.

Her hands now became aware of where they were, flat against the wall of hard muscle. Though he still held her tightly against him, she managed to find a sliver of room and slid them up and down, reveling in the feel of him, inhaling his clean scent from the recent bath. Once again, that low growl came from deep within his throat. His hands moved from her waist and cupped her buttocks, sending a jolt of desire through her as he kneaded them.

She became aware of something else. His manhood. It rose, hard and firm. Cassiana stilled, terrified by the thought of him entering her. Of the pain it would cause. She broke the kiss and stared up at him, willing him to release her. Those shockingly green eyes looked down on her, filled with heat and passion. His sensual lips curled into a lazy smile.

"I'd hoped we would suit," he said softly. "Now, I know we will."

Landon kissed her once more, this time, feather soft. His hands fell away, releasing her. Quickly, Cassiana stepped back, her lips already missing his. She found herself breathing hard, her breasts rising and falling as rapid as her heart beat.

"Why don't you return to the great hall?" he suggested. "I'm sure it's close to the evening meal." He studied her a moment. "Better yet, you might wish to return to your bedchamber and compose yourself before you see others."

She stared at him, confused for a moment. "I'll take your advice, my lord."

"Landon," he reminded again, this time a wisp of a smile playing about his lips.

"Landon," she confirmed, enjoying hearing his name spoken aloud by her.

She was only a few steps away when he called her name. She turned, not knowing what to expect.

"Thank you," he said. "I know it can't be easy for you. Losing your father and brother. Having a complete stranger arrive and claim you and your home as his. But you have made me feel welcomed. I hope . . . I hope . . . that our union will agreeable to you."

Cassiana found herself speechless and merely bowed her head before retreating from the solar. She raced to her bedchamber and closed the door, leaning against it for support. Her fingertips touched her lips in wonder, knowing his mouth had been there a short while ago. She reached and brushed them along her ear, remembering how he'd toyed with it. Her breasts ached, feeling heavy, aching for his touch. In fact, she couldn't think of a place on her body that didn't long for his hand. His mouth. His tongue.

A war raged within her. Part of her wanted to continue to behave cold and haughty toward him. This man was a usurper, invading her home and taking everything within it—including her—as his. Yet, he held the parchment that entitled him to do so. Her father had died and no more Campion sons remained as his heir. The king merely asserted his rights in awarding the estate to another. Knowing Briarwood's value as one of the largest estates in England made Cassiana very aware that Landon de Blays had done something remarkable to earn his reward. With the land also being so close to the Scottish border, she knew King Edward must not only think Landon brave but also incredibly trustworthy for him to give Briarwood to the knight. It took a man of exceptional intelligence and character to hold land so precious and important to England's protection. That their king had seen Landon fit to become the Earl of Briargate was statement enough of how dearly he viewed the knight.

Knowing the faith King Edward placed in Landon allowed Cassiana to let her guard down and accept her fate without further protest. She was thrilled to be allowed to continue to live at her home. More importantly, Landon was beginning to see she had value beyond what ordinary females displayed. Though reluctant at first, she saw her future husband becoming aware of what she could contribute.

Her husband . . .

That had been something she'd never dwelt upon. It had never been her dream to wed a man and bear his children. Even knowing that Tobyn searched for a bridegroom at her request had been something she would deal with months, if not years, down the road.

Landon de Blays' arrival changed all that. For some reason, the war between England and France had come to a standstill and her future had arrived in the shape of a man she wished would kiss from now through Doomsday. If she craved his kiss this much, what would love play be like between them?

Readying herself to go downstairs, Cassiana inhaled deeply and released the breath slowly. Once more, she felt calm and in control.

Until the next time Landon ventured to kiss her.

LANDON REMOVED THE bath sheet from his waist and draped it over the edge of the wooden tub. He dressed slowly in the borrowed clothes, unsure of the feelings that Cassiana Campion had stirred within him. He hadn't meant to kiss her. He hadn't planned on touching her until their wedding night. That had all changed the moment she sat near him as he bathed. Custom dictated that she aid him in his bath but he had gruffly told her he could manage on his own. The thought of her bent near, his eyes feasting on the round globes of her breasts as she scrubbed him, had caused him to keep her at arm's length. Only he regretted telling her so and compromised by saying she could help him wash his back. Cassiana's nearness and then her soothing touch had caused him to throw all good judgment out the window. Seating himself, Landon slipped into his own boots and leaned back, contemplating the last few minutes with the woman who would soon be his wife.

She had never been kissed before or if she had, her partner hadn't kissed her properly. Nevertheless, what she lacked in knowledge she'd made up for with a breathtaking enthusiasm. Shyness wasn't a trait that applied to this noblewoman. Cassiana had allowed him to lead until she understood what to do. Then she asserted herself, almost bringing him to his knees. Eventually, he'd stepped up and taken control again but it surprised him how little it had taken for him to fall under her spell.

He'd always been generous with a lover but Landon found himself wanting to please her beyond anything he'd done in the past. He recalled her fingers splayed on his bare chest and the dizzyingly slow movement as she began moving her hands up and down him. Oh, they would be well matched in the bedchamber. He had no doubt of that after having kissed her and seen how she responded.

Cassiana had surprised him in other ways, as well, especially with her temper. Landon admitted he'd pushed aside much of what she'd said—and she hadn't liked not being taken seriously. He appreciated that she spoke up for herself. Her intelligence was obvious. Whether he cared to admit it or not, this daughter of the house seemed to know a great deal about the estate and how it was run. In truth, she would be the best tutor he might have.

If he could concentrate long enough and keep his hands off her.

Already, Briarwood's steward and captain of the guard had offered

Landon their high opinions of her. Tobyn—and even Nicholas—had done the same. All in all, it seemed as if Landon had achieved not only an earldom and a valued estate, but one that included a beautiful, clever, desirable woman as his wife.

He only wished he hadn't agreed to waiting two weeks to wed.

Rising, he stroked his bare face, now shorn of its heavy stubble, and eyed the door to the bedchamber. Landon moved toward it and entered. The room was spacious, as large as the solar, with a bed large enough to rival that of the king's. A table rested next to it and another table stood in a corner, two chairs placed next to it. On it sat a chessboard. Idly, he wondered if Cassiana played chess. She probably did, even better than he. Smiling, he thought about challenging her to a game, wondering what their wager should be.

Before he left the solar, he went to his clothes on the floor and removed his most prized possession, one that he'd never mentioned to another. He studied the ruby brooch, remembering the last thing his father had told him when he placed it in Landon's palm.

Give it to the woman you love.

He wondered if—or when—he might gift it to his new wife.

Landon made his way downstairs after hiding the brooch at the bottom of the chest that contained the former earl's clothing. As he descended the staircase, he heard noise coming from the great hall and saw people pouring into it from the outside. He followed the group and headed for the dais, where Cassiana already sat.

"May I join you?" he asked.

"Certainly, my lord," she said formally, her features schooled and showing no emotion.

As he sat, he leaned toward her, his lips brushing her ear. He sensed her tremble and found himself satisfied.

"I thought you were going to address me as Landon." He drew back and contemplated her.

"I will do so in private," she said primly. "While others are present, even if they cannot hear our conversation, you will be Lord Landon.

Or my lord."

He reached for her hand under the table and entwined his fingers through hers. It pleased him to hear her sharp intake of breath.

"What are you doing?" she asked, her eyes widening.

Landon looked down at her lap and back into her eyes. "I believe I am holding your hand. The hand of my future countess."

"What if someone sees?"

"What if they do?" he countered, teasing her as he watched her brown eyes flicker with more amber now. "Did your parents never hold hands?"

"I . . . I don't remember."

Landon shrugged. "Not all wedded couples do. Hold hands, that is."

"Did yours?" she asked curiously.

He stiffened. "Nay. Never."

He released her hand and looked out over the great hall. Suddenly, her hand rested atop his, wriggling until their fingers were once more interlaced. Landon turned and faced her.

"I think I like holding your hand," she said boldly.

He laughed, relaxing at the contact between them. "Likewise, my lady."

Landon lifted their joined hands and, never taking his eyes from hers, kissed her fingers. Suddenly, all conversation died in the great hall. He saw the startled look on Cassiana's face and turned to survey those gathered. With her hand still in his, he rose and urged her to do the same.

"Good people of Briarwood," he began. "I am Landon de Blays, formerly of King Edward's royal guard, and the new Earl of Briargate."

A pleased murmur sounded throughout the room.

"I have already met a few of you—Sir Adam and Sir Baldwin. Hobart. Messina. They have been most welcoming and I appreciate their kindness. I realize I am a stranger to you and that you are in mourning, both for your liege lord and Sir Tobyn, but I hope that you will find me to be a fair, considerate lord. I look forward to meeting everyone seated in the great hall and those who live beyond the walls of the castle."

Landon turned and bowed his head in acknowledgement of Cassiana before looking out at the room again. "The king knows how blessed Briarwood has been to have Lady Cassiana all of these years. He wishes for her to remain and she will—as my wife."

Once more, he raised her hand to his lips and brushed a kiss across her knuckles as the room erupted in cheers.

"You certainly know how to introduce yourself," she murmured.

Landon smiled. "And I cannot wait to introduce you into the ways of love, my lady." He squeezed her hand and released it and then raised his arms high. "Wine for everyone," he shouted. "The best Briarwood has."

More shouts of approval exploded.

"You certainly know how to make yourself a popular liege lord," Cassiana remarked as she seated herself, a blush staining her cheeks. "With our wedding in a few weeks, we're going to certainly need to purchase more."

"Two weeks, Cassiana. 'Tis all I plan to wait."

She grinned at him. "I thought you said you would wait, what was it? *A great length of time.* Aye, that's what you said, I believe." Her eyes twinkled with mischief.

Landon laughed heartily. "You are too clever for your own good, my lady."

Her brows arched. "Someone's going to have to keep you in line and teach you how to be an earl, my lord."

He eyed her approvingly. "I'm glad that someone will be you."

Cassiana looked at him a long moment. "I am also glad that it will be me, Landon."

"Fire!" a voice shouted, and Landon watched a man race into the great hall and toward the dais. "Fire! At the drying barn!"

CHAPTER TEN

C ASSIANA SPRANG TO her feet as Landon did.
He grabbed her about the waist and lowered her from the dais, telling her, "You are familiar with what to do. Give the orders. I'll see them carried through."

"To your stations!" she cried as the mass of people present stood, recognizing the danger that beheld them all.

Lifting her skirts, Cassiana raced from the great hall and out the doors of the keep. Hurrying down the stone staircase, others passed her, heading in various directions. She ran through the baileys and out the already opened gates, trusting that the drills she'd put the people through would let everyone know what to do. Her nostrils filled with the acrid smell of fire and she prayed frantically that they would be able to save some of the harvest.

The drying shed stood a couple of hundred yards away from the wheat fields, on the opposite side of the road. She saw the right side of the building smoking as flames licked it and leaped toward the sky. The wattle and daub structure contained a thatched roof and it was this roof that concerned her most. If the fire spread throughout it and then the roof collapsed, all of the collected wheat would be lost. She would be hard pressed to feed her people and the nearby town of Stony Eastbridge, which depended upon Briarwood for its grain supply.

Men and women appeared, swinging buckets in both hands, both from the castle and nearby cottages, where tenants always kept buckets filled with water outside their own doorways in case of fire. Cassiana kept calm, directing everyone where to go as they lined up and buckets were passed from person to person. Soldiers with firehooks appeared and Landon took charge of that group, leading them close to the barn as he snagged a hook from a man. The soldiers divided as some began to use the hooks to pull the thatch to the ground, while the remaining half pounded at the sides, collapsing the structure where it had yet to burn.

Everything went as they'd practiced. Some worked at putting out the fire. Others, once the walls were knocked down, gathered sheaves and trotted out with them, placing them in carts that had arrived, drivers hurrying away from the smoke and flames. Cassiana had no idea how long they worked until the threat ended and all flames died out. Her eyes stung and her throat burned from breathing in the bitter smell of smoke. All around her, people slumped to the ground, fatigued from their intense effort. She hurried from group to group, checking to see if anyone was injured. Malkyn, their healer, gathered those who needed tending, telling Cassiana that only a handful had suffered mild burns, though many coughed from inhaling the waves of black smoke that had poured from the building.

She noticed Landon making his way through the crowds, touching shoulders, offering words of comfort and encouragement, until he finally reached her. Wordlessly, he opened his arms and she walked into them. He wrapped her against him, his hand stroking her head, murmuring words she didn't bother listening to. All she knew was he was here, with her, holding her, keeping her safe.

Finally, he released her. "We must check on the harvest. See what was lost."

Numbly, she nodded. Leading him away from the smoldering ashes, she said, "The fire didn't touch the fields. We still have two days of wheat to harvest. That is good news."

Landon nodded, placing an arm about her shoulders. "Most of the sheaves were stored on the left side of the shed. The fire burned through the right wall and first consumed two large carts that must have ferried the wheat from the fields. It took a while to burn through those and the oxen that were stabled there. In truth, I believe very few sheaves were lost. It could have been much worse."

Cassiana sighed. "It was an exceptional harvest this year. Hobart and I were surprised at the numbers. Even with what was lost before we arrived, I believe the people saved enough to still make our harvest successful."

Hobart greeted them. "I've begun a count, my lady, my lord. If you'll give me a few more minutes, I'll be happy to give you an idea of how many sheaves were saved."

"Go ahead, Hobart," Landon told him. "We'll speak with you soon." He led Cassiana back to the place where the barn had stood. Cupping her cheek, he said, "I must address our people."

He parted from her and shouted for everyone to gather around. Once the crowd settled down, he addressed them.

"You fought as bravely today as any people I've ever seen. Fire is a devastating enemy but thanks to Lady Cassiana, you were prepared to do your duty. From what Hobart tells us, most of the autumn harvest was saved."

Cassiana saw the relief spread through the crowd of soldiers, servants, and tenants alike.

"The first thing that must be done is to quickly rebuild the drying barn," Landon said. "Our English weather is prone to rain. I'll divide groups into teams, including our soldiers, in order to rebuild the structure as quickly as possible. If we work without stopping, replenishing with new workers every few hours, the structure should be completed in two days' time."

"What about the harvest, my lord?" a voice called out. "We still have wheat to gather in the fields, at least a couple of days' worth."

"Then I'll have our soldiers and the castle's servants, led by our carpenters, build the shed. The rest of you will collect the wheat from the fields. By the time you finish, the barn will be completed and the remaining tying and winnowing can occur."

"Why should a soldier have to build a shed?" called out a disgruntled man.

"Come forth, soldier," Landon commanded.

Cassiana recognized one of their newest hires come and plant his feet in front of Landon, an air of arrogance blanketing him.

"Your name isn't important to me," Landon said, his tone icy. "For you are no longer a part of Briarwood. Collect your gear and leave at once."

"But I—"

"There is no *I*, man. There is only *we* in a time of crisis. If this wheat harvest is not collected in time, we starve. Together. I will not let that happen. The people of Briarwood will work as one community and guarantee our success. You are no longer a part of us and are dismissed. Forever."

Reluctantly, the soldier looked around to see if he had any support—and found none. He stormed off as the crowd watched him in silence.

Landon looked to the group and found Sir Adam, motioning him over.

"Sir Adam, you, I, and Lady Cassiana will work out a temporary schedule that will assure that Briarwood's roads and people are protected but we will suspend training for the next few days until things are back in good shape."

"Aye, my lord," the captain said firmly, approval of Landon reflected in his eyes.

"Sir Baldwin?"

"Here, my lord." The knight stepped forward.

Once more, Landon gave this knight orders to work with Malkyn to gather the wounded and see them back to the keep and then called forth others, one after another. Soon, Cook had enough hands to help her feed the workers around the clock and the carpenters laid out plans for a new barn. Soldiers were dispatched to cut and haul the wood. Hobart reported with an early estimate of what had been saved. Everyone dispersed, ready to do what they could to contribute to right things at Briarwood.

Cassiana observed Landon throughout, her admiration for him growing. He proved a natural leader and quick thinker. The new earl rallied everyone to a collective cause and had his people ready—even eager—to please him.

She moved toward him as he sent the last person off.

"Are you all right?" he asked, concern for her shining in his eyes.

"I am," she said firmly, not wanting him to waste time worrying about her when so much had to be done.

He lifted a stray curl from her cheek and rubbed it between his fingers before pushing it back from her face. "You were magnificent," he said.

"What?" His words startled her.

"You took charge from the moment the man cried *fire*. You remained calmed as you directed others what to do. 'Tis obvious you have practiced for this very kind of disaster for every person knew his role and acted swiftly, without panicking." His eyes gleamed in approval. "Because of you, this incident went from being a catastrophe to a mere inconvenience."

Cassiana shook her head. "I may have drilled the people in what to do but you, my lord, took charge and guided them. As a true liege lord should."

Landon's hands captured her waist, his thumbs rubbing back and forth, causing butterflies to explode within her belly. "I suspect we have mutual admiration for one another, my lady. I can see you will make a formidable countess. I certainly plan to let the king know how pleased I am with his choice for me."

He pressed warm lips to her brow in a tender kiss and then pulled her against him, holding her a long moment. Cassiana's cheek pressed against his gypon, sensing the beating of his heart against it. Despite the tumultuous events of the last hour, contentment spread through her.

She couldn't wait to wed this man.

AS PROMISED, THE drying shed was completed on time and the last of the wheat taken from the fields and bundled into sheaves. Everyone at Briarwood had pitched in and made the impossible occur. Because of that, Cassiana had told Landon that they should go forth with the harvest home celebration as they broke their fast in the great hall.

"What's that?" he inquired.

"Once the autumn harvest is stored in the shed, 'tis been our custom to celebrate bringing in the sheaves."

"How is that done?"

"We give the people a day of rest before the tying and winnowing continue. There's food and music. Dancing. Games. A true day of rejoicing, seeing the harvest is safe and that bread will fill the tables through the next year."

"Hmm. Sounds like a wedding celebration to me. Minus the actual ceremony."

Cassiana felt her cheeks heat. "True, but it doesn't involve our neighbors. And you don't need fine attire to attend. That reminds me, I need to measure you. We've been so busy the past few days, I haven't begun on any kind of wardrobe for you. While I have cloth stored to complete most of what needs to be sewn for you, I haven't the material for our wedding finery. That will require a trip into Berwick-upon-Tweed." She thought a moment. "And we still have yet to issue invitations to our neighbors. Those missives must go out now that we have messengers available who can ride and carry them to their destinations."

Landon gave her a long, heated look, causing her toes to curl. "It seems you're telling me that our two weeks to prepare is only starting now."

"I'm sorry for the delay but who knew we would be fighting a fire and having to rescue our crop?"

"I'll give you two weeks from today," he said grudgingly. "No more."

"Then come to the solar with me. I'll need to measure you. I won't have time to make everything for you. We have a seamstress for that."

"Shouldn't she be the one to measure me?" he asked.

"Nay." Already Cassiana felt possessive of this man and didn't want another woman's hands upon him.

She had him stand still and took his measurements, promising that she would pass them along.

"We should go to the city today. That way, we can purchase the cloth you seek. Wine for our wedding and anything else we need for it or this harvest celebration."

"I'd like that. If you'll see to gathering some men to escort us and find a dozen carts."

"That many?" he asked, though she knew from the light in his eyes that he teased her.

"If not more," she retorted. "I'll have to think on it. In the meantime, I'll have Hobart write out brief missives asking our neighbors to the wedding. Two weeks from today if that suits you."

"It does." Landon paused. "I will write to the Mandevilles, though.

I would like Nicholas and Katelyn to come a few days before the rest of the guests arrive."

Cassiana supposed since he and Nicholas Mandeville were friends, Landon wanted to show off his estate. They might also take time to discuss defense of the border.

"I'll let Hobart know so that he will not include them in the group."

"How many neighbors are we thinking of inviting?"

"There will probably be fifty or so in attendance."

"That many?"

She grinned. "You are a very important earl in the north. They'll want to see who the king's sent and make up their own minds about you."

"'Twill be good to meet the men who will stand with me to defend England," he agreed.

"I'll meet you at the stables. You'll need a horse." She thought her father's steed might do and then decided Tobyn's mount would be a better choice for him. "Have a stableman bring you Orion. 'Twas my brother's horse. Orion is only three years old and he has fine bloodlines."

While Landon readied the men, Cassiana made a quick list of items she wished to purchase and confirmed it with Cook. Next, she retrieved a small purse from her bedchamber and tied it about her waist. Returning to the solar, she went to the bedchamber and pushed on a panel that led to the treasure room. Entering it, she opened a chest and counted out a goodly sum of coins which would pay for their purchases. Finally, she made her way to the records room to speak to Hobart about writing and sending out the invitations to her wedding.

"Put aside whatever you're doing," she told the steward. "I would like the missives to be brief and go out by noon. We need to give our neighbors plenty of time to make their way to Briarwood for the festivities."

"I'll begin at once, my lady." He hesitated.

"Go on," she encouraged. "You know you may always speak freely with me."

"Only that I am very pleased for you. I have known you since you were a small girl. Lord Landon is lucky to have you as his bride but you, too, are fortunate that the king sent such a capable man to lead Briarwood."

"Thank you, Hobart."

Cassiana left the records room. Several times over the past two days, various people had expressed the same sentiments to her. Landon had won everyone over with his leadership in a crisis and his continued interest in everyone around him as Briarwood returned to normal. She understood how important it was for a liege lord to have his people's confidence. Landon de Blays had earned it from all.

Especially her.

Not only did Cassiana believe Briarwood was in good hands, she knew she was, too. She exited the keep, looking forward to spending the day with the man who continued to intrigue her.

In many ways.

CHAPTER ELEVEN

L ANDON STOPPED FIRST at the training yard, where Sir Adam already stood upon the raised platform. Soldiers streamed into the yard, weapons in hand, ready for the day's training to commence after a break the past two days.

"Ah, my lord, I'm happy you are joining us," his captain of the guard said.

He climbed to stand beside the knight. "I can think of no place I'd rather be more than in the yard. Getting to know Briarwood's men and assess their skills is something I've looked forward to. However, it will have to wait a day."

Sir Adam frowned. "The men will be disappointed. Those who journeyed to Flanders and France and saw you in action there have shared with the others what a skilled swordsman you are. The men have looked forward to your leadership."

"I promise you that today is an exception, Sir Adam. My bride wishes to shop for supplies for both the harvest home celebration and our wedding feast."

The captain grinned broadly. "Our men can wait. Lady Cassiana should always be first and foremost and the people are especially thrilled to hold the harvest home celebration after the disaster that befell the wheat crop. You'll have need of a guard to escort you to Berwick-upon-Tweed."

"That's why I came to see you. I'm sure half a dozen men will do on horseback. The lady insists 'twill take a dozen carts to bring home what she needs. I'd prefer soldiers driving those, as well."

"You are wise to be prepared, Lord Landon. Though the city rarely sees any type of mischief these days, I find it better to come with more men than needed than be found with too few."

"If you'll choose the men, have them meet me at the stables," Landon said. "I will do so in the future once I learn more about them. When I return, I would speak with you about the training schedule and other matters. How many men are posted on the wall walk. The number and frequency in which the roads are patrolled. And how many spies Lady Cassiana has watching the seas."

"Oh, she told you about that?"

"Sir Baldwin did. An excellent idea, seeing as how close we are to the coast." Landon inhaled deeply. "I seem to smell a bit of salt in the air even now."

He excused himself and went to the stables, asking for Cassiana's horse and Orion to be saddled. Soon, the men Sir Adam selected came and saddled their own horses, while others took more from the barn to hitch to the carts that would go into the city.

"Lord Landon?"

He turned and saw a young man of about ten and two. "You must be Justin Cecil."

"I am, my lord. I was squire to Sir Tobyn. Lady Cassiana thought I might be squire to you."

"She mentioned this to me. We go into Berwick-upon-Tweed for supplies. Saddle your horse if you wish to accompany us, Justin."

The boy's eyes lit with eagerness. "Right away, my lord."

Soon, the drivers and carts had assembled and the escort stood ready. Landon saw Cassiana approaching and stood a bit taller. He took pride in this woman, not only for her comely looks but her sharp intelligence. The people of Briarwood held her in high esteem—as did he.

"May I help you mount?" he asked as she joined him.

"Aye." She walked to the tall bay and stroked the horse's neck fondly. "How's my Tressa today?" Cassiana kissed the nose of her horse, surprising Landon, before taking the saddle horn. She placed her foot in the stirrups and he boosted her up then mounted Orion.

The party trotted through the bailey and out the gates. Landon made sure he rode next to Cassiana as the guard fanned out and surrounded them and the carts.

"How far is the city?" Landon asked.

"By horseback, usually an hour," Cassiana replied. "Going more slowly, thanks to the carts, it will add another half-hour to our journey. I would venture at least two hours or more on our return since the carts will be filled."

They had only gone about a mile when her horse faltered. Cassiana pulled up on the reins as Landon dismounted. Cassiana followed suit.

"Your horse has thrown a shoe," he told her, retrieving the horseshoe and examining the hoof. "Justin, come here."

The squire rode up. "Aye, my lord?"

"Take Tressa back to the castle and have the blacksmith reshod her hoof." When he saw the boy's shoulders sag, he added, "You should easily be able to catch up to us at the speed we're going."

"You mean . . . I may rejoin you?"

"Of course." He tossed the reins and Justin caught them. "Don't rush her," Landon warned.

"I won't, my lord."

He looked to Cassiana. "Would you care to ride with me? It would save time instead of returning to the stables for a new mount."

"Certainly, my lord."

He swung into the saddle and then lifted her, settling her in front of him. His arm went round her waist and brought her snug against him.

"Move forward," he commanded.

Landon enjoyed the ride to the city much more after that. With every breath, he inhaled the subtle scent of lilac, which he'd noticed from being near her. Having her body rubbing against his brought ideas of sweet fantasies that he would be sure to make a reality come their wedding night.

They followed parallel along the Tweed River to town and arrived all too soon for him, passing through the entrance of the city's gates. Cassiana drew out a small parchment and unfurled it, studying it carefully as they traveled through the teeming streets. Landon looked over her shoulder and saw it contained a list of the items she wished to buy. Immediately, he swore under his breath.

"Is something the matter?" she asked, glancing back at him.

"I don't have much coin," he admitted. He'd saved most of what the king paid his guard, which was meager. It certainly wouldn't buy everything on her list.

"I gathered monies from the treasure room before we left. We have plenty with which to make our purchases," she assured him. "I should have shown you where the chests with coins are kept. Remind me to do so upon our return."

Continuing down the main thoroughfare, he had to steer clear several times of dozens of pigs foraging in the streets. Many city dwellers kept pigs as easy food to slaughter and more than often let them run wild, not possessing space to pen them up.

As they neared the center of town, Cassiana wanted to walk through the stalls so he dismounted and handed her down. Going from booth to booth, she purchased various items, haggling with expertise as she bartered.

"You are a true master when it comes to closing a deal," he said, his admiration growing for her once more.

"Would you care to try? I need some spices. You can bargain at those two stalls."

Landon did his best, going from one to the other and back again until he secured what he thought was a fair price for pepper, cinnamon, and saffron.

"How did I do?" he asked.

Cassiana cocked one eyebrow. "Not bad for a first attempt. In the future, though, I'd leave the bargaining of goods for the keep to me."

They left the market area and she had the others wait outside as she took Landon inside a large shop. Everywhere he looked, he saw bolts of cloth in an array of colors and textures.

"We'll find everything we need here for our wedding attire and for your pants and tunics. You'll also need a cloak or two."

"I've never had a cloak—much less two," he mused aloud. "My armor was warmth enough."

"You are Earl of Briargate, Landon. Let me see to your needs."

In truth, every place they'd stopped, she'd made sure to introduce him to the merchant or seller as the new earl. Landon saw instant respect in the eyes of many, merely because of his title. He began following her about, collecting the bolts of material she handed to him until the stack was so high he could no longer see above it.

"Take it to the counter," she ordered briskly. "I'll be done soon."

He rested the material on the counter and introduced himself to the man standing behind it. The merchant's eyes danced with glee as Cassiana returned and set down several more bolts. Then she began bargaining with him and drove a hard one. Landon wondered if she had been allowed to draw up battle plans and lead men in a charge, how quickly England's enemies might have fallen in defeat.

Finally achieving the prices she wanted, Cassiana paid the man in full. As the merchant took her purchases to the waiting wagons, she told Landon, "My father always believed in paying everything he owed at the time of purchase. Too many noblemen take advantage of others. They wait for a bill of sale to be drawn up and delivered and then wait far too long to compensate the seller."

"Your father had the right idea," Landon agreed. "I will model myself after him."

Their last stop was at a wine merchant's shop. It amazed him the variety that was available. Cassiana took her time selecting each vintage, pointing out to him the different attributes of each wine. Once more, she proved a fount of knowledge. Landon looked forward to all he would learn from her in the coming years.

"Have we everything?" he asked as their men loaded the casks onto the remaining carts.

She consulted her list again. "Aye. We need to stop for some refreshment, though, since we missed our noon meal. There's an inn a few blocks from here. We can stop there and have something to eat and drink."

They caravanned to the inn she'd mentioned. Landon left two soldiers outside to guard their belongings and appointed another soldier and Justin, who had returned from escorting Tressa to the blacksmith, to eat swiftly and switch off with their counterparts, knowing it would please the boy to be entrusted with responsibility. Landon also spied something down the street that gave him an idea.

Following Cassiana inside, she told the innkeeper what she wished served and the men gathered around several tables in the tavern. As they waited for their food to arrive, the soldiers began telling stories on each other and about Briarwood. Cassiana joined in several times. From her comments, it was obvious she spent a great deal of time with them and he saw the respect they had for her in the manner they addressed her.

Once their meal arrived, he urged her to eat quickly. "We have an errand just the two of us need to see to," he said.

"That sounds rather mysterious, my lord." Her eyes twinkled and she dug into the roasted meat with gusto.

After the two of them finished, he told the others, "Take your time. Lady Cassiana and I have one more purchase to make. We'll be back in a while."

Leading her outside, he slipped her hand through his arm. "It's not far. We won't need Orion."

He took her several shops away and paused at the door.

"A jeweler?" she asked, her nose wrinkling in confusion.

"Aye. You'll be needing a wedding band in less than two weeks."

She rewarded him with a brilliant smile, one that made him think he might sail over the sun and moon with ease.

Entering the shop, he noted a man behind the counter showed another buyer his wares.

"Looks as if we'll need to browse a bit."

Landon watched as Cassiana perused what lay in the cases while they waited. Finally, the jeweler was free to wait on them.

"We need to view wedding bands," he told the balding man. Looking to Cassiana, he asked, "Do you prefer silver or gold?"

She looked perplexed. "Either, I suppose. I have never worn any kind of jewelry."

"Let me show you what I have, my lady," the merchant said. "I'm sure we'll be able to find something to your liking."

He brought out a tray of rings and Cassiana inspected them thoroughly. She lifted one and held it to the light and then slid it onto her finger. After letting it rest on her hand a few moments, she removed it and tried on another. After three exchanges, she found the one she liked.

"This is the ring, Landon. I'm sure of it." A slim band of gold sat on her finger.

"You don't want it adorned with any other jewels?" he asked.

"Nay. It . . . feels right."

The jeweler winked at her. "A lady always knows what she wants." Looking to Landon, he asked, "Is there anything else I might show you, my lord?"

There was—but he didn't want Cassiana to know about it.

"Nay. Not now. Mayhap in the future."

She counted out the coins from her small purse and handed them to the jeweler. As he tucked them away, she wandered off, idly perusing other items in the shop.

As the man took out a cloth to wrap the ring, Landon said softly, "The amber pendant. Wrap that, as well. Separately."

While the merchant did as Landon asked, he counted out the money to pay for it from his own purse hanging from his waist. It was important to him that he buy her something with his coin. Not coin from the previous earl, though Landon realized it all belonged to him now. Instead, he wanted to give Cassiana something from him alone. The amber pendant had caught his eye because it reminded him of the shade her eyes turned upon occasion. He looked forward to giving it to her, mayhap as a wedding gift. Something made him hold back in giving her the dragon brooch. That could wait for another time.

Landon handed over the monies and received the two packages in return. He joined Cassiana and they returned to the inn, where he fetched the men so they could return to Briarwood. Once more, he took her up into the saddle with him, holding her close, hardly believing that this beautiful, intelligent woman would soon carry his name.

When they arrived at the castle, Cassiana ordered the carts to be driven to the keep. The soldiers were to take the goods inside and she would see everything distributed to its proper place.

They cantered to the stables and as Landon pulled her from the horse, she asked, "Did you like Orion?"

"He's a fine horse. I would be proud to accept him in your brother's memory."

"I want to check on Tressa. Would you like to come with me?"

The way she asked, Landon knew she wished for his company. "Let me remove Orion's equipment and rub him down. I'll be there shortly."

Instead, she followed him to Orion's stall and talked with him as he cared for the horse. Everything seemed easy and natural between them. To think that he hadn't known her a week ago and now she was to be his wife. A mellow feeling spread through him, knowing he was ready to settle into not only being a landed earl but a married one, as well.

He heard the others who'd gone with them come and care for their horses but as they headed toward Tressa's stall, Landon realized they were finally alone. As Cassiana bent her horse's knee to inspect the new shoe, he decided he wanted her to have the pendant now. Stepping into the stall, he caught her wrist as she released the horse's foot and pulled her to him.

Her eyes widened and then a slow smile graced her lips. Landon bent and brushed his lips against hers, a surge of longing running through him. It surprised him when her hands locked around his neck and pulled him down closer to her. He captured her waist and spun them around, stepping with her until her back touched the wall. His body pressed against hers as his hands held her in place and his tongue parted her lips. He slipped it inside, tasting her sweetness. Her goodness.

Cassiana remembered the lessons from before and responded. She broke the kiss and then took the tip of her tongue and ran it along his bottom lip. Hot desire shot through him. Boldly, she invaded his mouth, as sure as any general who had marched into war. She took; he gave. He took; she gave in return. One kiss blended into a dozen. Landon released her waist and ran his fingertips up and down her arms slowly, over and over, until she trembled. He cupped her face and tenderly kissed every inch of it. Her brow. Her eyelids. Her cheeks.

The tip of her nose. He feathered kisses along her jawline and dropped his lips lower, to where her pulse beat rapidly in her throat.

His hands longed to cup her breasts. Landon fought the urge and then gave in. The pad of his thumbs ran across her stiff nipples and she gasped. As he kneaded one breast, he slipped his hand inside her cotehardie and cupped the other. A low moan escaped her lips. He raked a nail across her nipple and she sucked in a quick breath.

Landon brought his hands back up and cupped her face again, knowing he must stop before being carried away. He kissed her one last time, slow and deep, branding her as his.

Lifting his lips from hers, he said softly, "I have something for you."

Cassiana gave him a wry smile. "I can feel it."

He realized his cock had come to full attention and pressed against the apex of her legs. "Not that." Giving her a sly smile, he said, "That's for later."

Landon stepped back, giving them both room to breathe. He retrieved the cloth from the jeweler's.

"I wanted you to have something from me. Before we wed. Not something bought with the Earl of Briargate's coin. A gift from me. To you."

He pressed the folded material into the palm of her hand. "Open it."

Cassiana did, staring at the pendant a long time, so long that Landon thought she didn't like it and couldn't decide how to tell him of her dislike.

"If you'd rather have something else—"

"I wouldn't." She looked up at him, tears swimming in her eyes. "No one has ever given me a gift before, much less a valuable piece of jewelry." She smiled. "But I will wear this with pride every day because it comes from you."

Relief swept through him. "The color reminded me of your eyes.

When you're angry or excited, the amber in them consumes the brown. Here, let me put it on you."

Landon lifted the chain and stepped behind her. Cassiana moved her braid aside and he pressed a hot kiss to the nape of her neck. Then he unhooked the chain and lowered the pendant over her head. Once it was in place, he fastened the clasp.

She lifted the stone to her lips and pressed a kiss against it. Looking to him, she said, "I will kiss this every day I place it around my neck for it will always remind me of this moment and how I feel for you."

Landon raised his thumb and brushed it back and forth against her full, bottom lip. "And how is that?"

Cassiana's mouth trembled as she said, "I think I love you."

CHAPTER TWELVE

C ASSIANA HADN'T MEANT for those words to slip out. Immediately, she said, "Forgive me. I misspoke."

She brushed past Landon but he caught her elbow and spun her so that she faced him. Her eyes dropped to his boots.

"Cassiana. Look at me." His voice caressed her like a soft summer breeze.

Stubbornly, she kept her head down, unwilling to let him see how vulnerable she was at this moment.

His hand remained clasping her elbow while the other took her chin in hand and raised it until their eyes locked. In his, she saw doubt.

Landon's hand slipped to cup her cheek, his palm warm as he searched her face.

"You must think me rather foolish," she began. "To make such an outlandish statement when we've only known each other a short time."

"You are the least foolish person of my acquaintance," he said softly. "Other than our king, you are the most intelligent person I have met. I am honored to be the man who will wed you."

"I don't know a thing about love," she said hesitantly. "I've never really seen it before. All I know is my heart grows tender every time you come near. I'm filled with a yearning inside that seems ready to explode at any moment. I pine for your kiss. Your touch. If you left, I would become incomplete."

Landon enfolded her in his arms and held her as if she were the most fragile thing on Earth. Cassiana closed her eyes, soaking in his warmth, feeling secure and calmed. Finally, he released her, sliding his hands down her arms slowly until his fingers entwined with hers.

"I, too, have never experienced love. My parents rarely spoke to one another. How they tolerated being close enough to produce two children still amazes me." He paused, a haunted look appearing in his eyes. "I fear once I tell you who I truly am that you may not feel any affection toward me—and I wouldn't blame you."

Landon fell silent. Cassiana didn't urge him to speak. Obviously, what he wanted to tell her was something difficult to put into words.

"My father committed treason against the crown," he said abruptly.

His words caused her to go cold inside.

"I was very young when it happened, not even old enough to foster. I cannot venture a guess as to why he did so. I don't know if it was something my mother drove him to do. Even as a child, I could see how much she despised him. Mayhap, he was trying to prove something to her—or himself. I'll never know.

"The king's men came for him. The sights and sounds of that night still bring terrifying nightmares. Father was executed for his crimes against England. My family was torn apart. All my life, I've striven to prove I am not the man my father was. That I am loyal and a faithful servant to king and country."

Landon's eyes blazed intensely. "I don't know if I am worthy of your love, Cassiana. I do promise you that I will do everything I can to be a good husband to you. I will care for the people of Briarwood and protect them—and the north—from any threat."

To know Landon was the son of a traitor struck her hard. Allegiance to the crown was driven into the minds and hearts of every northerner, especially knowing the danger of invasion from Scotland by land or France by sea could occur at any moment. She couldn't fathom a man who would plot against the king, trying to destroy the core of England. Landon's father had been such a man, weak from greed or pride or some other sin.

And Landon was his son.

This traitor's blood ran through the man who stood before her. The new Earl of Briargate. The man she would be bound to, on Earth and in Heaven, once they'd wed.

His eyes bored into her, uncertainty in them. Landon hadn't needed to tell her of his past. If she revealed what she knew, he would be judged harshly. Cassiana couldn't help but think of how kind Landon seemed. How he put others above himself. How much he wanted to be a good earl and see Briarwood succeed.

In that moment, she determined to consider only the man before her.

"I cannot allow what your father did to color your view of yourself, Landon. Nor mine. You were but a small boy and unformed in your ways."

"You say this even though my father rebelled against everything in his knightly code. And you now know his blood flows through me. How can you think to love me, Cassiana, when I am so unworthy?"

She looked at him steadily. "We are not our fathers or mothers. We can look to our parents as an example of what to do or disregard their actions and learn to stand on our own. You exemplify everything a knight should be, Landon. You will be a true defender of the north and a good liege lord to your people."

"Thank you," he said. He brought her hand to his lips and pressed a fervent kiss upon it. "I will always seek your guidance, Cassiana. Your heart is with your people." Gazing at her longingly, he added, "I hope someday that I may earn your respect. And your love."

When she started to speak, he placed a finger against her lips to silence her.

"Speak no more of love tonight. If the seed has been planted within you, then let me water it with tender words and strong actions. If a year from now you believe love remains, only tell me then. And I will do the same."

Landon's mouth pressed against hers briefly in a chaste kiss, as if they sealed a bargain between them.

"Let me escort you to the keep. You have quite a bit of goods to put away."

Cassiana tucked her hand through his arm and allowed him to lead her home.

LANDON LEFT THE great hall, eager to reach the training yard and see his men in action for the first time. His new squire fell into step with him.

"How long have you fostered at Briarwood?" he asked Justin.

"Five years," the boy replied, looking warily at him and then glancing away.

"Is your home in the north?"

"Aye." The word came out sullenly.

"Do you enjoy going home to visit with your family?"

Justin's look turned defiant. "I do. My father is a staunch supporter of the king. He expects me to be the same."

"As we all are," Landon said.

They continued on without further conversation. Landon found Justin's attitude a bit odd but then thought of the boy's age. He remembered that time in his life, when his voice changed and his emotions raged out of control and his limbs seemed to go every which way except where he wanted them to.

Arriving at the training yard, he witnessed the soldiers assembling, weapons in hand as they broke off in pairs to spar with one another. Justin parted company from him and went to the butts, where the archers practiced. Landon joined Sir Adam on the platform. The knight nodded coolly and his gaze returned to the men.

Landon watched various pairs engage in combat, picking out a half-dozen from the many gathered that might benefit from individual instruction. For the most part, his soldiers seemed more than capable with a sword and he took pride in that. After an hour, Sir Adam had them practice with weapons beyond a sword, turning to clubs and maces and then war hammers. Landon moved from the observation platform and studied the soldiers from different angles, intervening a few times to make a suggestion.

An odd feeling seem to hover over the yard. The men continued their training but he sensed everyone present watched him surreptitiously. Returning to Sir Adam's side, he decided to ask the captain about it.

"Is there something going on with the men that I should know about?"

Sir Adam shrugged. "Not that I know of, my lord." The captain's eyes continued to sweep across the yard.

"When we finish for the day, I would like to meet with you in the solar. As I mentioned yesterday, I want to become familiar with the men and the schedules in place."

The knight finally turned and made eye contact with him. "It isn't necessary, my lord. Everything is running smoothly. I don't think you need to make any changes."

Landon bit back a sharp retort and tamped down the anger that rose in him. "I didn't say I would make changes, Sir Adam. I merely wish to acquaint myself with how things are run."

His captain faced him. "Briarwood runs just fine, my lord."

He saw mistrust in the knight's eyes and defiance in his stance. "By the Christ, man, what goes on that I'm not privy to?" he shouted.

All activity in the training yard ceased. Every eye focused on the pair standing upon the platform.

"We don't need some Judas to tell us how to keep Briarwood safe!" countered Sir Adam. "You come strutting in here as the new earl when all along you've a betrayer's blood running through your veins. The north has no need of traitors, *Lord* Landon. So you can take your fancy new title and wile away your days in the solar. I'll not be having the likes of a serpent in *my* training yard."

The man's words landed as an unexpected blow to Landon's gut. Only Cassiana could have revealed this information to Sir Adam. He glanced around the training yard, seeing each soldier's dark look directed toward him, daring him to contradict their captain's words. It cut Landon to the quick, knowing his future wife had betrayed him, turning his men against him this way.

He faced the hundreds of soldiers who glared up at him. Landon had never felt more alone in his life, seeing distrust on every face. For a moment, he was that small boy again, afraid and alone, being kicked about by Despenser as he licked the man's boots clean. Still, he must confront the accusation now, while every man-at-arms was present.

"'Tis true. My father was a traitor."

A low rumble passed through the yard as the men stirred, pressing closer.

"I barely remember what he was like as a father since I was so young—but I will tell you what I do remember. His head, resting on a pike, for all of London to see. To jeer at. To spit at. To laugh at."

Murmurs filled the training yard. Landon pressed on.

"From the moment he was taken into custody by the king's men, I have fought to climb from the black hole that man forced me into. Because *my sire* committed treason, people have always looked at *me* as suspect. As the boy whose father thought to topple a king. I tell you, men of Briarwood, that is not who I am. Adelard de Blays' blood may run through my veins but I have done everything in my power to distance myself from him and his despicable actions.

"I've made it my mission in life to prove my trustworthiness to our king. I have fought and bled for the crown and the people of this great nation. I have risked life and limb, over and over again, to demonstrate my fealty. King Edward himself watched me grow up and saw I was willing to do anything for him and England."

Landon paused, hoping his words might sway the crowd but still seeing doubt linger.

"Do you think our king would appoint a traitorous rebel to serve in his royal guard? To protect him? His wife? His children, day in and day out? Nay, I tell you. Our king saw many times through the years what I am truly made of." He paused. "I am not the weakling my father was. I will defend Briarwood. The north. The king. All of England. I will guard all of these with my sword and shield to secure our people's safety and happiness.

"Any man who doubts that, step forth. Challenge me now and I will defend myself as a point of honor. I will show you what I am truly made of."

Landon leaped from the platform, his eyes searching those gathered before him, daring anyone to come forth.

"I will." A broad-shouldered soldier with fair hair took a step forward. "Once a traitor, always a traitor. The king may have forgiven you, but blood tells. And bad blood can never be forgiven—nor forgotten."

Whirling, Landon grabbed a sword from the soldier standing nearest him. His challenger raised his own weapon and advanced toward Landon.

CHAPTER THIRTEEN

C ASSIANA ADMIRED THE new shed that had been constructed and where all of their autumn harvest now rested. Hundreds of workers now participated in the tying and winnowing. Those sheaves that had already dried were being removed from the barn, where in open air the grain was threshed and then separated from its outer casing. She passed among the people as they used sieves to separate the grain from the chaff, placing the heads of wheat into the sieve and then tossing them in the air. The wind blew away the chaff today. If it died down, women stood by with sheets, which they would waft to mimic a breeze.

This process would take another week before the grain could be milled into flour, which they would use to make bread in their bakehouse. Some grain produced would be sold to those who lived at Stony Eastbridge so that the villagers would also be able to bake bread throughout the winter and into spring and summer.

Even though the winnowing would continue for a week or more, she was pleased at the progress so far and glad that plans for the harvest home had continued. The celebration would begin tomorrow afternoon and last into the night. She looked forward to introducing

Landon to the custom.

As she made her way back into the castle grounds, Cassiana thought about how he'd bared his soul to her the previous day, trusting her to know the very worst about him. She'd offered her heart to him but he hadn't wanted to accept it until she fully knew his background and what he came from. Even then, he told her to hold her tongue and keep her heart intact for a year. Only then would he hear her declaration of love.

She didn't need a year to know that she loved this man. Still, she would honor his request and not speak of it. For now.

Since their soldiers were training as a group for the first time today with Landon, Cassiana decided to look in and see how the exercises progressed. If she knew their men, they were probably going out of their way to impress their new liege lord with their fighting skills.

"My lady!" Justin came running toward her.

She stopped and waited for the squire to reach her. No doubt he carried a message from Landon, wanting her to join him in the yard to see the men at work.

Justin skidded to a halt. "They'll kill him!" he got out.

"What?" Her skin prickled with an uneasy feeling. "What are you talking about?"

"Lord Landon," the boy said. "He's challenging everyone in the yard. He's already taken on a dozen men and they still keep coming at him."

Fear gripped her. "Why?" she asked.

"They know he's a traitor," Justin said simply.

"Lord Landon is no traitor," Cassiana said firmly. "How dare you spread such gossip!"

"But he is. Everyone was talking about it this morning. He finally admitted it to the men but said he wasn't like his father. That he would protect—"

Cassiana didn't hear the rest of what Justin said because her feet moved without warning. She lifted her skirts and ran toward the training yard. She entered it and saw a mass of men yelling angrily in a tight circle. The clang of steel reverberated through the air. She fought her way to the front, pushing soldiers aside until she reached a point where she could see the action.

Landon fought with a sword raised high, sweat pouring from him, blood dripping from several wounds along his limbs as Tarquin slammed his own weapon down against Landon's blade.

"What is the meaning of this?" she demanded, stepping close to the pair.

Tarquin's eyes glinted with satisfaction. Landon looked at her wearily. Neither man spoke.

"I won't ask a second time why you all jeer at your liege lord," Cassiana said, glancing about the group, now silent. "Tell me. What goes on?"

Sir Adam stepped forward. "Word passed among the men last night and this morning that the earl . . . is a traitor. That his father betrayed the crown. That his treachery will infect us all and he'll lead the Scots against us and England when the time is right. We'll all die, thanks to this bastard."

"Are you mad?" she accused the knight. "You, of all people, Sir Adam, believed rumors and lies?"

The knight stood firm. "Lord Landon admitted as much, my lady."

Her eyes narrowed. "He proclaimed he was an agent of Scotland and would lead Scottish whoresons against Briarwood and England?"

The captain's face turned red. "Nay, my lady. He told us of his traitorous father. We all know bad blood begets bad blood."

Anger raced through her veins. Cassiana turned and plucked a sword from the man on her right. Holding the hilt in both hands, she moved menacingly toward Tarquin. Surprise jolted the knight and he stumbled back a few paces.

She turned in a circle, glaring at her soldiers, holding nothing back.

"You've all gone mad," she proclaimed. "Lord Landon is a hero. How many of you saw him fight bravely against the French? You came home with stories of his courage and prowess and bragged to everyone at Briarwood how proud you were to have him as our new earl."

Soldiers started nodding mutely.

"You saw him in action, leading us as one people when our stores of wheat were threatened and we might have starved this winter. You know from his very lips that he served as a member of King Edward's royal guard, the finest group of knights in all of England. Men who implicitly hold the king's trust and guard him and the royal family, including his heir. Do you think our king is a fool and would allow a viper in his midst? Would the King of England bestow a fine property such as Briarwood upon a man who would mutiny against him?"

Cassiana raised her sword high. "Nay, I tell you. This man, Landon de Blays, the Earl of Briargate is a fine man. The finest I have ever known—and that includes my beloved father. If anything, he will protect us from our enemies even better than my father did. And look what you've done. You've gone against the very man and title you swore to protect. How many of you challenged him? Beat him down until he grew weary? And yet look at him. He would fight every man here, until his last breath, all because he loves you."

She glanced to Landon, breathing heavily, fire still in his eyes. "He is the only man I would trust to lead Briargate. If you fight Lord Landon, you fight me, as well. Come on, then," she taunted. "Who dares lift a hand against my future husband and me? I call you out, here and now. If you are not for us, you are against us. I will not tolerate any disrespect."

Cassiana circled around, seeing shame on the faces of those present.

Sir Baldwin stepped away from the group and paused in front of her.

"A man should be judged by his actions and character," the knight said. "I have seen firsthand how valiantly Lord Landon fought the French. I have spoken with him several times. He is a man of honor, who exudes every portion of the knightly code."

Baldwin dropped to a knee. "I pledge my life and loyalty to Lord Landon, Lady Cassiana, and the people of Briarwood."

A ripple occurred as the crowd all began to take a knee. Cassiana noted Tarquin was the last to move. She lowered her sword to her side and reached a hand to Landon. He took it. She squeezed it and through the grime and sweat, she saw he gave her a faint smile.

"To Lord Landon and Lady Cassiana!" cried Sir Baldwin.

"To Lord Landon and Lady Cassiana!" the soldiers echoed.

Landon looked to Sir Adam. "Continue with the exercises. We will meet in the solar after the evening meal as planned." He dropped the sword in his hand and staggered away.

Cassiana released her weapon and his hand so she could fasten an arm about his waist as Landon draped his arm over her shoulder. They moved slowly from the yard in silence, Justin following. Once they reached the keep, the squire got on Landon's other side and helped her take him inside, leading him slowly up the steps until they reached the solar.

"Have the kitchen bring hot water for a bath, then find Malkyn and send her to us," Cassiana ordered.

"Aye, my lady."

Landon stumbled inside and fell into a chair. She pulled off his boots and placed them under the chair.

"What were you thinking?" she asked.

"That you betrayed me," he said simply. "That I'd lost the confidence of our men. That I needed to prove to them my worth." He sighed, tilting his head back and looking to the heavens. "Nothing has changed for me. Nothing ever will. I may have a title now, but people still see me as my father's son."

She took his hand in hers, aware of the cuts and bruises on it. "I would never betray you, Landon. *Never,*" she said vehemently. "I have no idea how anyone found out about your past but it didn't come from me."

He gave her a crooked smile. It looked as if it pained him to do so. "I know that now. Look at how you bravely defended me, sword in hand as you faced every man-at-arms in the yard. No one has ever believed in me the way you do, Cassiana."

"The king does," she responded. "Else he never would have made you a part of his guard." She gently kissed his knuckles. "Give them time. Be true to yourself. They will come to know who you are."

A sob burst from him. "I have tried for so long to be a good man. To ignore the gossip. To erase the memory of my father." Landon wiped away a tear that fell. "He was a good father to me, Cassiana. Gave me a sword and instructed me on how to use it. Taught me to hunt and fish. I'll never understand why he did what he did. 'Tis hard to reconcile in my mind the man he was with me and the face he showed to the world."

"You loved him," she said. "He was your father." She pressed another kiss upon his hand. "You'll distance yourself from him. You'll take your place among the leading noblemen of the north. Our soldiers and people will come to know you, Landon. The man you are and always will be."

"You are a balm to my soul, woman." Landon pulled her into his lap and winced. "If I get blood on you and ruin this pretty cotehardie, then I'm sorry."

He kissed her tenderly. She framed his face with her hands and then pushed her fingers into his thick hair. She was the one who chose to deepen the kiss, wanting to show him that she believed in him.

A knock sounded on the solar's door. Cassiana broke the kiss and climbed from his lap. "Come!" she called.

Malkyn entered. "I see there are cuts and bruises to be seen to, my lord," she said brusquely. "Some wounds, too, according to young

Justin."

"I've sent for hot water," Cassiana explained. "Once Lord Landon has bathed, you'll be better able to tend to his injuries."

"I'm fine," Landon complained. "I've no need of a healer."

Malkyn's brow shot up. "So you don't need anyone to tend to that slice on your arm? Or how about the blood that drips from your chest or thigh? My lord, I must see to your wounds so they don't become infected." She gave him a wise smile. "I wish for you to be my liege lord for many years to come. To father many sons and daughters and die of old age after decades as the Earl of Briargate. Do I make myself clear?"

"Women," muttered Landon. "Do what you must."

The hot water arrived and Cassiana mixed in scented oils to it, while Malkyn added herbs that she said would cleanse and promote healing. The two women efficiently bathed Landon together. Cassiana was grateful for the older woman's company. If she'd had Landon to herself, she might have pounced on him and his cuts would have gone untreated.

Once salve had been applied to his bruises and cuts and two wounds stitched closed, the healer excused herself. Landon lay in the bed, exhausted.

"Sleep, Landon. You need to build your strength," she said.

"As long as you don't let me sleep through the evening meal," he growled. "I plan to face everyone in the great hall tonight and meet with Sir Adam afterward."

"As you wish."

"Come lie with me," he said, his words slurring from the herbs Malkyn had him drink. Cassiana knew some of them were meant to help him rest.

She went to the other side of the bed and drew the curtain aside before climbing in next to him. Resting her head on his shoulder, she placed her hand on his chest and curled up against his side. Landon put his hand over hers. Before she could urge him to sleep, his eyes closed and his breathing evened out. She lay next to him, watching him slumber, relishing the feel of him against her.

It angered her that he'd confronted so many men, one after another, in an effort to show who he was. Cassiana could only hope their people would accept him after today's events. She'd meant every word she'd told the crowd. She believed he would be a finer lord than her father had been. An innate goodness permeated this man to his core.

He slept until the evening meal hour approached and she woke him.

"It's time for you to dress."

Landon looked her over. "You should change, my lady. Your cotehardie did get blood on it and it's rumpled from lying abed in it."

She stood and helped him swing his feet to the floor. "I will return in a few minutes."

Heading to her bedchamber, she discarded the stained cotehardie, doubting she'd ever get the blood out of the pale yellow cloth. Changing into a new one of mint green, she took the time to unbraid and comb her hair before re-braiding it.

Cassiana returned to the solar and found Landon dressed in one of two outfits that had been completed for him by their seamstress. One side of his face was slightly swollen, the eye now black. His sleeves and pants covered where his own men's swords had nicked and pierced him.

Landon offered her his arm and they proceeded to the great hall. She believed it only right to prepare him for what lay ahead.

"The people have been loyal to the Campions for generations," she began. "It may take them time to come around. They will—just as the soldiers did today. I don't want you to be disappointed if your reception is less than ideal."

"I understand," he said quietly. "It doesn't make me any less anxious, though."

Cassiana came to a halt. Her eyes searched his, seeing his apprehension and vulnerability, knowing how hard it would be for him to enter the great hall.

"You are the future of Briarwood, my lord. You are the right person to lead the people. You must believe in yourself. As I believe in you."

Doubt flickered in his eyes. "You barely know me, my lady."

"I know you are loyal to king and country. That you fought bravely for England. That the king has faith that you are the man who can keep Briarwood on the right path and defend it from any enemies."

Cassiana paused and then said, "I choose you, Lord Landon. I support you. The people will come to understand your goodness. Trust them."

Her words obviously bolstered him for he stood taller. "Thank you for believing in me."

With that, he moved them down the stairs and toward the great hall. They paused on the threshold and she saw everyone had already arrived and was seated. When the people caught sight of them, a hush fell over the room. Cassiana held her breath, wondering what stories had been spread by the soldiers of what occurred in the training yard this morning.

Then as a group, the soldiers of Briarwood stood—and applauded their liege lord.

Landon acknowledged their recognition with a curt nod and led her to the dais as every remaining soul followed suit. She gazed across the standing crowd, applauding and cheering, and her heart told her all would be well.

CHAPTER FOURTEEN

C ASSIANA COULDN'T BELIEVE that her wedding would occur in three days. The castle's harvest home celebration had gone even better than expected. Though Landon's wounds were still fresh, he'd participated in the feasting and dancing with nary a complaint. From her visits to the training yard since then, all seemed well with the men. More than a few of them had made a point to apologize to her for their behavior. She'd directed them to her future husband, saying no apologies were due her—only to Lord Landon.

"My lady, Lord Nicholas has been sighted from the wall walk," Messina said.

Putting aside her sewing, Cassiana made her way downstairs. Landon came out of the records room, where he'd been sequestered with Hobart all morning. The two men had spent several hours going over various ledgers the past week and Landon seemed comfortable now discussing the estate's business.

Cassiana greeted him and said, "Messina just informed me that Lord Nicholas' party will arrive soon. Would you care to greet him with me?"

"I would."

Landon's warm smile made her tingle inside. Soon, something would come of all those tingles. He hadn't kissed her since the day she'd stepped up with a sword in hand to defend his name and honor. He'd thanked her and given her a brief kiss in the solar but hadn't touched her since.

It was driving Cassiana insane.

She'd never longed for a man's touch. She wondered if her mother had experienced anything similar toward her father. It was hard to remember how they'd behaved toward one another since so many years had passed after her mother's death. Cassiana rarely saw her parents together when she was young. It seemed her mother gave birth to a new babe every year so they must have spent some time together.

But did her father make her mother feel as if she were the only woman in the world? That's how Cassiana felt when Landon looked at her. Kissed her. Touched her. She recalled the one time when his fingers brushed against her breasts. How they'd swollen and ached. How her nipples pebbled in need, yearning for him to stroke them.

Soon, it would come to pass. She only hoped she wouldn't disappoint him. He had lived at the world of the royal court and she assumed, because of his good looks, that he'd had his pick of any number of ladies. Cassiana could only hope she wouldn't compare poorly.

Together, they descended the stairs to stand at the foot of the keep, awaiting the arrival of their first wedding guests. Cassiana supposed they would do this together many times over the coming years. It pleased her that Landon was friends with Nicholas Mandeville. The Earl of Northmere was a superb leader and wielded much influence in Northumberland. If he championed Landon, she knew the other northern nobles would do the same.

She looked forward to meeting Nicholas' wife. No invitation had been extended to his wedding and Cassiana had heard rumors that the wife first married the father and then, by proxy, the son. Her curiosity about the woman had grown over time after others had shared that Katelyn Mandeville had a sharp mind and was the most beautiful woman in all of Northumberland.

Suddenly, the thunder of hoof beats sounded, growing louder as the escort party entered the bailey and came to a halt in front of the keep. She spied Nicholas in the center and gave him a wave. He returned it and dismounted, going to the horse next to him. Cassiana caught a glimpse of the woman riding it, her hair black as night and her skin white as pearls. Nicholas set her on the ground.

Landon broke away from Cassiana and Nicholas met him. The two men greeted each other, huge grins on their faces, and then Landon rushed to Katelyn Mandeville's side. His arms went around the beauty. A sharp pang of jealousy shot through her.

How well did Landon know Nicholas' wife?

She watched as the pair clung to one another, a sick feeling washing over her.

Nicholas joined her, kissing her hand. "You look wonderful as always, Lady Cassiana." He paused. "And distracted. Why the frown?"

She'd been looking over his shoulder and quickly tore her eyes away. "No reason."

He glanced back. "You'd think the two of them hadn't seen each other in a decade, when it was only June."

"Oh?" she said, trying to avoid staring at the stunning beauty who now held Landon's face in her hands and cooed over him.

"Aye. Kate came to see me off when we sailed to Flanders with Morley. We ran into Landon at the harbor."

"You did?" she said stiffly as she watched Katelyn Mandeville slip her hand possessively through Landon's arm, resting her head on his shoulder.

Nicholas took Cassiana's arm and turned her toward him. "You don't know, do you?" he asked.

"Know what?" Her belly churned painfully.

"That Kate and Landon are brother and sister."

"What?" she gasped.

"They were separated when Kate was five and Landon was almost seven. Kate was banished to some awful nunnery. Landon searched for her for years until he found her." Nicholas smiled. "Then she came to me and I inherited Landon as a brother-in-law and friend."

"That means Landon . . . is the king's cousin," she stammered.

"Aye."

Cassiana held tight to her skirts. To think of how Landon's father was executed for treason against his own kin—and that Landon was related to the king himself. The news overwhelmed her.

At that moment, Katelyn Mandeville broke away from Landon and came toward Cassiana. The noblewoman threw her arms around Cassiana, hugging her tightly before releasing her. Immediately, Cassiana looked down and saw from the small, rounded bulge that Nicholas' wife was with child.

"I know we've just met but I'm thrilled that Landon is marrying you. I've heard so many wonderful things about you, my lady, and have looked forward to meeting you for some time. To think now that we will be sisters-in-law! We have so much to talk about. Oh, I do hope we will become good friends."

Cassiana stared at the enthusiastic beauty, seeing how remarkable the resemblance was between brother and sister. Both were tall and had the same thick, dark hair and a similar nose and mouth. Lady Katelyn also possessed the same brilliant green eyes that Landon did.

"Would you like to come to the solar?" she offered. "I can have food and drink brought up."

"That would be lovely," Lady Katelyn said.

"Not us," Landon proclaimed. "I want to show Nicholas a few horses in the stables and the drying shed we recently completed."

Nicholas slapped Landon on the back. "After that, we should go for a ride so you can show off some of your property."

The two men set off and Cassiana invited the soldiers from the escort party to return to the keep for bread and ale once they situated themselves in the barracks. Then she led the noblewoman upstairs. They'd barely seated themselves when Messina appeared with a tray. Cassiana thanked the servant and poured wine for them.

"We saw some of your land on the way to the castle," Lady Katelyn noted. "You have quite an impressive property. Nicholas told me your father had been ill for some time and that you managed the estate. You've done such a nice job."

"Thank you. Father was injured in battle several years ago and became bedridden. Much fell to me since my brother Tobyn was away fostering."

"And your mother?"

"She passed on when I was a girl. What about yours?"

Lady Katelyn bit her lip.

"Oh, forgive me," Cassiana said quickly. "I only learned when you arrived that you and Landon were siblings. I gathered he and Nicholas were friends but I had no idea you were related." She paused. "Landon has told me of your father's transgression against the crown. Nicholas mentioned to me that you were separated as children because of it. I'm sorry I asked about your mother. If it's too painful to speak of, we can discuss more pleasant things."

The noblewoman snorted. "Anything would be more pleasant to discuss than my mother." She took a sip of wine and then ran her fingertip around the rim of the cup, a contemplative look on her face. "My mother and I were sent to the Convent of the Charitable Sisters in Essex. She took her vows and eventually rose to the position of abbess."

Lady Katelyn stood and began pacing the room. "Mother Acelina thrived on the power her position brought. An abbess possesses as much power as a mighty nobleman. She kept me hidden in the convent for years and then thought to sell me to the present king."

"Sell you?" Cassiana shuddered.

"Aye. I was nothing more than a bargaining chip for her. Fortunately, Landon discovered me in time and took me away from her and the hateful nuns who showed me no charity over the many years I lived with them. I consider the mother I once knew gone. Dead and buried."

Cassiana rose and slipped her arms about Katelyn Mandeville, hoping to comfort her.

"Thank you for sharing a part of your story that is so painful," she said. "I'm glad Landon found you and, that after so many years of separation, you'll live close enough to see one another often."

Lady Katelyn wiped a tear away and kissed Cassiana's cheek. "You are as kind as you are beautiful, my lady. My brother is fortunate not only to gain a title and land but a generous woman as a wife. Please, call me Katelyn."

"And I am Cassiana."

They returned to their seats and their wine.

"Landon told me that the only women he respected were his sister and the queen," she shared. "I suppose he did not have a good experience with the women at court while he was in the royal guard."

"Once Landon was taken away, he spent his entire life at court."

"He hasn't spoken much about his past."

"Aye. The old king and the Despensers were quite cruel to him but Prince Edward—now our king—took a liking to his cousin and adopted him as a little brother since he had none. Landon has lived through all the political intrigue at both the French and English courts and witnessed the king's mother and her lover depose her husband. He and King Edward are quite close. I know Landon thinks very highly of Queen Philippa but I agree with him about women at court. Most of them are not to my liking, though a few ladies-in-waiting were kind to me during my short stay at Windsor Castle."

"I have never been to court. I probably never will go. It sounds as if I haven't missed much."

"Nay, Cassiana. To be honest, I am glad to be so far north and away from all the politics. Enough of such mournful topics. Let's speak about your wedding. Can you show me your dress?"

"Let me show you first what your brother will wear. I've sewn it myself."

Cassiana led Katelyn into the solar's bedchamber and revealed the splendid golden tunic she'd embroidered with blue leaves.

Katelyn held it close, inspecting the stiches. "You have a fine hand and Landon will look superb in this."

She escorted Katelyn to her own bedchamber and brought out the cotehardie she would wear for her vows.

"The castle's seamstress finished it only yesterday. I'm quite pleased with her work."

Katelyn fingered the gossamer material. "Oh, you will look like an angel in this. Have you decided how to dress your hair? I must say, it's the most extraordinary color I've ever seen. There's as much red as there is gold blended together."

"What do you think I should do with it?"

They talked about various ways to style it. Katelyn unbraided Cassiana's hair and combed it out, trying different ideas.

Finally, Katelyn said, "I think you should wear it down. With a gold circlet."

"I have no circlets." She fingered her amber pendant. "This is the only jewelry I've ever owned. Landon gave it to me as an early wedding gift."

Katelyn took the stone in hand and glanced up at Cassiana's face and back again. "It's a perfect match to your eyes. My brother did well." She smiled with satisfaction. "Oh, you are going to be a beautiful bride. And I cannot wait until you have children. Our sons and daughters can be raised together."

"Do you have any babes?" Cassiana asked. "Beyond the one you carry now."

"We have a boy, Ruston, who turned a year old last month," Katelyn revealed. "This is my first time away from him. He's into absolutely everything, walking and babbling constantly. I knew it would be hard to keep up with him during all the wedding activities so I left him at Northmere."

"Then Landon and I will have to visit so I can meet him."

"Landon would like that. He's very good with Ruston. I know he will make for a fine father."

A look of sadness crossed her face and Cassiana knew she thought of her own father.

"Landon said that your father was very good to you," she said gently.

Katelyn blinked away tears. "He was. That's what makes it so hard to reconcile whatever occurred. It was so long ago. Whoever knew the truth about the matter is long dead or would never dream of speaking up and admitting knowledge of any plot. Still, Father passed along his love of horses to me. I never ride that I do not think of him."

They returned to the solar and chatted amiably for a few hours until the door swung open and Landon and Nicholas entered.

"You look thick as thieves," Katelyn proclaimed.

Nicholas went to his wife and pulled her to her feet. "Wouldn't you like to know what we've been about?" he said, his eyes gleaming with mischief.

Katelyn wound her arms around her husband's neck. "Oh, I'm sure I could wheedle it out of you."

Nicholas chuckled. "Oh, I know you could, Kate. You always do." He drew his wife to him and gave her a long kiss.

Cassiana had never seen a couple so open with their affection in front of others. It startled her—and made her slightly envious. She felt her cheeks heat and glanced to Landon. He took her hand and led her to the hearth.

"They are madly in love," he said quietly. "I thank the Christ every day for bringing such a good man into my sister's life. She had many hard, lonely years but Nicholas—and Ruston—have brought her much joy."

Landon drank her in, a hungry look in his eyes. "You bring me joy, Cassiana."

Her heart raced at his words. "I hope we will be as happy together as they are."

Landon squeezed her hand. "I have a thought. Many wedding guests will arrive in the next day or two. Then the ceremony and feast will occur. You will be busy from all the entertaining and probably tired by the time our wedding night arrives."

Cassiana's mouth grew dry. "So, what thought do you have?"

Landon gave her a devilish smile. "Mayhap, we should enjoy our wedding night tonight. When there are no distractions and no fatigue. What do you think, Cassiana? Will you come to my bed tonight?"

CHAPTER FIFTEEN

C ASSIANA WENT ARM-IN-ARM to the great hall with Katelyn as Landon and Nicholas trailed behind them. The couples went to the dais and enjoyed a hearty meal and then moved around the room once the trestle tables had been shoved aside, introducing the Mandevilles to others.

After an hour, Landon said, "Why don't we four retreat to the solar and share some quiet time before we retire?"

"I would love to get off my feet," his sister said.

"And so you shall." Nicholas swept his wife into his arms and led them from the hall upstairs to the solar.

Landon offered Cassiana his arm and she watched the couple in front of them. They seemed more in love than was humanly possible. She yearned to experience what they had and hoped that would be possible with the man by her side.

They seated themselves around the fire and Landon added another log so that it blazed.

Katelyn held her hands out before it. "I love a roaring fire. I'm not sure I'll ever get used to how cold the north is."

"'Tis only October," Nicholas reminded her. "You know how cold the wind will blow down from Scotland come the New Year." He gave her a smile. "Never fear, Kate. I'll keep you warm."

They spoke of the upcoming wedding and various guests who would attend. Nicholas and Cassiana shared stories with the other two about many of those who would soon arrive at Briarwood and then he and Landon told about some of the fighting they'd seen in France and how glad they were that the truce had been called.

Suddenly, Katelyn sat up, putting a hand on her belly. "Someone just woke up and is kicking like mad."

Nicholas leaned over and placed both his hands against her. Then his face lit up. "That is a strong kick. Like a horse that hasn't been broken yet."

"It seems fiercer than when Ruston rested inside me," Katelyn said.

Her husband grinned. "Then that's proof enough 'tis a girl. One as feisty as her mother," he teased. "You look tired, love. Mayhap we should end our conversation and put you to bed. It's important you get your rest."

Cassiana rose. "I can show you where your bedchamber is. It's a few doors away from mine."

"I will escort you all where you need to be," offered Landon.

They left the solar and Cassiana indicated which bedchamber had been reserved for the Mandevilles. "Let me know if you have need of anything."

"I'm sure Kate and I will be fine," Nicholas assured her, opening the door and tugging his wife through the portal. "Thank you for your hospitality. We've enjoyed ourselves today. Goodnight to you both."

Cassiana loved how Nicholas was the only one to call his wife Kate. She watched the door shut and then felt a rush of nerves pump through her, knowing what was to come. Landon took her hand and led her to her own bedchamber.

"Do we part here, my lady? Or do we extend our time together?" He bent and brushed a kiss against her cheek.

Her response was to open the door. Taking his wrist, she pulled him inside and closed the door behind her, resting her back along it to steady her trembling legs.

Landon's eyes gleamed in anticipation. "So, you aren't coming to my bed?"

"Nay, my lord—you're coming to mine," she said saucily.

In response, Landon stepped close, his body trapping hers. He cradled her face in his hands gently, as if he held the most fragile of glass within them.

"You're certain?"

"Aye," she said softly, her eyes closing as she willed him to kiss her.

His lips touched hers in a sweet kiss that lingered on and on. She opened to him and he accepted her invitation, his tongue mating with hers as his fingers swept into her hair. They kneaded her scalp as his tongue stroked hers. Cassiana's hands went to his chest, slowly rubbing up and down along the sleek muscles until she linked her hands behind his neck. Landon's body pressed against hers, his heat stronger than any fire she'd stood before. His fingers raked through her locks a final time and then went round her waist, encircling it.

They kissed for a long time. The blood rushed through her, making her own body heat with desire. Landon broke their kiss, his lips trailing down her throat. A steady throb began between her legs and she felt herself grow moist there. She ran her fingers through his hair, enjoying the sounds he made in the back of his throat.

Then his tongue licked its way from her throat to the top of her breast, traveling tantalizingly slow along its curve. Cassiana's hips moved instinctively, pressing against Landon's length.

"I want more," she said huskily.

"More of what? This?" he asked, allowing his tongue to cross back along the curve again.

She shuddered. "Aye. And even more. Don't ask me what. I know not. I only know I want it. With you."

He raised his head, his gaze boring into her, as if he could see down to her very soul.

"I want what Nicholas and Katelyn have," she said breathlessly. "I want you to look at me as he does her. I want you to kiss me. Touch me. Possess me. I want to be yours, Landon de Blays. Tonight. Always."

His green eyes glowed. "I have never wanted a woman as I do you, Cassiana. I want you in this moment and every one that follows."

With that, he swept her off her feet so fast that she became dizzy. Taking her to the bed, he set her back on her feet and slowly peeled her cotehardie from her. He took his time, the silk rustling faintly as it finally pooled at her feet. Landon lifted her from it and then picked up the dress, resting it over the back of a nearby chair. Then he bent and caught the hem of her smock and pulled it up and over her head, tossing it aside.

Cassiana stood in only her hose and shoes as his eyes roamed over her naked body.

"You are so beautiful," he said hoarsely. "I'm not sure I deserve you—but I want you all the same."

He pulled back the bed curtain and had her sit on the mattress so he could remove her boots. Her heart raced so that she thought it might burst from her chest. Landon untied the ribbons at her knees and eased her hose down her calves, his fingers burning a trail along her bare skin. Now, she was totally unclothed. Cassiana thought she would have been embarrassed but his admiring glances made her feel bold instead.

Landon took her hands and helped her rise from the bed and then he pulled back the bedclothes. Strangely, he retrieved her smock and smoothed it across the bed and then told her to lie down atop it. She did so and then stifled a giggle as he doffed his garments so quickly it made her head spin.

He started to climb onto the bed and she said, "Nay," sharply. He froze, uncertainty in his eyes.

"You have changed your mind. I understand." He lifted his knee and stepped back.

"Stop," she ordered crisply.

Landon looked at her, confusion evident on his face.

Cassiana grinned. "I merely wish to admire you, my lord. You did not give me an opportunity to do so."

He began laughing softly as she drank him in. The broad shoulders. The muscled chest with a matting of fine dark hair that tapered down toward his growing manhood. Narrow hips. Large, powerful thighs. He looked every inch the warrior that he was.

And he was to be her warrior. Forever.

"All right," she finally said. "You may join me."

A low growl sounded as he pounced on the bed and took her in his arms. The minute their bare flesh touched, anticipation rippled through her.

"So, you enjoy teasing me?"

"I wasn't teasing you. I just wanted to see all of you. Now, I want to touch you."

"Not before I can touch you," he replied.

His head dipped to her breast and his tongue circled her nipple, taunting it without touching it. Cassiana felt vibrant tingles moving through her, the ones that were ever present each time this man caressed her. Then the tip of his tongue came to rest on her nipple and she moaned from the pleasure. He dragged it across and around, up and down, until she thought she might scream. Landon moved to her other breast and gave it equal attention, laving and sucking it, causing the pounding between her legs to go wild.

His hands began to roam along her sides, dipping along the curve of her hip and back up. She sighed as they continued to move while his tongue did magical things across her body. Then his hands slid along her thighs, stroking them lightly, driving her to a frenzy.

"I think you need to touch me," she gasped.

"I am touching you," he murmured against her skin.

"Nay. I mean . . . oh, I'll show you."

Cassiana grasped his wrist and brought his hand to rest atop the curls at the apex of her legs.

"Oh, there," Landon said, his tone wicked as his eyes gleamed.

"It's calling for your attention," she said, her voice small.

"Then I must respond to this call," he declared.

Landon ran a finger along the fold, causing her hips to rise. Then he pushed it inside her.

"Oh, my!" A ripple of awareness ran through her.

"My, indeed," he murmured as his mouth moved on hers again and his finger stroked her. Another joined it and she whimpered. His tongue mimicked the action of his fingers, slow then fast, then agonizingly slow again. She felt something unnamed build within her. The throbbing began to pound like a drum and Cassiana writhed beneath him.

"Let go, love," Landon urged. "Give in to the pleasure."

"Oh!" she cried and then called his name over and over as sunshine burst inside her and spread warm waves of rays from her core outward. She rode the wave, cresting, cresting, and finally falling from the dizzying height of Heaven back to Earth. Cassiana didn't know if she could ever lift a hand again. A wave of lethargy blanketed her.

Then Landon hovered above her. "You're ready for me, sweetheart."

He thrust into her and Cassiana gasped, nearly flying from the bed. Landon eased her back into the pillows as she started to tell him she'd changed her mind.

"'Twill never hurt again," he reassured her, kissing her temple and then her brow. "It only does the one time. Love play from now on will be joyful."

He hadn't moved since he first entered her. She felt him swelling inside her, afraid, regretting ever having let him come to her bed. Then he moved slightly and she realized the pain didn't linger. In fact, what Landon did felt good. Very good. He moved again—and it felt even better.

"Are you all right?" he asked softly.

"Aye."

This time when he entered her, Cassiana met him with her body. They began a slow, sensual dance that became more heated as time went on. Within minutes, it became frenzied. She clawed at his back and kissed him hungrily. Once more, the same feeling built within her as before. This time, she recognized it and kept rising toward him, knowing what would overtake her.

The explosion occurred again and that wonderful heat radiated through her as she clung to him. Landon, too, seemed to experience something similar. He collapsed atop her and quickly rolled to the side to take his weight off her. He kissed her deeply, the kiss filled with promise of what all their tomorrows would be. Cassiana held tight, never wanting this moment to end.

Finally, they pulled apart, each breathless, their eyes roaming as they both studied one another's face.

"No regrets?" asked Landon.

"None," she assured him. "None at all."

She lay in his arms and her eyelids grew as heavy as her limbs. Though she wanted to stay awake and relish the feel of his hard body against hers, his arms holding her close, she lost that battle and tumbled into sleep.

Something awoke her. It was his lips pressed against her brow. She latched on to his forearm.

"Where are you going?"

He chuckled. "I thought I should return to my own bed. If I stay, I might continually wake you throughout the night."

Cassiana cocked an eyebrow. "You think that would be a bad

thing?"

His palm cradled her cheek. "You're sore. You need to rest."

"I'd rather engage in love play again," she told him, running her nails lightly down his chest.

Landon slipped back into the bed and made love to her once more, slow and sweet, worshipping her body. When they came together again, she marveled at how she hadn't known this existed.

No wonder Nicholas and Katelyn looked at each other the way they did.

Finally, he told her he was leaving for good. "Rest, sweetheart. I will see you in a few hours."

Landon looked at her exactly as Nicholas looked at his wife. Cassiana smiled.

Life with this man would be good.

Chapter Sixteen

C ASSIANA WOKE AND stretched lazily. She was a woman now—in every way. One who loved a good man and would soon wed him.

She rose from the bed and then saw the smear of blood on her smock. So this was why Landon had placed it under her. She hadn't realized she would bleed when he breached her maidenhead. Going to the basin, she took a cloth and cleaned a bit of dried blood still on her thighs. The quick pain had been worth every moment she'd spent in his arms. Cassiana wondered if they might enjoy a repeat performance tonight. She didn't see why not.

A thought occurred to her and she picked up her small hand mirror. She studied herself from different angles but could see no changes. Now, if she could only stop herself from running through the keep and shouting for joy, no one need know that she'd begun married life a few days early.

Once she was dressed, she opened her door and found Landon waiting in the corridor.

"I thought I might escort you to mass." His eyes raked over her, causing her cheeks to heat.

"I'd like that."

They walked to the stone chapel where they would be wed and entered. Landon's shoulder and upper arm rested against hers as Father Peter entered and began the service. Cassiana fought wicked thoughts throughout mass, all of them involving her future husband and what she wanted to do with him. After mass ended, they returned to the great hall to break their fast. Nicholas and Katelyn joined them on the dais.

"I would love to see some of the keep and beyond today," Katelyn said. "Not having been raised in the nobility, I'm constantly seeking advice for how other women manage things. I would love to see how your kitchen and bakehouse are organized."

"I'd be happy to show you around," Cassiana told her.

The men headed for the training yard after the meal ended and the two women spent an hour touring the keep.

"Would you care to see my herb garden?" Cassiana asked.

"Of course," Katelyn said with enthusiasm. "And your chickens. I have a fondness for them and goats. I cared for them at the nunnery. They were my only friends." A brief shadow crossed her face.

She took the noblewoman's arm. "You have a new friend in me, Katelyn. And a sister. Together, we will keep Landon in line."

They wandered through the garden and Cassiana pointed out several herbs that grew especially well in the north.

"I also buy some herbs that don't thrive well in these cold climes when I visit Berwick-upon-Tweed. Being a port city, they import all kinds of goods. Mayhap we can meet up there sometime and shop together in the market."

"I'd like that," Katelyn said. "On to the chickens!"

As they walked arm-in-arm, Katelyn said, "You look different today."

Cassiana stopped in her tracks. "No. I couldn't," she insisted. "I viewed myself in the mirror today. No one should be able to tell."

Katelyn's slow smile spread. "It's the way you looked at Landon this morning and how he did the same. Do you love my brother, Cassiana? And have you celebrated your love privately?"

Her face flamed. "Aye," she confessed. "We did last night. It was Landon's idea but if I'd known what love play was like? I would have suggested it before then."

Katelyn laughed. "I'll ask again. Do you love Landon?"

Cassiana nodded. "I did so even before we came together. I told him and he refused to listen." She paused. "When I spoke the words of love was when Landon had the courage to tell me of his past. Of his father's transgressions. He told me he hoped to earn both my love and trust."

Her friend sighed. "Landon has spent a lifetime trying to make up for our father's sins. I'm sure he doesn't believe himself good enough for you."

"I know he is worthy," she said passionately. "He's the best man I have ever known. He told me never to mention love again. That if I felt the same in a year, then I could say the words. I do love him, Katelyn. I wish I could tell him but I must respect his wishes."

Her future sister-in-law smiled. "Just because you aren't to speak the words doesn't mean your actions cannot convey your feelings for him. I promise you, Cassiana, you can let my brother know how much you love him. With every glance. With every gesture. With every touch. He'll know."

They continued on their tour until they reached the training yard. Usually, the sound of many swords clashing against one another rang out. In this instance, Cassiana only heard a pair who sparred. Cheers suddenly broke out, followed by a collective groan.

"I want to stop here a moment," she said, an uneasy feeling spreading through her.

She led Katelyn inside the yard. The wad of men was so thick they would never be able to see what went on so she took Katelyn to the dais where Sir Adam stood observing the action. The knight offered both of them a hand up and Cassiana turned to see who was fighting.

It was Landon and Nicholas.

Though the October air was cool, both men were stripped to the waist, sweat glistening on each of their perfect physiques. They must have been at it for some time. Her mouth grew dry as she watched them spar with one another for a few minutes. Even to one unfamiliar with warfare, it would be obvious that each man was a skilled warrior. Both moved with a fluidity and range that few possessed.

"I've seen enough," she announced to her companions and allowed Sir Adam to help her and then Katelyn from the platform.

The women left the area. Katelyn said she needed to rest for a bit. Cassiana walked with her back to the keep.

Before Katelyn went inside, she said, "I know that was hard to watch. I hate thinking of Nicholas fighting."

"We've been fighting the Scots most of my life. I've lost brothers in battle." She shivered. "But seeing Landon fight seemed . . . different."

"War is different when we send away the men we love." Katelyn sighed. "The most difficult thing I've ever done is when I accompanied Nicholas in June to Berwick-upon-Tweed. He was leaving to fight for the king in Flanders and France and I insisted on going with him to the coast to tell him goodbye. I stood there with Ruston in my arms and the hint that I might carry another of my husband's babes in my belly. I thought I would come undone having to let him go. 'Twas even harder than killing a man and that has—and always will—haunt me."

Cassiana put her hand on Katelyn's arm. "You've killed?"

"Aye. To get back to Nicholas. I was kidnapped by Scots and held for ransom less than a month after we'd wed. It's a long story but only know I loved Nicholas with all my heart—and we hadn't yet coupled."

"Even though you were wed?"

Katelyn nodded. "I knew I would do whatever it took to return to him. That included killing a man." She shuddered. "But 'twas worth it. Those few days away from Nicholas let me know I never wanted to be parted from him again. I will always carry the guilt of what I did but I'll never be sorry for doing what it took to get back to the man I love."

She embraced Cassiana. "I'm so tired from all of our walking. We'll talk later."

Katelyn entered the keep and Cassiana decided to check on the milling. It surprised her that Landon's sister had killed a man, but somehow she understood why. If anyone ever tried to separate her from Landon, she would go to the ends of the Earth in order to be reunited with him.

Going to the stables, she had Tressa saddled so she could ride to the river. For many years, Briarwood's mill had been close to the fields and powered by wind. Her great-grandfather had decided to build a watermill instead, using the nearby Tweed River to supply the power. He'd believed water more reliable than wind and had been proven correct. Cassiana had studied ledgers from decades before and those after the estate began milling with water power. Production began strong and had only increased over time.

All the tying and winnowing had been completed at this point so milling was the last step before turning the grain into flour. She couldn't imagine what it had been like in olden times when the people had to use a mortar and pestle to grind the grain by hand. It was hard enough to do that with the herbs she collected from her garden. To think that an entire autumn harvest had been milled by hand was unimaginable.

People buzzed with activity around the mill. Cassiana looped Tressa's reins around a nearby bush and entered the hectic atmosphere of the mill. She'd always learned best by seeing things herself so she strolled through and watched production in motion. William, who was in charge of the Briarwood harvest, caught her eye and waved.

She returned the greeting and continued to observe the milling for half an hour.

Finding William again, she motioned him to follow her and then went outside where they could converse more easily.

"How goes the milling?" she asked, already knowing his answer.

"Very well, my lady. You will be pleased with the yield."

William proceeded to walk her through everything that had been accomplished and when he expected to finish.

"I'm pleased with the progress. Remember, though, the day after tomorrow will be my wedding and no work will occur. I want everyone at Briarwood to celebrate my union with Lord Landon."

William smiled. "We are all looking forward to the feast, my lady. The people already think highly of our new earl."

Cassiana returned to Tressa and rode to the stables. A groom took the reins and she headed toward the keep, thinking the noon meal grew close.

She saw soldiers streaming from the yard ahead toward the keep and was surprised when one turned in her direction. He made his way toward her and as he drew closer, she recognized the man as Tarquin. She hadn't spoken to him since the summer, when he'd been a part of the men who'd sailed to Flanders. Cassiana had told the knight then that she would wed another. A part of her felt ashamed that she'd let this man kiss her and ply her with false compliments. She straightened her shoulders and continued, determined not to converse with him.

He came to stand directly in front of her, halting her progress.

"You wish to speak to me, Sir Tarquin? I don't believe we have anything to discuss."

"I think we do, Cassiana."

She took a step back. "Please refrain from using my Christian name, sir."

"You used to let me," he said softly. "You also used to enjoy my kisses."

Cassiana hadn't but she didn't want to hurt the man's pride. Glancing over his shoulder, she saw no one else in the area. For the first time, she felt a chill of fear.

"I'm to wed Lord Landon in two days," she said briskly. "He is the man whose kiss I will enjoy and the only one to call me by my given name."

Cassiana took a step forward to go around him but Tarquin's fingers curled around her arm.

"Wait."

She tried to shrug him off but his fingers tightened.

"Unhand me," she ordered.

"I will—if you stay and listen to what I have to say."

"All right."

The knight's hand fell to his side. "Lord Landon isn't the man you think he is."

"How do you know what I'm thinking? It's none of your concern anyway."

"Landon de Blays could have saved your brother. He didn't."

His words were like a slap in the face.

"What?" she hissed. "I have no idea what you're talking about."

Tarquin held out a hand to silence her. "I was there, fighting by Sir Tobyn's side. Oh, you would have been proud of him, Cassiana. Your brother became a man possessed that day. I'd never seen him swing his sword with such passion and skill. He cut down one French soldier after another. Your father would have enjoyed seeing his son in action.

"But like all of us, after many hours in battle, he began to tire," Tarquin continued. "I saw Tobyn finish off a man while I fought another, only a handful of feet from him. Landon de Blays was nearby. A French bastard raised his sword at your brother, who was unaware the man approached from behind. Sir Landon stood and watched Tobyn being struck down. He never lifted a sword to defend him."

The knight shook his head in disgust. "If I hadn't seen it with my own eyes, I wouldn't have believed it. A knight refusing to come to the aid of a fellow knight." Tarquin rubbed his chin. "By the time I dispatched the man I fought, your brother had fallen in combat and died. Landon de Blays had moved on."

Pity filled Tarquin's eyes. "I thought you should know exactly who you will wed. The kind of man he is. One like his father. A man who has no loyalty or code of honor."

Numbness filled Cassiana. She knew Landon had met Tobyn. He'd told her they'd spoken at length on the voyage to Flanders. Why wouldn't he have come to Tobyn's aid?

Unless Tobyn told Landon that he was the last Campion son and only heir.

Landon had revealed that Tobyn mentioned that he looked for a husband for her. What if Landon deliberately allowed her brother to be struck down—and then had then asked his cousin to award him Briarwood—and her?

She stumbled away from Tarquin and was sick. The man she loved—the man she had given herself to—was vile and untrustworthy. Then the anger set in, a spark that began to build. Cassiana wiped her mouth on her sleeve and lifted her skirts. She ran blindly toward the keep, needing to confront Landon. By the time she reached it, her rage boiled over.

Entering the great hall, she saw Landon stepping up to the dais to join Nicholas and Katelyn. She hurried toward him, seeing red.

As she reached him, he glanced down to offer her his hand but stopped in his tracks. Before he could say anything, Cassiana glared up at him.

"Why did you let my brother die?"

Chapter Seventeen

C ASSIANA'S ACCUSATION STUNNED Landon. He froze, seeing the fury in her face.

What was she talking about?

"You—"

"Careful, Cassiana." Nicholas had sprung into action and grasped her elbow. In a low voice, he said, "'Tis never wise to air grievances in front of your people. If you need to confront Landon, do so in private. Not while the great hall is filled with others listening to your every word."

Cassiana turned to Nicholas and hissed, "I *will* see Landon. Now."

"Why don't you go to the records room?" Nicholas suggested. "It's close by and will afford you the privacy you need."

She turned back to Landon and scowled at him. Through gritted teeth, she said, "Follow me. No delays."

Taking a deep breath, she schooled her features and masked her anger. Nicholas released his hold on her and, head held high, Cassiana walked from the room. Every eye followed her and then conversation broke out.

"Go to her," Nicholas urged Landon. "See what caused such an outburst. It seems out of character for her, especially knowing how well the two of you suit."

Katelyn touched his sleeve. "Remember that she loves you. Listen to whatever she has to say."

Landon left the dais and headed to Hobart's office. He couldn't imagine what would have turned Cassiana against him in such a short space of time. What they had shared together last night had proved to him that love truly did exist. That he might actually be worthy of such a woman. That they could share a lifetime of love. Raise a family. Work alongside each other to continue to build Briarwood. He loved her with every fiber of his being and would be desolate without her.

Landon arrived at the records room. The door stood open. He entered and closed it behind him, not wanting anyone to overhear whatever complaints she flung at him. Cassiana's back was to him, her arms wrapped around her protectively. He didn't speak. He had nothing to say. He waited for her to make the first move.

Finally, she turned to face him. Angry tears ravaged her face. "What else haven't you told me?" she accused, her tone deadly. "What else are you hiding from me?"

"I don't understand."

"You told me you were nothing like your father but you're not to be trusted. You are disloyal. Dishonorable. You could have saved him!"

Landon closed the distance between them and clasped his hands around her upper arms. "What are you talking about? What has changed between us?"

"Everything." Cassiana's hands grabbed his wrists and tore his hands from her. "Don't think you can kiss your way out of this. I want answers," she demanded.

An ache filled his heart. It was as if he'd already lost her. Dully, he said, "If you will but give me the question, I will provide the answer you seek."

She retreated to a corner and crossed her arms again. Landon sank into the nearest chair, unsure if he could stay on his feet.

Cassiana wiped her tears away and took a calming breath. Then her eyes bored into his as she said, "I have just learned that you saw my brother fall."

Landon nodded. "I did," knowing the story would cause her unnecessary pain.

"You admit it."

"Aye. I was on the next ship. I called out a warning—"

"Nay. You lie. You didn't," she spat out.

He frowned. "I did." He thought back to the incident. "The French ships were all lined up, sitting side by side, so close that you could leap from one to the next as the fighting raged on. I was on one deck and your brother was on the ship beside me. I saw . . . a French soldier coming for Tobyn and tried to alert him."

Cassiana rushed toward him. "You didn't. You were alongside him and you deliberately did not engage. You refused to come to the aid of a fellow knight. A man you say you liked. You *let* him be killed."

Her hand was a blur and then he felt the slap against his cheek.

Landon stood quickly, his face stinging as much as his pride. "You are wrong," he said firmly. "I don't know who's tried to poison you against me. It did not happen as you say."

He raked his hands through his hair in frustration. "I glanced to the next deck. Tobyn had just disposed of a man. A Frenchman did raise his sword behind Tobyn's back. I cried out, hoping to alert Tobyn or the English knight who fought next to him. I never understood what happened."

He sank into the chair again. "The soldier fighting beside Tobyn turned and saw what unfolded. He intentionally kept his sword by his side—and smiled. *Smiled!* When I saw the danger Tobyn was in, I jumped from my ship to his." His voice broke. "I didn't reach him in time. I was too late."

Landon's head fell as he recalled the moment of horror and help-lessness. Raising his eyes to Cassiana, he continued. "I was too late to save Tobyn—but I sent the bastard that killed him straight to Hell. By then, the man who'd failed to come to Tobyn's aid had vanished. He'd disappeared amidst the brutal fighting."

He swallowed. "I'm sorry I never told you that I witnessed To-byn's death. You were already in pain hearing about his death. I didn't want you to know that he might have lived, had the soldier next to him supported him in battle."

Cassiana's jaw dropped as understanding about something un-known to him dawned on her face. She burst into tears and crumpled to the ground. Landon picked her up and sat with her in his lap and she sobbed loudly. He stroked her back and her hair, murmuring words of comfort, but she cried even harder. As he held her, he wondered who might have spread such vicious lies about him. He realized the only man who could have done so was the one who had been present. The only other witness that would recall seeing Tobyn's death. The soldier who had purposefully turned his back on Tobyn Campion.

That man was at Briarwood.

Fury sped through him, striking as fast as lightning. Someone had tried to taint Cassiana's opinion of him by altering the true events. But why? What would a soldier at Briarwood have to gain by the death of the earl's son in battle?

Cassiana's face had been buried in his chest. She now lifted her head, her eyes red and swollen.

"I will kill him," she snarled.

"Who?" Landon demanded. "Who wished to turn you against me? For what purpose?"

Her eyes sparked with anger. "Tarquin Grosbeck."

Landon had to think a moment to put a face to the name. Briar-wood had close to two hundred soldiers but he thought he knew the knight she mentioned. The man had average skills and hadn't stood out in any way during Landon's brief time at the estate.

His hands cradled her face. "Tell me."

Her lips trembled. "I will. I hope you won't think less of me."

Landon managed a chuckle and thought to lighten the dark mood. "Well, you certainly seemed to think less of me a few moments ago."

His words caused her face to crumple. "I'm sorry for doubting you, Landon. I've been such a fool."

He gave her a brief kiss of encouragement. "I hope you will never doubt me again. I realize my association with my father colors everyone's view of me but I mean it, Cassiana. I have done everything in my power to distance myself from him. I would never betray you or hurt you in any way."

"I jumped to conclusions, though, and believed the worst of you. I said such awful things to you." She began to weep again.

"No more of that," Landon ordered. He wiped her tears away with his thumbs. "Tell me."

She wound her hands around his neck. "I've only kissed one man besides you and that was Tarquin Grosbeck."

A flare of jealousy sparked within him. "Do you love him?" he asked, afraid to hear her reply.

Her eyes widened. "Nay," she denied vehemently. "Never. Tarquin showered me with compliments and we kissed a few times. I thought it bland, to be honest. Then, just before he traveled with Tobyn and the other Briarwood soldiers to board Morley's fleet, he revealed the purpose behind the attention he gave me."

Landon's gut told him what Cassiana would say next but he remained silent. Better to let her relieve herself of the burden she'd carried.

"I knew the time had come for Tobyn to prepare to manage Briarwood on his own, especially with Father close to death. I understood Tobyn would never be comfortable running the estate with me looking over his shoulder, though."

"So, that's when you asked him to find you a husband?"

"Aye. I told Tarquin he mustn't kiss me again for I was soon to be wed. He countered by asking me what would happen if Tobyn fell to the enemy in France. The thought horrified me but I told him the king would name a new earl once Father passed since there would be no heir."

Her nails dug into his back. Landon felt the waves of anger coming off her.

"Tarquin pointed out how my father would soon die and that I must urge him to petition the king to allow me to control Briarwood upon his death."

"Let me guess," Landon ventured. "Grosbeck offered to wed you so that he might become the next liege lord of Briarwood."

Her eyes filled with pain. "He never cared for me. Tarquin merely flattered me into thinking he desired me so that he could use me to gain control of what he truly wanted—Briarwood."

Landon's fingers stroked her long neck. "I'll never be able to identify him with certainty. The battle at Sluys raged for hours and dusk began to fall. The man I saw who ignored helping Tobyn was covered in blood and filth, as all of us were. I only glimpsed him for a moment and when I saw he refused to help Tobyn, I concentrated on reaching your brother. This man, whom I believe to be Tarquin Grosbeck, melted away.

"I will say this. The only man who would have even noticed that I was close to Tobyn—that I tried to stop the French swordsman from attacking him—would most likely be the man who fought beside your brother and disappeared after neglecting to intervene and help him."

"The very man who just now tried to turn me against you," Cassiana said, her voice shaking with emotion. "Tarquin sought to drive a wedge between us, thinking I would refuse to marry you, and that would give him another chance to weasel his way into my life." Her lips trembled. "Tarquin told me I didn't know the man you truly were. He was wrong. I know exactly who you are, Landon. What you are made of. Whether you want to hear it or not, you are the man that I love. The man I trust with my life. The man who will continue to protect me and his people. I beg you, Landon. Forgive me for taking Tarquin's word as truth. For questioning who you are and what we have. I will never do so again."

Cassiana pressed her mouth to his. Desire exploded within Landon. He wrapped his arms around her, his mouth slanting across hers, his tongue pushing inside her mouth and consuming her. He kissed her long and hard, needing to possess her, to make her his. To erase any questions she might still have. Finally, he broke the kiss, shivering as he did.

"Never doubt me again, Cassiana. Never doubt that I will always be true to you. And never, ever doubt that I love you."

He kissed her again, gently this time, hoping his kiss rid her of any uncertainty.

This time, she broke the kiss and looked at him with hope in her eyes. "You love me? Truly?"

"With a passion that will never die. I promise to always be by your side, no matter what. I love you, Cassiana Campion."

"I love you more, Landon de Blays."

He grinned. "Then I will let you prove it to me tonight. In my bed this time." Scooping her up, he stood and set her on her feet. "For now? We deal with Tarquin Grosbeck. Together."

Landon entwined his fingers with hers and led her to the great hall. As they entered, a hush fell over the room. Hand-in-hand, they returned to the dais. Relieved murmurs swept through the room.

"Nicholas, Katelyn, would you please join us in the solar?" Landon asked.

"Of course," they both replied.

Landon took Cassiana to the first table on the left, where his captain of the guard sat finishing his meal.

"Sir Adam, I would request you come to the solar at once. With Tarquin Grosbeck accompanying you. He may not come quietly," Landon warned.

"I'll see that he is delivered, my lord" the knight promised. He looked to his companions.

The entire table of soldiers stood.

"Come, my lady," Landon said.

They joined Nicholas and Katelyn, who waited for them outside the entrance to the great hall. No one spoke as they ventured upstairs.

Once they arrived, Landon said, "I wish for you to act as impartial witnesses since you are not residents of Briarwood."

"What's this about, Landon?" Katelyn asked, concern written across her face.

"We'll speak more once I've dealt with a soldier," he said. "Please, have a seat."

The women sat and Landon and Nicholas stood behind them. Landon placed a hand on Cassiana's shoulder. She looked up at him and nodded encouragingly.

He'd deliberately left the door to the solar open and heard the approaching footsteps. From the sound of it, Sir Adam had involved several soldiers to escort Grosbeck to them. Landon thought that good. They would hear what occurred and spread the word afterward.

The group of men arrived, Sir Adam leading the way and Sir Baldwin bringing up the rear. In the middle was Tarquin Grosbeck. Two soldiers held tightly to him as he struggled, with another two nearby in case he broke from their grasp. Landon saw the knight had been disarmed.

"My lord," Sir Adams said, bowing his head and then stepping aside.

"Release him," Landon ordered, his eyes boring into Grosbeck's as the ring of knights tightened about him.

The soldier looked around in desperation and saw he had nowhere to go. He accepted his fate and stood tall, sneering at Landon.

"You are the knight who broke his code. Who deliberately turned his back in the heat of battle and let Tobyn Campion be struck down," Landon began. "You swore to protect the Campion name and yet sacrificed your liege lord's son to the enemy. All because you wanted to wed Lady Cassiana and control Briarwood."

"You have no proof of that, de Blays," countered Grosbeck. "I say *you* are the man who neglected to come to Sir Tobyn's defense and allowed him to be struck down and killed."

"Nay," Sir Baldwin called out, stepping from behind the group of soldiers. "I wasn't far from Lord Landon at that point in the fighting. I heard him shout a warning and then leap to another ship. I witnessed him arrive a moment too late to save Sir Tobyn. He cut down the French swordsman who killed Sir Tobyn with a single blow. Lord Landon did everything in his power to save the boy, not cause him harm."

Turning to Cassiana, Sir Baldwin said, "I swear this on my oath as a knight, my lady."

"Why didn't you tell her this before now?" Grosbeck complained.

The knight wheeled to face Grosbeck. "Because Lady Cassiana had lost her last brother and her father. What good would it have done to share with her the details of how Sir Tobyn was cut down? She didn't need any more heartache. The king had already commanded that Lord Landon receive Briarwood and the lady. I knew he would be a strong liege lord and make her a good husband."

Sir Baldwin turned back to Cassiana. "Things move quickly in battle, my lady. I did not see Tarquin Grosbeck's lack of action. I can only attest to Lord Landon's bravery. I also know of his goodness and that he would never lie. If he says Grosbeck acted in such a manner, then it is fact."

Landon squeezed Cassiana's shoulder. "What would you have me do with him, my lady? How would you see him punished?"

"I want him off Briarwood lands. We will announce to our wedding guests what this man did. How he acted deceitfully. No lord of the north will ever trust you to be in their service, Tarquin Grosbeck."

Cassiana stood and went to stand in front of the shamed knight. "Collect your gear and your horse and be gone, man. If you're ever foolish enough to be seen by any of us again, 'twill be your death."

She returned to her seat and the guard of soldiers escorted Grosbeck from the solar. Sir Baldwin remained behind and came to Cassiana.

Kneeling before her, he said, "I am sorry for your brother's death, my lady. Sir Tobyn fought bravely against the French." He stood and exited the room.

Landon let out a long breath. Men humiliated such as Tarquin Grosbeck had been were dangerous. His eyes met Nicholas' and they nodded at one another.

Landon would need to be on constant watch against this new enemy.

CHAPTER EIGHTEEN

C ASSIANA AWOKE TO her wedding day. Guests had arrived for two
days, up until late last night, keeping her busy introducing them
to Landon and making sure everything ran smoothly. She'd hired extra
hands from the village to help with cleaning and preparing all of the
bedchambers and to help cook the meals prior to the ceremony and
the feast afterward. Just thinking about all the effort that had been
expended made her doubly glad that they had already consummated
their marriage. Her only regret was not having spent last night in
Landon's arms. He told her it was best to keep to their own bedchambers, telling her they had a lifetime of love play ahead.

Word had spread of Tarquin Grosbeck's banishment from Briarwood. The knight would find no lord to serve in Northumberland. He
would have to make his way far south to outrun the gossip and
rumors about him. It angered her that she had actually believed
Tarquin's words for a moment and wrongly accused Landon. Thank
the Christ, he'd been able to harness her fury and help her to see the
truth before she caused irreparable damage between them.

A smile spread across her lips. The one good thing that had come
from the incident was that Landon had openly declared his love for

her. He'd told her again several times, both in and out of bed, the past two days. Her future husband was proving as affectionate as Nicholas was with Katelyn. Mayhap more so.

A knock sounded at her door and she went to answer it. Messina stood waiting, holding a tray with something for her to break her fast.

"We've brought hot water for your bath, my lady, and something for you to eat and drink."

The servant directed a line of servants to enter, each carrying two buckets. As Messina prepared her bathwater, mixing hot and cold water and adding a heady vanilla oil, Cassiana ate quickly. Once the servants were gone from the solar, she removed her clothes and sank into the scented water. Messina washed Cassiana's hair for her and then scrubbed her from head to toe, just as she had when Cassiana was a child.

"Stand, my lady." Messina held a large bath sheet up and wrapped Cassiana in it. "Sit by the fire and let me comb your hair while it dries."

She allowed the older woman to fuss over her, closing her eyes as the comb ran through her long locks.

"Your mother would be very proud of the woman you've become."

"I hope so. I wish she could have been here for this day. Do you know . . . I mean . . . did my mother love my father?"

"They respected one another. Of that I'm certain. Love, though? Nay." Messina patted her shoulder. "You are one of the blessed, my lady. Fortune has smiled upon you and Lord Landon. Everyone at Briarwood can see the love between you. You will make many fine babes in the years to come."

A light rap sounded at the door.

"Come," Cassiana called.

Katelyn Mandeville entered the room, carrying something in her hands. As she approached, Cassiana recognized what she held.

"I brought you this circlet," her friend said. "I think if you leave your hair down and top it with the circlet, my brother will be most pleased with your appearance." Katelyn offered it to her.

Cassiana held the thin band up, admiring it. "It's lovely. Thank you so much for letting me borrow it for the wedding."

"Oh, 'tis a gift," Katelyn assured her. "I think the gold will suit your hair well."

Messina excused herself and the two women chatted while Cassiana's hair finished drying.

"I'm so happy that Landon is starting a new life with you. I know it was hard on him when the king stripped him of his future title and land. To know he has a new home, with a woman he loves, goes beyond anything I could hope for him."

"I do love him, Katelyn. Very much. I never dreamed I would be able to remain at Briarwood as its countess, much less have the love of a good man."

"Landon showed me his wedding finery last night. I think, more than how the cotehardie turned out, he was pleased that you'd sewn it for him yourself and not a servant," Katelyn confided.

"It was a labor of love. Landon has forgotten all about making us wait a year to declare our love. He's already told me many times that he loves me."

Katelyn took Cassiana's hand and squeezed it gently. "He will do so every day of your life. I can tell you that when you have a child, your love for one another will grow even more." Her hands went to her belly and she rubbed it affectionately.

Cassiana watched as Katelyn's cotehardie moved without warning. "'Tis the babe?"

"Aye. A very active one. I do hope we have a girl, for Nicholas' sake."

"He truly wants a daughter? Most men prefer sons."

"Nicholas loves Ruston but he is a man who would love any child of ours. Landon will be the same, I'm sure." She paused. "Let me check your hair. It's probably time for you to begin dressing."

Cassiana allowed Katelyn to take over and soon she wore her new velvet cotehardie of midnight blue, embroidered with gold. Katelyn fluffed Cassiana's hair and it spilled about her shoulders and down past her waist, the reddish-gold a stark contrast to the deep blue of her gown. Katelyn set the gold circlet atop Cassiana's head and stepped back.

"You are a bride everyone will admire. The most beautiful one I've ever seen." Katelyn retrieved the hand mirror and allowed Cassiana to view herself.

Her eyes were more amber than brown and her skin had a rosy hue to it. The circlet gave her a regal look.

"Wait. I forgot my pendant."

"I'll place it around your neck," Katelyn offered.

Once it rested against her breasts, Cassiana was satisfied. She and Katelyn chatted about the upcoming babe and funny things that Ruston was now doing until a strong knock sounded and Nicholas poked his head in.

"Are you ready?"

Cassiana had asked the nobleman to escort her to the chapel and give her away since she had no living male relatives. Nicholas would also serve as the best man to Landon, standing beside him in support during the ceremony.

He came and helped Katelyn rise, pressing a soft kiss on her brow. "I'll see you at the chapel." She left the room.

Nicholas gave her an appreciative glance. "You make a stunning bride, Cassiana. We are both lucky to have landed a de Blays as our soul mate. If only there were more of them to spread around the north," he mused.

"Thank you for accompanying me today, Nicholas. It means much to me and to Landon. He values your friendship."

"We are family now, Cassiana. Or we will be within the hour. I am happy to escort the bride to her bridegroom."

Nicholas offered her his arm and they made their way from the solar to outside the keep. A group of musicians joined them, playing a merry tune as they led her through the bailey to the chapel. Everywhere Cassiana looked, she saw smiles from their invited guests and the many workers, servants, and soldiers of Briarwood who'd come to witness their union. The crowd parted to allow the musicians through and she and Nicholas remained close behind them.

Then she caught sight of Landon, tall and impossibly handsome in his own cotehardie of rich gold interwoven with dark blue. Cassiana had reversed the colors she wore and thought they would be a matched pair as they made their vows to one another. Her heart began thumping wildly as they approached Landon, who stood at the steps of the door leading into the chapel. Nicholas handed her off to her bridegroom and took his place by Landon's side.

Her bridegroom's hand enveloped hers in warmth as his eyes shone down at her in love. In that moment, Cassiana knew perfect happiness, knowing she loved and was loved by the best man in all of England. Life with Landon de Blays would only get better with each passing day.

"Are we ready to begin?" asked Father Peter.

"Aye," she and Landon answered, finally tearing their eyes from one another and looking to the priest.

Father Peter began the ceremony, asking them if they were of age and if they were related in a way which might prevent them from wedding in accordance to law. They had previously determined among the three of them to skip the question regarding parental consent since the king had commanded they were to wed.

The priest explained to those gathered that no dowry would be required from the bride since Lord Landon, by virtue of the king's expression, had been awarded everything at Briarwood.

Father Peter began his brief homily, which would be followed by the exchange of their vows and Landon placing the wedding band on Cassiana's finger. She tried to listen to the priest's words but every thought in her mind was of the man who held her hand and how happy he made her.

A sudden commotion sounded behind them. Father Peter fell silent and stared out across the crowd, his lips pursed in displeasure with the interruption. Cassiana saw three riders had arrived near the back of the crowd. Her eyes were drawn to the first man. She gasped.

Tobyn was alive!

Somehow, Landon—and Sir Baldwin—were wrong. Tobyn hadn't died at Sluys. They'd only thought him mortally wounded. Happiness flooded her. Then she realized if Tobyn were back from the dead, Landon was no longer the Earl of Briargate.

Tobyn Campion was.

Murmurs from those in attendance began to swell as Tobyn threaded his way through them. Cassiana glanced and saw the other two men who accompanied him had also dismounted and followed. One was a priest. The other, she didn't recognize. Then Tobyn came to stand before her.

It wasn't her brother.

From a distance, he'd been the very image of Tobyn. Up close, though, she saw subtle differences. This man was older than Tobyn, probably a few years older than she was. He was slightly taller and his frame more filled out. While his hair had the same deep red tint in sunlight, his eyes were blue, unlike Tobyn's brown ones.

Who was this stranger?

"Are they wed?" he demanded, looking at Father Peter.

"Lady Cassiana and Lord Landon are about to speak their vows."

"Then I'm in time," the man said, relief sweeping across his face. He faced her. "Greetings, Cassiana. I am your brother—Collin Campion."

She gasped. "What?" Landon's hand tightened around hers.

"I am your older brother. Actually, your half-brother. From our father's first marriage," the stranger revealed, his eyes watchful.

"*First* marriage? My father wed . . . twice?"

He snapped his fingers and gestured toward the priest, who stepped forward, a parchment in his hands. They trembled as if he had the palsy.

"I am Father Barnard, my lady. I can testify that Sir Collin speaks the truth. I married his mother and father a score and six years ago in Durham. He is the issue of their marriage. I bear the proof of their union."

Cassiana reeled. She was three and twenty, the first of her parents' children. If what the priest said was true, then Collin Campion was her half-brother. Merely looking at him alone told her he was a Campion but the priest's word, along with the document he bore, was proof enough.

The third in their group spoke up. "I am Reynard Payne, Baron of Newfield. My estate is situated on the border of Durham and Northumberland. 'Twas my sister, Juetta, who married Sir Darwin, the man who became the Earl of Briargate."

"Why don't I know of this marriage?" Cassiana asked, her mouth dry.

"They wed in secret," Lord Reynard said. "Your grandfather was ill and your father returned home to look after the estate right after he received his knighthood. After several months, Sir Darwin became the new earl and returned for his bride." Lord Reynard's face fell. "By then, Juetta had given birth to Collin. She died only hours later."

His words caused her mind to reel. "I don't understand why Father didn't bring the babe home to Briarwood," Cassiana said. "The boy would have been his heir."

"Because Uncle Reynard told him I was dead," Collin interjected.

Lord Reynard continued the tale. "I was angry my sister had wed without permission. We'd always been close. Her death affected me a great deal. I didn't want to lose the only part left of her so I told your father that Juetta and her babe had passed. He believed me and returned to Briarwood. We never saw him again."

Collin Campion said, "Uncle Reynard raised me. I always knew who my birth father was. Uncle Reynard told me when the Earl of Briargate passed, it would be time for me to claim my lands and title. I am here now for that very reason." He looked to Landon. "I've heard the king made you the new earl. That will change now since I am the rightful heir to Briarwood."

Campion reached for Cassiana's arm but she pulled away. "Landon may not be the earl but we will wed all the same."

Her half-brother's eyes glittered in anger. "*I* am the Earl of Briargate," he ground out. "As the earl and your closest male relative, 'tis my right to make the decision when and whom you wed." Collin looked to Landon. "Tell me, Lord Landon, do you hold claim to any other titles?"

"Nay."

"I suppose that makes you Sir Landon. And do you own any properties?"

"I do not."

Cassiana sensed the tension running through Landon since their hands were still joined.

"Under no circumstances would I see myself giving permission for a mere knight with no title and no estate to wed my sister. After all, where would the two of you go? You don't even own a bed to sleep in."

Campion's low laugh caused a chill to run along her spine. He looked around at the crowd and said, "Good people of Northumberland, no wedding will take place today. Feel free to join me and my sister in the great hall. We will celebrate that I come into my rightful inheritance this day."

He swung around and addressed Landon. "As for you, Sir Landon, I wish for you to leave my estate at once. Gather your things and be gone."

CHAPTER NINETEEN

R AGE COURSED THROUGH Landon. If he'd had his sword by his side, he might have drawn it and run it through this man. Losing the earldom and the estate pained him.

Losing Cassiana would destroy him.

Knowing he had no recourse at the moment, Landon raised their joined hands and pressed a light kiss upon her knuckles. "Farewell, my lady. May life bring you everything you could wish for." He released her hand and saw the fire blaze in her eyes and then she banked it, her face now placid.

She turned to the new earl and said, "Sir Landon's belongings are in the solar. With your permission, my lord, I will see them packed up so that he might vacate Briarwood."

Campion waved a hand dismissively. "A servant can do that."

She smiled graciously. "Not nearly as efficiently and quickly as I can. Please, go to the great hall for the celebration. I will join you once all traces of Sir Landon have been eliminated."

Cassiana turned and walked away with dignity, the crowd parting to allow her through. Landon began to follow her.

Katelyn stopped him, placing a hand upon his sleeve. Worry filled her face. "We will wait for you at the stables, Landon. You must come to Northmere with us."

He nodded curtly and moved away from the chapel, seeing Cassiana ahead of him. He hurried up the steps of the keep and found her waiting for him inside the door.

She clasped his hand and pulled him toward the stairs. "I tried to buy us time together so we can come up with a plan. Should I leave with you now?"

As they ascended, he tried to keep the despondency that had begun to blanket him from his voice and said, "You should remain at Briarwood. There's very little we can do."

"What?" She stopped, shock evident on her face. "You will not fight for me?"

He cupped her cheek. "I will leave straight for Windsor and make my case to the king. Only he has the authority to override any plans Campion may have for you."

Landon tugged her up the remaining stairs and toward the solar. As they went down the hall, he said, "Legally, you are under Campion's guardianship and he may choose the man he wishes for you to marry without input from you."

"He cannot make me say the vows," she snapped.

"Actually, he can," Landon revealed. "If you refuse to repeat the priest's words, he could merely wed you by proxy to the man he selects."

"Nay! I would enter a convent and pledge myself to God before I allowed myself to be wed to any man other than you."

They reached the solar and entered. He looked about what had already become a home to him. His eyes flickered toward the bedchamber, thinking of the things he had done with Cassiana in the large bed. Grief threatened to swallow him whole. Still, he masked it, not wanting her to know how desperate he felt their situation was.

"I will ask my cousin to allow our marriage to take place as planned. Edward might be feeling generous and award me a new property and title if one is available. If he doesn't, I'm certain he would be eager to take me back into his guard. The queen is fond of me. She would find a place for you in the royal household, most likely as a lady-in-waiting to her. We would be assigned a room at court."

Cassiana's eyes lit up. "All we need is a bed."

Landon gripped her shoulders. "Watch what you say from now on. You won't know if Campion has any spies or where they might be. He might have brought soldiers from Newfield—or even servants— with him. Don't let him know of our feelings toward one another."

"Why?"

"You are the one who once told me that knowledge is power. Collin Campion seems the type of man who might use the knowledge of our love against us. If anything, feign indifference toward me."

"I understand." She looked about the solar. "Gather your clothing. He also seems the type of man who would shred anything you left behind."

"I want to ride light. I'll only bring a change of clothing with me. I'll give my armor to Nicholas to take to Northmere."

"Nay, leave it—and your other clothing—with me. Take it to my chamber now. I'll give you gold to make your trip south."

While Cassiana retrieved coins for him from behind the hidden panel, Landon took every possession he owned to her bedchamber, including the parchment that awarded him his earldom. She joined him there, giving him a small pouch filled with coins. He slipped it under the cotehardie he wore, afraid if he left it in the small purse attached at his waist that Campion would stop him and demand its contents. He only had a few pieces of silver in it, all that was left after he'd purchased the amber pendant she now wore.

"Let us say our goodbyes here in private," he said. "If you don't care that I'm leaving, you wouldn't see me off outside."

Determination filled her face as she placed her palms against his chest. "Have faith, Landon. We are meant to be man and wife. My heart tells me so. God would not have brought us together only to rend us apart so cruelly. I will pray daily to the Blessed Virgin to intervene and resolve our problems."

Landon cradled her face between his hands, memorizing everything about her. Then their lips met in a searing kiss, one that he would remember in the days and nights to come.

He only hoped it wouldn't be their last.

Cassiana was the first to pull away. She lifted his hand, palm up, and pressed a tender kiss in its center. "I love you, Landon. I will wait for you. As long as it takes."

"Love was a word with no meaning. Until you came along," he replied. "I love you, Cassiana."

With that, he broke away from her and scooped up the extra set of clothes he would take on his journey. Hurrying from her bedchamber, Landon descended the stairs and passed the great hall. He stopped, seeing it was only a quarter full. Those who dined did so in silence. He glanced to the dais and saw the three intruders seated upon it. Collin Campion had taken the spot Landon had once sat in. Their eyes met, Campion's full of triumph. He raised a cup and then drank from it.

Landon left the keep. A voice called out to him. Turning, he saw Messina.

She caught up to him and handed him a small bundle. "Here, my lord. Something for you to eat on the road."

"Thank you, Messina. You have always been kind to me."

"We are all sorry, my lord. I know Lady Cassiana must be heartbroken."

Landon's throat grew thick. Instead of replying, he gave the servant a nod and continued walking briskly to the stables. Many horses were being saddled as wedding guests left Briarwood. No one met his eyes. He couldn't blame them.

Nicholas joined him. "Kate and I are ready to leave. I insist you come with us."

"Nay. I leave directly for Windsor."

"You plan to petition the king for Cassiana's hand and Briarwood?" his friend asked.

Landon shook his head. "Briarwood is lost. I accept that. What I won't accept is losing the woman I love."

Nicholas gripped his shoulder. "Then Godspeed, Landon. Our prayers are with you."

Katelyn rushed over and threw her arms about him. Her tears fell onto the cotehardie Cassiana had sewn. Landon tipped his sister's chin up.

"I go to our cousin now. I hope he will still allow me to wed Cassiana. Pray for me, Sister."

She kissed his cheek. "Be safe, Landon. I love you."

"And I you."

He watched as Nicholas helped Katelyn onto her horse. Then saw a groom bringing Orion to him.

"We will miss you, my lord," the stable hand said as he gave Landon the horse's reins.

"Whose horse is that?" a voice shouted.

Landon turned and saw none other than Collin Campion striding toward him, a smug look on his face. Landon gripped the reins in his hand, willing himself not to pummel the new earl into unconsciousness.

"You!" Campion cried, pointing at the young groom who'd brought Orion to Landon. "What's the name of that horse?"

"Orion, my lord," the groom said nervously.

Campion marched to him, his nose almost touching the groom's, and said, "Think very carefully before you answer me, boy. What you say will determine if you still have a place at Briarwood."

The young man swallowed hard. "Aye, my lord."

"Again. What's the name of that horse?"

"Orion."

"And did Sir Landon arrive on Orion when he came to Briarwood?" Campion demanded.

The groom swallowed again. "Nay, my lord. He walked from Berwick-upon-Tweed, as did the other soldiers who returned from France."

Campion took a step back, cocking his head to one side. "So, from what you say, Orion is a Briarwood horse. Who did he belong to before Sir Landon claimed the animal as his own?"

"Sir Tobyn. Lady Cassiana gave Orion to Lord—Sir Landon since he had no mount."

The new earl dusted his hands together. "Then Sir Landon will leave as he came. I'll have no horseflesh of mine taken by him." Campion turned and headed toward the keep then changed his mind. He returned to stand before Landon.

"Empty your purse," he commanded.

"Why?" Landon asked, knowing exactly what the earl did.

"I want to see if you are leaving with any of my monies."

He opened the purse and dumped the contents into his hand. Lifting it, he showed Campion. "This is what I came with."

"Good." The nobleman strode away without a backward glance.

The groom went to Landon, shaking his head, anguish obvious on his face. "I'm sorry, my lord. I've a wife and child to feed."

Landon handed the reins back to the man. "You did the right thing."

Nicholas hurried to him. He handed Landon the wedding band that was to have rested on Cassiana's finger. "You never know when you might need the ring and I may not be there when you do. Take my mount, Landon," his friend urged as Landon slipped the ring into his purse. "You need to reach the king as soon as possible. I can ride with Kate."

"Are you sure?"

"Of course." Nicholas threw his arms about Landon and pounded him on the back before pulling away and swinging up behind his wife.

Landon mounted his friend's horse and rode with the escort party from Northmere through the castle grounds and out the open gates. When they reached the main road, Landon gave a wave and turned south while the others ventured north. He urged the horse into a gallop.

He couldn't reach his cousin fast enough.

CASSIANA MADE SURE all of Landon's things were tucked out of sight. She wouldn't put it past her half-brother to glance into her bedchamber. Inhaling a long breath, she expelled it slowly, feeling calmer than she had. The smart thing would be to join the earl in the great hall and pretend to celebrate with him. Though it was the last place she wished to be, she remembered Landon's words. She would give this new relative nothing of herself.

As she left her chamber, she met Messina and two other servants in the corridor.

"I will see that the solar is cleaned beyond expectations," Messina assured her. "New bedclothes. The chamber pot emptied. There will be no trace of Lord Landon once we are done."

"Sir Landon," Cassiana corrected. "Please, Messina. Be careful. I fear this new earl has a quick temper."

"Aye, my lady."

Cassiana went to the great hall and saw only a handful of people gathered there. She assumed most of the wedding guests had left directly after Campion confronted her and Landon. Most of the people of Briarwood had chosen not to come to the feast in their new lord's honor, a risky move on their part. At least Campion didn't know any names yet so he wouldn't know who was present and who was missing.

She went to the dais and found her half-brother absent from his own feast. Only his uncle and the priest that accompanied them dined at the long, raised table.

Joining them, she asked, "Where is my brother? I was looking forward to conversing with him."

"He went to the stables. He'll be back shortly," Lord Reynard said.

She didn't pursue why he would do so, only hoping Landon had already left by the time Campion arrived and no confrontation had occurred between them.

Minutes later, the earl returned and came to sit next to her.

"Your solar is being cleaned as we dine, my lord. I think you will find everything to your satisfaction. If not, let me know and I will immediately address your concerns."

"Please, we are brother and sister," he said. "You must call me Collin."

"All right," she agreed. "It's still hard to imagine my father had another child—another wife—before my mother. It's a little upsetting."

His hand covered hers unexpectedly. She took pride in the fact that she didn't flinch.

"I know you've lost everyone dear to you, Cassiana. Your parents. All those brothers. Never fear. I am here now. I will take care of you."

"Thank you, Collin. I am relieved to hear that."

She tried to force down a few bites, not wanting him to grow suspicious. Instead, she asked him many questions as servants brought out course after course, trying to glean information that might prove useful. She learned of his childhood and his love of horses. That he preferred using a sword over a pike. He boasted of his prowess as a hunter. None of that interested her. Then she casually asked how close he was with Lord Reynard.

"He disgusts me," Campion said vehemently, his tongue loose

after so much wine. "I could have grown up here, known to all as the heir apparent. Instead, he selfishly kept me with him all these years. I wasn't even allowed to foster."

Leaning close to her, he said, "Uncle thinks I'll be an ally to him." He chuckled. "My only allegiance is to myself. And my lovely sister, of course."

Cassiana hoped to use the knowledge of a rift between the two men to her advantage, especially since the older man had no idea how his nephew truly felt.

Suddenly, Campion asked, "Why did you say that you would wed Sir Landon, even though he wasn't the Earl of Briargate?"

Cassiana knew all his talk had been to lull her. Then trap her.

Looking directly into his eyes, she said coolly, "Father always impressed upon me how important it was to honor a commitment. That my word was my bond, the same as a knight's would be. Though we weren't betrothed, the king had ordered us to wed. I had agreed to this with Sir Landon after reading the missive he brought from the king. I'd given him my word, Collin. I thought I must do so to honor what had been spoken between us."

She shrugged. "Frankly, I am glad you forbade us to wed." Cassiana raised her cup of wine and took a long sip, knowing she had to choose her words carefully in order for Campion to believe her.

"You are?" Campion leaned forward. "I'm intrigued. Explain yourself."

"Why would you be surprised? You were right in pointing out that Sir Landon came from nothing. In fact, after I read the king's missive and agreed to the marriage, I discovered that his father was a traitor to the crown and executed for treason. I had strong doubts about wedding him. Blood usually tells, you know, but the king had commanded it. I am not one to negate what our king wishes."

"Interesting." Campion leaned back. "I didn't know about de Blays' past."

"He is a cousin to the king. I'm sure King Edward will find Sir Landon another property and a different bride." She took a sip of wine and motioned for more to be brought to her.

Campion studied her. "You seem . . . indifferent."

"I'll admit that Sir Landon was quite handsome," she confided. "I knew I would have beautiful babes with him. He wasn't suited to run a property, though, especially not one the size of Briarwood. He's been a soldier his entire life and knows nothing about property management or how to care for our people."

"And you do."

Cassiana nodded. "I did help my father some once he became bedridden. Of course, I am merely a woman, my lord. You will find others can help you more than I can. Hobart is our steward and has been for many years. Sir Adam Crane is the captain of our guard. Men such as these will be able to guide you as you become familiar with the workings of Briarwood."

"I see." He pursed his lips. "May I ask how old you are?"

"Three and twenty."

"Why weren't you wed before now?" he asked curiously.

"When Mother died, I raised my five brothers. Then Father's wounds from a battle with the Scots were so serious that I took to nursing him for several years. I spent most of my days in his sick room. As you know, he only recently passed. Tobyn had plans to betroth me once he returned from the wars in France." Cassiana allowed her gaze to fall to her lap. "When he was killed in the fighting, I didn't know what would happen to me. Or Briarwood."

Campion placed an arm about her and pressed a kiss to her temple. She fought the urge to shrink away.

"I am here now, Cassiana. I will take care of you. And Briarwood."

CHAPTER TWENTY

L ANDON HAD ONLY ridden a few minutes when a rider emerged from the woods to his right. He signaled Landon to stop. Warily, he approached and then recognized none other than Baldwin Gifford.

The knight glanced both ways and said, "I took the shortcut through the woods, hoping to intercept you, Lord Landon. Will you enter them with me? I don't think we should be seen together."

For a moment, Landon hesitated. Was this man here at Collin Campion's bidding, trying to confirm where Landon rode? Though the knight had been loyal to him when he was Earl of Briargate, his loyalty would now lie with the new earl. Then he decided to give Sir Baldwin the benefit of the doubt. The soldier had stepped forward and offered proof to Cassiana of how Landon had tried to save Tobyn. That act alone had earned trust.

He nodded and steered his horse from the road. Baldwin followed and then dismounted once they could no longer see the road for the trees. Landon did the same.

"What was so urgent that you needed to speak to me in secret?" he asked.

"Our conversation definitely needed to be held privately. I know I am breaking my oath to the Campion family by even being here—but something troubled me enough that I believed I should seek you out."

The knight looped his horse's reins around a low lying branch. Landon followed suit and then faced Baldwin.

"I fostered with the Baron of Newfield. As did Lord Darwin. Darwin was two years older than I but we became close in our many years together at Newfield. He did not wed Juetta Payne. Of that, I'm certain."

"Why do you say that? Collin Campion is the very image of Tobyn. For a moment, I thought both you and I were wrong or that Tobyn returned from the dead, so strong was the resemblance between the two."

Baldwin raked a hand through his graying hair. "First, Darwin was betrothed and had been from the age of ten and two. A betrothal is legally binding so even if, by some chance, he did marry Lady Juetta? Their union would not have stood."

"If what you say is true, that means Collin Campion is a bastard. Unable to inherit his father's title and lands," Landon concluded, feeling a glimmer of hope.

"Darwin thought he might have lain with the lady, though it was totally out of character for him. He was a most principled man." Baldwin paused. "Let me explain. 'Tis a bit complicated."

He seated himself on a fallen log. "We never saw Juetta Payne with the rest of her family. Her brothers and sister were always present. At mass. Dining in the great hall. But Lady Juetta remained a mystery. Sometimes, I caught a glimpse of her from a parapet as she looked down on us in the training yard but she never made an appearance."

"Why not?"

Baldwin shrugged. "Rumors abounded. That she was disfigured. Crippled. Mad. No one knew for certain. Then during one May Day celebration, the last Darwin participated in before he left for Briarwood a week later, we all had too much to drink. Darwin disappeared in the merriment. I thought nothing of it until he didn't return to the barracks. I lay awake, waiting for him, worrying as time passed.

"Just before dawn, he stumbled in, unsteady on his feet. I met him and led him back outside. Thrust his head in a trough of cold water to try and help him clear his head. Then I asked him where he'd been."

The knight stared off, as if trying to remember the exact conversation. Finally, he said, "Darwin could always hold his drink, better than most. He told me he thought someone had tampered with his cup, though. His head and body seemed to separate. He left the festivities and passed out somewhere along the way back to the barracks. When he came to, he was lying in a bed. With a beautiful young woman. She was naked atop him and kissing him. He could only remember bits and pieces—but he did recall her whispering a name into his ear.

"*Juetta.*"

Landon's mouth fell open. "She somehow . . . seduced him? This unseen woman?"

"Darwin's memory of the night faded quickly as he came to his senses, much as when a dream vanishes in the light of day. He did recall Juetta saying something about how she longed for a child and hoped he gave her one." Baldwin sighed. "It wouldn't surprise me if Reynard Payne had something to do with the incident."

"So, you believe this child is Collin Campion, and he's Lord Darwin's bastard."

"I do, Lord Landon. That would make you the rightful earl. There's more, though. Something's off about the priest that came with them."

"Father Barnard?"

"Aye. Father Bennett was the Newfield priest during all my time there. Said mass daily. Officiated at all weddings. I never heard of this Father Barnard, much less why he would be the one to have supposedly wed Darwin to Lady Juetta." Baldwin scratched his chin. "Besides, there's something familiar about him. As if I've seen him before."

A plan began to form in Landon's head. "Thank you for sharing what you knew from the past with me, Sir Baldwin."

"I thought you would head south and to the king to petition him for Lady Cassiana's hand despite Campion's harsh words toward you. All of us at Briarwood are quite fond of her. We can see the great affection between the two of you." The knight looked at him hopefully. "Mayhap, you could call at Newfield since it's on your way. I don't know if you could discover more than I've told you, but it's worth a try to find proof that Collin Campion is not the legal heir."

Landon clapped the soldier on the back. "I'll head for Newfield now. Be careful. If you fostered there, Lord Reynard might recognize you. If he or Campion thinks you might know something that could hurt their scheme to take Briarwood, you could be in danger."

"I had no beard when I left Newfield and a head full of dark hair." Baldwin smiled. "With my graying hair and beard, I'm sure I look much different from my younger self. Still, I will take your advice and ask to be relieved of my duties in the training yard. By not serving as Sir Adam's second-in-command, I can blend in with the other soldiers at work."

"You are an excellent soldier, Sir Baldwin. Why didn't Lord Darwin ever make you his captain?"

"I told him not to," confessed the knight. "When it came time to name a new captain of the guard, Darwin wanted me in the position. While I am an accomplished knight, I knew Sir Adam's leadership skills would serve him better as our captain. I'm happy to step in when needed."

"You have been a faithful servant to the Campions. I hope the next time we meet will be under better circumstances."

Landon freed his reins and mounted his borrowed horse.

"Godspeed, Lord Landon," called Sir Baldwin as Landon rode away with hope in his heart.

CASSIANA DRESSED FOR the day and, as usual, went to mass. It pained her as she crossed the threshold to the chapel, knowing she'd stood there the day before with Landon by her side. They were supposed to speak their vows and then walk inside the chapel hand-in-hand for the rest of the nuptial mass. This morning, they should have awakened side-by-side, newly wed.

Instead, she entered alone, wondering how far Landon had traveled yesterday. The gossip had reached her regarding Campion demanding that Orion stay at Briarwood and how Nicholas Mandeville had offered Landon his own horse. Anger seethed at how petty her half-brother was. He acted in a confident manner but she believed he was filled with doubts regarding his abilities.

Cassiana didn't bother listening to what Father Peter had to say. Her constant prayer, echoed over and over in her mind, appealed to the Virgin to make things right. To keep Landon safe on his journey to the king. To see the two of them wed. She didn't care where they lived, as long as they could be together.

As Cassiana left mass, she noticed none of the Newfield arrivals had been present. She found Campion and his uncle already on the dais. The priest who'd accompanied them was missing.

Seating herself, she smiled sweetly and said, "I missed you at mass this morning, Collin."

He shrugged. "I needed to see Father Barnard off."

"He's already left for Newfield?"

"Aye. He's needed there. Briarwood already has its own priest."

Cassiana looked to Reynard Payne. "And how long might you stay with us, my lord?"

"I'm not sure. I want to make sure Collin is settled in with his new duties before I depart."

She didn't need an experienced nobleman guiding Campion and

decided to appeal to her half-brother's vanity.

Touching his sleeve, she said, "Oh, Collin seems most intelligent, my lord. I know he will have no trouble making any decision. After all, Briarwood is now his. He should do as he pleases with it."

A scowl flashed across Payne's face. He lifted a cup of ale and downed it.

Her words had the effect she wanted, though. Campion turned to his uncle.

"Cassiana is right, Uncle. I am a grown man. You have raised me well. I can manage my new estate and people without your constant advice."

Payne bristled at the rude remark. Cassiana saw he restrained from lashing out but it took a great effort to do so.

"You may leave today," Campion suggested. "Please give Lady Druscilla my best."

The nobleman stood abruptly. He bowed to them and left the dais.

"Your uncle seems upset," she said. "I wonder why."

Campion brushed her comment aside. "Uncle Reynard still thinks of me as a child. I am a grown man, though, with my own estate. One much larger than his. I fear he's become jealous of all that I now possess."

She patted his arm. "You don't need anyone telling you what to do."

"You're right about that." Campion tore off a piece of bread and chewed thoughtfully. "What did you say the steward's name was?"

"Hobart. I can show you where the records room is once we finish breaking our fast."

"Good. I have urgent correspondence for him to see to. It must be sent out today."

Cassiana thought she'd already pushed him enough for now. She could always seek out Hobart and find what the correspondence regarded.

"After you finish speaking with Hobart, mayhap I could show you about your estate."

He flashed her a smile. For a moment, her heart stopped. She could see pieces of Tobyn and her other brothers in this man. She mustn't let that influence the way she thought of him, though. He was her enemy. One who'd parted her from Landon.

"I'd like that. I'll meet you in the stables once I have spoken to the steward."

"Then I'll meet with Cook. Do you have any favorite dishes, Collin? I'm sure she would be happy to make them for you."

He suggested several to her and they went their separate ways. Men always seemed to be placated by food in her experience. She and Cook arranged what to serve for the next several days and then Cassiana walked to the stables. She could tell others observed her but none were willing to meet her eyes. She supposed if they did, she would see the pity in theirs. It hadn't been a secret how she and Landon felt about one another. He'd also won over the residents at Briarwood and she knew everyone at the estate must be sad for how the situation had turned out.

Cassiana asked for Tressa to be saddled, telling the groom that she and the earl would be riding together. When the stable hand appeared, he led both Tressa and Orion. She swallowed hard, thinking how magnificent Landon had looked atop the horse.

She waited until her half-brother appeared, a spring in his step.

"You seem very happy," she noted.

"I am happy to be riding with my newfound sister on my property," he replied as he helped her mount Tressa and then climbed upon Orion. "Lead the way, my lady."

They walked their horses through the bailey. Cassiana named everyone they passed, from carpenters to blacksmiths to squires.

As they went by the training yard, she said, "Briarwood's captain of the guard is Sir Adam Crane. He's a Northumberland man and had

Father's confidence."

"I'll make my own judgment of him," Campion said quickly.

Cassiana wanted to protest, thinking Sir Adam might be replaced, but thought better of it. Her half-brother's moods seemed to change swiftly.

They cleared the castle's gates and picked up the pace. She showed him the fields where their crops grew and took him to the mill, where they stopped and spoke with William. Afterward, they rode through the countryside, seeing livestock and where the horses were trained, and saw many of the cottages dotting the land.

"I call on our tenants at least once a week," she shared.

"Whatever for?"

She hid her dismay. "To build a relationship with them. I see that their needs are being met. It's important to know them and their families."

Campion snorted. "They are the ones who should see that my needs are met."

"As their liege lord, you are responsible for their protection," Cassiana pointed out. "We are close to the Scottish border and the sea. The threat of invasion is always present."

"Is there a nearby village?" he asked, changing the subject.

"Aye. Stony Eastbridge lies next to the sea and is only a couple of miles from us. Would you like to see it?"

"I would."

Cassiana directed them east. The smell of salt and fish grew stronger as they neared the village. She told him a little about each shop and suggested they stop at the inn for something to eat and drink since they'd been out a good part of the day and had missed the midday meal.

The innkeeper himself brought them steaming bowls of fish stew and tall tankards of ale. She chatted with the man, asking about his wife and their newborn son, telling him she would look in on them in a few days.

"My wife will be pleased to see you, my lady," the innkeeper proclaimed and excused himself.

"He should have been more deferential toward me," Campion complained once the man left. "I am his superior. As an earl, he should have treated me with more respect."

Once again, Cassiana kept silent. If she defended the innkeeper, it might cause trouble for the man—or for her.

They finished their stew and when it came time to pay, Campion simply walked out. Shocked, Cassiana dug into her purse and handed over a coin, receiving a grateful smile.

Outside, Campion helped her remount Tressa and then climbed on Orion.

"Are you going to pay him?" she asked, tired of remaining quiet.

"I may. He should consider the fact I even stopped at his establishment to be payment enough. If the Earl of Briargate eats there, so will others."

"Father always paid in full," Cassiana said. "He understood that working men needed every coin to survive."

Campion's eyes narrowed. "I'm not your father."

"He was your father, too."

"My uncle was father enough to me." He paused, studying her so long that she grew uncomfortable with his gaze. "I will pay when and where I choose. You're not to question me again, Cassiana. Do you understand?"

"Aye, Collin," she said meekly.

They returned to Briarwood and left their horses at the stable. Campion said he wanted to visit the training yard and strode off in that direction. Cassiana asked a groom if Lord Reynard had departed and was told he'd left several hours ago. She found it interesting that a rift had already occurred between uncle and nephew and hoped without Lord Reynard guiding him that it would take Campion longer to take action. She was already worried about his temper and how it might affect the residents of Briarwood.

Heading back to the keep, she decided to speak to Hobart since Campion was busy with their soldiers. Her gut told her he would not approve of her checking up on him, much less learning what he'd directed Hobart to do.

Cassiana went directly to the records room and found Hobart hunched over a parchment, scribbling away.

"Am I interrupting?"

The steward looked up. Something in his eyes made her wary. She shut the door and sat in the chair before his massive desk.

"Campion is in the training yard so you may speak freely. Tell me about the correspondence he wanted sent out so quickly."

Hobart's distress was evident. "My lady, you won't like it." He shook his head. "I've spent all day copying the same message he dictated to me to go out throughout Northumberland. To every noble family, great and small."

"What message? Tell me."

"Collin Campion seeks a husband for you. And plans to sell you to the highest bidder."

CHAPTER TWENTY-ONE

L ANDON CANTERED INTO Old Smotley, the nearest village to
Newfield. He didn't want to head directly to the castle. He would
see what he could learn from the residents in this fishing village,
remembering Cassiana's motto that knowledge is power. The more he
knew about the situation before he visited Newfield, the better.

During the long hours of riding south, he wondered who he might
confront at the castle. If anyone would be willing to speak to him,
much less confirm anything Sir Baldwin had told him about Lord
Darwin's time at Newfield. More than anything, he wished to hear
about the mysterious Lady Juetta.

He saw several fishing boats some distance from land as he rounded a corner in the road and came upon a row of cottages, followed by
a small shop, an inn, and a blacksmith's shed. He decided to start with
the blacksmith first and steered his horse in that direction. Landon
regretted not learning the name of Nicholas' horse before he'd set out
on this journey. He was still grateful to his brother-in-law for providing him a mount. He knew both Nicholas and Katelyn worried about
him. His sister didn't need to suffer any anxiety in her present
condition. Landon could only pray his situation would soon be

resolved so that he could send word to Northmere.

"Greetings," a burly man with a thick, blond beard called as Landon approached.

He swung from his horse. "I'm journeying to London and hoped that you might have a moment to look at my horse's front left hoof. I want to make sure the shoe fits properly since I have such a long way to go. It seemed to be troubling him some for the last mile or so."

"I can look at all four, my lord." The blacksmith lay down his hammer and came forward as Landon looped his reins around a post.

The smithy lifted each hoof and inspected it thoroughly. "They're all in good condition but I'd have someone look at them once you reach your destination. 'Tis a long way to go and can be rough on a horse's hooves to travel so far."

"This is a beautiful area," noted Landon. "Did you grow up here?"

"Aye. And I'm raising two fine children here, a boy and a girl, four and two."

"I passed what I believe is Newfield a few minutes ago. I recently met the baron at a wedding."

"Did you now?" The blacksmith entered his shed.

"Aye. Someone accompanied him. I can't remember if he said it was his son or not."

"The baron's son is away, fostering south of here. 'Twas probably his bastard you met. Collin."

"Aye, that was the name. His bastard, you say?"

The smithy shrugged. "He claimed the boy as his but who knows? I heard from others, many years ago, that Collin was the brat of Lord Reynard's sister. The baron's raised him alongside his own son and two daughters."

The conversation died and Landon decided he would gain nothing further by staying.

He passed a coin to the man. "Thank you for looking at my horse. Is there any place nearby for a quick meal?"

The blacksmith pointed across the street. "The inn. My sister wed the innkeeper and she does all of the cooking. Mary's a better cook than our mother ever was."

"Then I will stop and eat there before I'm on my way. Again, I thank you. Might I leave my horse here?"

"Of course, my lord."

Landon ventured across the street and entered the inn. Only one other man sat at a table, sopping bread into the remains of a bowl.

"Good afternoon, my lord. Are you here for a meal or to stay the night?" a friendly voice called out.

He turned and saw a plump woman with the same blond hair of the blacksmith and said, "You must be Mary. Your brother told me you're a fine cook and I'm a hungry man. I'll eat anything you prepare as long as there's plenty of it."

Looking pleased, she said, "Have a seat, my lord."

Landon sat at the table perched next to the fire. Mary brought him a large tankard of cold ale and promised to return soon. When she did, it was with a side of mutton and a fragrant stew of cod, along with pears and cheese and an entire loaf of bread. By this time the other man had left, leaving only the two of them.

"Please, Mary, join me while I eat. I'm traveling alone to London. 'Twould be nice to share some company before I'm off again."

She sat on the bench opposite him and began chatting about the weather and people in the village. Landon allowed her to go on and as she grew more comfortable, he started asking a few questions. Finally, he steered her toward discussing the people at Newfield.

"Ah, Newfield's a big place. My cousin works in the keep as a servant."

"What does she say about the family? I recently meet Lord Reynard and his son, Collin, at a wedding up north."

Her nose curled in distaste. "Lord Reynard is hard to please and that's on a good day. The baroness is much kinder, as are her son and daughters. But Collin Payne?" Mary snorted. "He's vicious, that one. And not Lady Druscilla's son, if you get what I mean."

"He's Lord Reynard's bastard?"

"Aye. Brought up alongside his true children. The baroness had no say in that. Rumor has it the boy's actually Lord Reynard's nephew."

"Is that so?"

Mary shrugged. "My cousin tells me of a room at the top of the turret. No one's allowed in it to clean. Only Lady Druscilla and one old servant come and go from there. From what I gather, Collin Payne spent time up there when he was young. Not so much once he grew older. He's probably a score and five or six now. My cousin says he never goes to the turret anymore and has never spoken about it."

"Interesting," Landon mused.

He allowed Mary to talk more about her cousin and Newfield but learned nothing else useful.

Putting a last bite in his mouth, he sighed. "That was truly a fine meal, Mary. I'm glad your brother pointed me in your direction but I must be on my way. If I ever come north again, I will be sure to stop in Old Smotley simply to dine on your food."

She blushed. "Thank you, my lord."

Landon gave her a coin and a smile and left the inn. He retrieved his horse and continued through the village before doubling back and heading north again toward Newfield. He stopped in the woods and changed into his other tunic, not nearly as fine as the one he'd worn for his wedding. He wanted to appear more messenger than nobleman, though he was sure he'd be viewed as the knight he was. Once he reached the gates, he called up to the gatekeeper.

"I come from Briarwood and bring a missive for Lady Druscilla from Lord Reynard," deliberately not providing a name but knowing by using both the baron and baroness' names, he should be granted entrance.

As expected, the gates opened and he rode through.

The gatekeeper shouted, "Take your horse to the stables to be watered and fed. The keep is half a mile to the north of there."

"My thanks."

Landon found the stables and handed his horse off and then set out to the keep. Once inside, he explained to a passing servant who he was and why he was there.

"Follow me, my lord," she said after giving him a saucy smile.

They went upstairs and the servant knocked upon a door. When bidden to enter, she did so, signaling him to remain in the hallway. Moments later, she opened the door and ushered him inside as she left.

Landon saw a plain woman of two score sitting by the fire, her sewing in her lap. No one else was present, which suited his purpose.

"I'm told you have a missive for me." She set the sewing aside and held out her hand.

"I have no written message, Lady Druscilla," Landon began. "Actually, I've come for answers."

The noblewoman didn't look frightened. Instead, she appeared curious as she studied him.

"My best guess is that you are Lord Landon de Blays, former Earl of Briargate."

His pulse jumped. "You are quite astute, my lady."

She smiled. "I wasn't expecting you, my lord. 'Tis a bold move on your part." Her eyes, a lively blue, sparkled. "Have a seat," she directed. "I look forward to what you have to say."

Landon did as asked and said, "You did not accompany your husband and Collin Campion to Briarwood."

"Nay. I wasn't asked and wouldn't have gone if offered the chance. Why would I wish to see you robbed of what is rightfully yours?"

"You know this to be true?"

Lady Druscilla shrugged. "I'm happy to share what I know with you. My husband and Collin are dishonest men. Bastards of the worst kind. In Collin's case, quite literally."

Landon leaned forward. "I have so many questions, my lady, but I'm going to sit and let you speak."

"That calls for wine."

She stood and went to the table, pouring them both ample amounts in intricate pewter cups and then bringing the cups back with her. Offering him one, he took it and waited eagerly to hear what she might reveal.

"You might wonder why I'd be willing to speak openly to a stranger, especially when it smacks of disloyalty to my husband. Lord Reynard is a vile man. I've suffered under his heavy hand for more years than I can count. If I can help you reclaim what belongs to you and see him and Collin suffer, then I am the true winner in this game."

The noblewoman settled back into her chair, her wine in hand.

"Reynard has a twin sister. Juetta, Collin's mother. He and Juetta have always been close. From the beginning, though, something was off about Juetta. As she grew older, the family thought it wise to isolate her from others. She had a raging temper and would laugh uncontrollably for hours. Eventually, they settled her in a room in the north turret and charged a servant with her care. Juetta never appeared in public. Naturally, rumors ran rampant. I can tell you, she's quite mad."

Landon wondered why the baroness spoke of her sister-in-law as if she still lived, knowing the woman had died shortly after giving birth to Collin.

"Reynard always spent time with her. Being twins, they were close. Juetta decided that she wanted a child. Of course, by the time she was of age to wed, her parents knew she was mad and decided not to betroth her to any man. Juetta and Reynard hatched some plot between them. This was a year before I came to Newfield but after living here all the years, I've learned the bones of their scheme.

"Juetta used to watch exercises in the training yard and chose the man she wanted to father her child."

"Darwin Campion," uttered Landon.

The baroness nodded. "Reynard put something in the Sir Darwin's cup. Who knows what or how he got it. Nevertheless, he brought—more likely, dragged—Sir Darwin to his sister's bedchamber in the hopes that a child would result from their coupling. It did. From all accounts, Sir Darwin left Newfield shortly after this illicit encounter and never returned, probably none the wiser."

Landon frowned. "Your husband told us that Lord Darwin wed his sister, my lady. That Darwin returned to claim his wife after he gained his earldom and that he found Juetta had died in childbirth. Lord Reynard admitted lying to the earl and telling him that the babe—Collin—had died, too. The baron said he missed his sister dreadfully and wanted to keep a part of her with him."

Lady Druscilla sniffed. "What rubbish! I had wed Reynard by the time Juetta gave birth to Collin. Darwin Campion never set foot at Newfield and he never knew about the child. My husband and Collin lied to you about that."

She leaned forward. "That wasn't the only falsehood that came from his lips, Lord Landon. Juetta Payne is alive. I know—because I am her jailer."

CHAPTER TWENTY-TWO

L ANDON'S MOUTH GAPED as he absorbed what the noblewoman revealed.

Lady Druscilla drained her cup of wine and set it on the table. "I would offer to take you to see her but she is hostile to any visitors. Only a servant who has cared for her from childhood and I enter her turret room these days."

"Lady Juetta never leaves there?"

"Never. I bring her meals. Try to bathe her when she lets me. She'll go for weeks and rarely speak, making guttural sounds from howls to whimpers. Occasionally, she'll become quite talkative but her mind has deteriorated over the years."

"What . . . what kind of a mother was she to Collin?" Landon asked, wondering what it would be like for a child to be locked in a room with a mother gone mad.

"Childbirth was a greater ordeal to Juetta than most women. I tried to tell her what to expect but she wouldn't listen. Once she gave birth to Collin, she wanted nothing to do with him for the first few days. Finally, I convinced her to feed him so her milk wouldn't dry up." She sighed. "Juetta seemed to enjoy him when he was a babe. It was as if she played with a doll. She would dress and undress him, over and over. Feed him. Comb his hair. As he got older and less manageable, she lost interest in him."

The noblewoman stood and returned with the wine, pouring herself more. When she offered him more, Landon waved her away, wanting to concentrate on the rest of her tale.

"I gave birth to my first child three months after Collin was born. I would take my daughter to the turret room and rock her. Sing to her. I tried my best to show Juetta what a mother should do but the babe she thought she wanted was more trouble than she'd imagined. And then the day came when I finally had to take Collin away from her."

Lady Druscilla took another sip of wine to fortify herself. "The boy was almost two and growing very stubborn. I'd had hot water brought up so Juetta could bathe him. I remember I had a fierce cough that had settled into my chest. I turned away, coughing up phlegm, and heard Collin splashing wildly. By the time the coughing spell ended and I looked back, I saw Juetta held him under the water, trying to drown him. He was flailing—not splashing.

"That was when I brought him into the nursery downstairs. Collin never returned to Juetta's care again."

Landon couldn't imagine a mother trying to murder her own babe but he'd never known anyone unbalanced as Lady Juetta was.

"On occasion, Reynard and I would bring Collin to visit Juetta. The boy was terrified of her and, frankly, she didn't seem to care if he came to see her or not. When Collin turned seven, he told Reynard and me that he no longer would see her. That his mother was dead to him."

She rubbed her eyes. "That was about the time Juetta's anger began to rage out of control. She no longer wanted Reynard to stop by and visit with her. She would become feral if he or anyone else came and we had to restrain her many times. She does tolerate me for some reason and her old nursemaid. Nowadays, we are the only two who ever see her. Even then, it takes much out of me."

They sat in silence a few minutes. Landon had trouble taking in everything that had been said.

Finally, he asked, "Can you tell me about the priest that accompanied your husband and his nephew? I'm wondering why a man of the cloth would blatantly lie about performing a marriage between Lord Darwin and Lady Juetta."

"I can tell you that Father Bennett hasn't left Newfield. He is the only priest we've had since I've been at Newfield. Describe this priest."

Landon recalled Sir Baldwin mentioning the same name of Father Bennett, which confirmed the knight's memories.

"He was on the short side. Balding. About two score, with a small scar above one eyebrow. Father Barnard was his name."

She rolled her eyes. "That was no priest, Lord Landon. 'Twas our assistant steward playing the role of one. Barnard vanished when my husband and Collin went north to Briarwood. He returned earlier today. When I asked him where he'd gone off to, he grew nervous and said he'd been on secret business for my husband." She thought a moment. "Did he produce any kind of proof that the wedding had taken place?"

"He did," Landon confirmed. "I'm ashamed to say none of us asked to read the document he produced. We took him at his word, believing him to be one called to God." Anger coursed through him. "Did your husband plan all along for Collin to try and force his way into a false inheritance?"

Lady Druscilla grew thoughtful. "I don't think so. At first, he was merely pleased to have the boy. We raised Collin with our three children. He even carried the last name of Payne. Reynard put out that Collin was his bastard but those who'd known Sir Darwin could see how much the boy favored him. Most people guessed Juetta was Collin's mother. It's been an open secret at Newfield for many years."

She stood and began pacing the room. "My husband has not been a good manager of Newfield. He also has huge gambling debts. I believe the scheme to pass Collin off as Lord Darwin's legal heir began to formulate a few years ago, when Reynard's gambling began to rage out of control. Somehow, Reynard must think that Collin will pay him back for the kindness he showed the boy in raising him as his own son." Lady Druscilla shook her head in sorrow. "It will never happen."

"Why do you say that?"

"I fear Collin is touched by his mother's madness. Oh, he's not totally unhinged as she is. His temper, though, is volatile. The smallest thing can set it off. He has Juetta's arrogance and unpredictability, as well. Once he gains control of his own estate, he will quickly turn his back on my husband. Collin has always thought of himself, first and foremost."

Landon drew a deep breath. "I need to stop him, my lady. I know I'm asking much of you. Is there any way you can speak the truth and help me confront Collin? It would help if I could also get the false priest to confess his part in the scheme, as well."

Lady Druscilla paused in front of the fire, her back to him. Long minutes passed. Landon knew she fought within herself and could understand the turmoil. She was in an impossible situation—yet she was his only hope.

Turning, she said, "You've given me a choice of betraying my husband or seeing the truth come to light. I cannot in good faith go to God someday with this on my conscience. No amount of confession would clear my soul." She nodded, determination shining in her eyes. "I will accompany you to Briarwood and see that Barnard goes with us."

Landon stood and went to her, taking her hand and kissing it. "If you feel it's not safe for you to return with Lord Reynard to Newfield, you would be welcomed to remain at Briarwood."

A genuine smile lit her face. "That is beyond kind, my lord. What I would ask is that you provide me an escort to my older daughter's estate. I like her husband better than my younger daughter's. She will not turn me out. In fact, she has begged me to come to her for protection. I will be safe there."

Tipping the cup to her lips, she finished the remainder of her wine. "I will send for Barnard. We will tell him he's to accompany us to Briarwood. He's been at Newfield for many years. I'm sure Reynard threatened him with dismissal or worse if he didn't play along. Two of Barnard's children are grown and wed. His last child is quite simple and needs extra care and his wife passed a few months ago. Instead of me, would you be willing to take on Barnard and this son at Briarwood? Once he speaks out against my husband, he could never return here."

"I will be happy to put him to work at Briarwood and see that his son is cared for," Landon assured her.

"Wait here. I will have a servant locate Barnard and have my things packed and sent to my daughter's home. If it pleases you, we will leave at first light tomorrow for Briarwood."

Landon bowed his head. "Of course, my lady."

He went and stood by the fire, contemplating what would cause men such as Reynard Payne and Collin to swear upon such lies. Their words affected him and Cassiana directly but, indirectly, many more lives had been touched by this falsehood. He only hoped Cassiana was holding her own against the unstable pretender. He couldn't reach her soon enough.

Lady Druscilla returned to the solar with two servants who carried a trunk. They took it into the bedchamber and he assumed they were packing her things. Moments later, the man who'd called himself Father Barnard entered. The moment he saw Landon standing in the room, his steps faltered. He looked poised like a bird ready to take flight.

"I would stay where you are, Barnard," warned Lady Druscilla, her tone calm yet deadly. "You have much to answer for. If you flee, Lord

Landon will merely chase you down and beat you within an inch of your life."

The steward fell upon his knees. "Forgive me, my lady," he cried.

"It's not my forgiveness you need, Barnard. It's Lord Landon's."

Barnard began to weep. "He forced me to lie, my lord. He said if I didn't help him, he would turn me out without references or pay. I have a son, a special boy. A son who needs me."

Landon went to him and grasped his elbow, bringing the man to his feet.

"I cannot understand the lie but I do understand wishing to protect your son. You love him and wanted no harm to come to him. I'm willing to overlook your actions against me but you must help me in return."

"Anything, my lord," the steward said hastily.

"Then you will come to Briarwood with me and confront Lord Reynard and the man calling himself Collin Campion."

Barnard's eyes went wide. He sputtered, no words coming from his mouth.

"I will be there, Barnard. So will Lady Druscilla. The truth will come out—and then you and your son will remain at Briarwood under my protection."

"You mean it?" He glanced to Lady Druscilla and back to Landon.

"I do."

Relief swept over the steward. "Then I will be happy to journey with you, my lord. I felt a stain so black on my soul. I hope you—and God—might forgive me."

"I already have. The rest is for you to confess. Pack your things. We leave first thing tomorrow." Landon thought a moment. "Do you ride, my lady? Barnard, do you?"

"I enjoy riding, Lord Landon," the noblewoman said. "Barnard may ride with his son on one of the Newfield horses and keep it if he wishes."

"Thank you, my lady," the steward whispered.

"Not a word to anyone," Landon warned.

"I promise to keep silent, my lord." Barnard left the solar.

He looked to Lady Druscilla. "What about caring for Lady Juetta?" he asked.

She gave him a long look. "That will be my husband's problem."

Landon made a final decision. "I know you think it a poor idea, my lady, but I would like to meet Lady Juetta. If I see her alive with my own eyes, I can attest to that when we meet with your husband and his nephew."

Doubts flickered in her eyes but she said, "As you wish."

LANDON ACCOMPANIED LADY Druscilla up a narrow staircase that led to the turret room in which Lady Juetta resided. He wanted to bring her some little gift that might help ease them into conversation—if that was even possible. The recent frost had eliminated most of the flowers he might have picked as a bouquet so he'd asked for a small piece of wood and carved her a figure with his baselard before they'd eaten the evening meal.

An old woman hobbled down the staircase, carrying a tray. She paused when she saw them headed in her direction.

"Did she eat?" the noblewoman asked the servant.

"She did. More than usual. She even spoke to me some and she hasn't in weeks."

They let the servant pass and then continued to the top of the stairs. Hanging by the door was a set of keys that Lady Druscilla lifted.

"Let me go in first and see if I can smooth the way for you. I can't guarantee that she will see you, much less speak with you."

She placed the key in the lock and swung open the door. Stepping inside, she let the door remain partially open so Landon was able to catch a glimpse of the woman. Her hair was stark white, though her face seemed unlined except for a few lines about her eyes.

"Juetta, I've brought a visitor to see you."

A low guttural sound came from the prisoner's throat and then she erupted. "Not Reynard. I hate him! Go away, go away, go away!" She went to the wall and began pounding her forehead against it.

"Stop," Lady Druscilla said. "I know not to bring your brother here. It's a handsome knight that wishes to speak with you, not Reynard."

The madwoman moved away from the wall. Landon could see blood running down her face from where she'd bashed her brow against the stone.

"How handsome?"

"Very handsome."

Lady Juetta shrugged and plopped into a chair. Her head fell and she began humming off-key, wringing her hands in her lap.

Lady Druscilla turned and motioned to Landon. He entered the chamber and said softly, "Would you wait outside? I think she'll be more willing to speak to me if you're not present."

Reluctantly, the noblewoman agreed and stepped into the corridor, closing the door behind her.

Immediately, Lady Juetta's head popped up. An odd grimace twisted her lips awkwardly, as if she'd forgotten how to smile. She studied him carefully.

"You are handsome. But I won't couple with you."

"I didn't expect you to do so," Landon replied calmly. "I know you did that with Sir Darwin."

Her eyes lit up in recognition of the name. "You know Darwin?" she asked eagerly.

"Nay, but I have met his son and daughter."

Lady Juetta frowned. "I didn't know he had a daughter. I gave him a son. I thought I wanted one. With Darwin. I used to watch him in the training yard. Darwin stuck his thing in me and it hurt. It hurt more when the babe came out. He doesn't come to see me anymore."

Her rambling stopped suddenly. She twisted her finger around a lock of her hair and stared across the room at the wall.

"I'm sorry to hear that. Did you know Sir Darwin for long?"

"I only knew him in the Biblical sense, my lord," she said slyly and cackled.

Landon pretended to take in her words and then asked, "You never wed him?"

"Wed him? Nay. We were never married. We just lay together and made a child. Darwin left. He never came back. I just wanted his babe. He was a beautiful man. Collin was a beautiful boy. He was afraid of me, though." She gave him a knowing look. "They all are. Even Druscilla. Even though she pretends she isn't."

Lady Juetta leaned forward. "Do you know who she should be afraid of? Reynard. He beats her, you know," she said matter-of-factly. "He got smarter. She used to come to me with a blackened eye or split lip. Then no more. But I would see the pain in her eyes. I'd touch her arm and she'd wince. Push back her sleeve and see the bruises lining her pale skin. Reynard is evil.

"And they think I'm the one who's mad. He's much worse because he *likes* hurting people."

Landon couldn't help but think of how she tried to drown her own child.

He opened his palm and extended it toward her. She looked at the wooden figure a moment and then snatched it from his hand, examining it with care. As she turned it over and over, she began humming again.

"I thought you would like it. I carved it for you."

The noblewoman grinned. He could see several of her teeth were missing and her gums had blackened.

"This looks like me. When I was a girl. I was pretty, you know.

But not anymore."

"I thought since you'd birthed a son, you might want a daughter to play with."

"Play, play, play," she said in a sing-song voice as she moved from the chair to the floor. Then she wrapped her arms about her knees, the wooden figure still gripped in her hand, and began humming as she rocked back and forth.

Landon watched her slowly retreat from the world and go somewhere deep inside herself. At least he'd seen she was alive and would mention that to both Payne and Campion when he next saw them. When he returned to claim Briarwood.

And Cassiana.

CHAPTER TWENTY-THREE

C ASSIANA THREW BACK the bedclothes and dragged herself from her bed. She wasn't looking forward to another day of pretending to be empty-headed and pacifying her half-brother, as she'd done for the past few days as more and more so-called guests arrived. She'd innocently asked Campion who all these arrivals were, knowing full well they were the noblemen who'd come to purchase her. The fact that she knew and couldn't scream in outrage at the new earl had nearly driven her to murder.

Campion had assured her all of the noblemen who descended upon Briarwood were merely visiting at his invitation in order for him to get to know them better. He wanted to build relationships with his fellow Northumberland lords.

Or so he told her.

She dressed and braided her hair so she could go down for mass, something Campion never attended. She'd tried to gently explain to him that it set a poor precedent for the liege lord not to go to daily mass at his own chapel but he'd disregarded her words. At least the chapel was the one place, other than her bedchamber, that she could relax, knowing he would not be there observing her. She found him watching her several times and it made her very uncomfortable.

Stepping out her door, Cassiana saw Sir Garth Atwood lingering in the corridor. As she shut her chamber door, she greeted him wearily.

"Good morning, Sir Garth."

"And good morning to you, my lady." He gave her a ready smile, which she found tiresome. The knight was one of several men who'd followed her about ever since he'd come to Briarwood, trying to engage her in conversation and woo her.

"If you'll excuse me, I'm on my way to mass."

"I'll go with you."

The knight offered her his arm but Cassiana ignored it and started down the hallway without him. Suddenly, his fingers tightened about her upper arm and whirled her around.

"I am most desperate to speak with you, Lady Cassiana. It cannot wait."

She stared at him coolly. "Please release me, Sir Garth. I can't imagine what you might have to say to me."

"Only this."

His other hand tightened about her arm and he pushed her against the wall. His body pressed against hers as his tongue invaded her mouth, causing her to gag. She tried to knee him in the groin but had no room to maneuver. Her hands pushed against his chest, trying to knock him away. Unsuccessful, she did the only thing she could think to get him off her—and sank her teeth into his roaming tongue.

Atwood yelped and jumped back, surprise on his face.

"Well done," a voice said as applause began.

Cassiana saw Campion standing there.

"You bit me!" accused Atwood.

"You kissed me without my permission," she retorted. "Permission that I will never grant."

The knight looked to Campion, who said, "I will speak to her. Leave us."

Atwood stormed off. Cassiana remained motionless, dreading to hear what Campion would say next.

"Sir Garth is a pleasant fellow," he began.

"May we speak privately? In your solar?" she asked.

"Of course."

Campion reversed direction and returned to the solar, Cassiana following. He seated himself and indicated a chair for her to take. She did, trying to bank her temper before she spoke.

"What is going on, Collin? A gaggle of men have descended upon Briarwood."

He gave her a sly look. "Don't tell me you haven't figured it out. I thought you were more clever than that, Cassiana."

She glared at him. "They are suitors. For me," she admitted.

"Indeed. They include the best noblemen of Northumberland, from the most prominent families."

"I thought you wanted to get to know me."

He shrugged. "I know everything I need to know. You are a tremendous beauty from a powerful family. You need a husband. I'm in the process of finding you one, especially before your beauty begins to fade."

"I thought you offered me your protection!" she exclaimed.

"Part of that, dear sister, is marrying you off. You've been running Briarwood on your own for far too long. Oh, don't show me false modesty. I'm not sure what game you play but I do know you're as intelligent as any man and have managed this estate for several years. That means you're in my way."

"I'm no threat to you, Collin," she hurriedly assured him, desperately wishing she could placate him.

He assessed her. "I'm not so sure about that." Then he brightened. "Don't worry. I've narrowed down your new husband to Sir Garth and two others. I'll dismiss the rest of our visitors after they break their fast this morning and we'll go from there and see how the bidding goes."

"Bidding? Do you not understand how a marriage is arranged? The bride's family supplies the bridal price to the groom's. *You* are the one who offers a settlement, not the other way around."

"True," he agreed, "but because of your lovely face and luscious body, not to mention your fine pedigree, I have decided that *I* should be compensated for letting you go to another man."

"That's outrageous!" Cassiana cried.

"Mayhap it is—but I found plenty of men willing to pay for you."

She stood, her body trembling in fury. "No other man will have me," she told him.

"And why is that?" he asked.

"Because another man of my choice has already had me. I'm no longer a virgin," she proclaimed.

Campion leaped to his feet, anger pouring off him in waves. He slapped her so hard that it knocked her to her knees. Cassiana grasped the leg of the chair next to her, trying to steady herself while the flashes of stars faded. Then Campion yanked her to her feet by her braid, causing her scalp to scream in pain.

His hands dug into her shoulders and he shook her. "Who?" he demanded. "Who has sullied you?"

Cassiana spit in his face.

Campion turned bright red. He released her and wiped the spittle from his cheek with his sleeve. Then he struck her again. Pain exploded along her cheek. She bit her tongue and tasted blood.

Once more, his fingers captured her upper arms, squeezing so tight that she knew she'd find ten separate bruises along them come tomorrow.

"Was it de Blays?" he hissed.

"It doesn't matter who it was," she said, wanting to protect Landon. "I'm damaged goods now. No nobleman is going to pay you for me. In fact, I could be with child right now. You might as well send me to a convent and be done with it."

His grip tightened. "Nay. Not if I hurry and wed you today. No one need ever know you're no longer a virgin."

"I won't speak the vows," she said stubbornly.

"I'll make you," he promised. Campion thought a moment. "Who is that squire that's always following you about, doing your bidding? Justin, mayhap. That's his name, isn't it?"

Cold fear settled in her belly.

"How would you like to watch me torture him? Cut off each finger, one by one, as he screams in agony."

"He's only a boy! And he's done nothing wrong. No one would help you do such an abominable thing."

Campion's smile spoke of pure evil. "They wouldn't have to. I'd be happy to do it myself. Besides, who would speak out against me? I'm the Earl of Briargate. I can do whatever I want." He shrugged. "I could say I caught the boy stealing. Cut off both his hands, to start."

"You wouldn't," she said. But in her heart, Cassiana knew he would do that—and much worse.

"After punishing young Justin, if you still don't agree to wed the man of my choice, I could try and convince you again. Mayhap put down your precious horse? You seem to love the animal. I'd take a pike to it. Stab it again and again." He brightened. "I know. I'll blind the beast first. Then stab it before I burned the animal and served you horse stew. I'd make sure you ate every bite, Cassiana."

Nausea roiled through her. She didn't speak. She couldn't listen to any more of his vile ideas.

Campion seemed to understand that she was defeated. He released his hold on her and then touched her chin with a finger, raising it until her gaze met his.

"You will wed, Cassiana. Today. I will negotiate with the three men I have in mind and then have the marriage contracts drawn up. For now, return to your room. Do not leave it under any circumstances. If you do, I'll start with your horse and then the boy. Then Messina. And Hobart."

She stumbled from the solar and then ran to her bedchamber. She started to latch the door and then thought no good could come of that.

What kind of man would speak the way Collin Campion did, threatening innocents?

In that moment, she realized her half-brother was mad.

LANDON CUT A piece of cheese from the round before him and handed the slice to Stephen.

"What do you say to Lord Landon?" prompted Barnard.

"Thank. You." Stephen grinned and nibbled on the cheese. "Father. Can I go to the fire?"

"Aye, lad. Just be careful. Don't touch it."

"You have been very kind to my son," Barnard said as he watched Stephen cross the room and sit next to the fire. "It almost makes it worse, knowing what I did to you."

"Stephen is a kind young man," Landon said. "Though simple, he is sweet and friendly. I think he would be good working with animals. Mayhap feeding them. Milking the goats."

"He can learn," Barnard said. "Whatever you wish him to do, Stephen will try very hard to please you, my lord. The same with me. I am grateful that you will give us a home."

"You are doing me a favor, Barnard, by helping bring the truth to light. I think you will be happier at Briarwood than you were at Newfield."

Barnard nodded. "I know I will, Lord Landon."

Lady Druscilla came down the inn's stairs. She wore a cotehardie of pale rose and a confident look.

Joining them, she said, "Are we ready to unite and see that Briarwood is returned to Lord Landon?"

"Aye, my lady," Barnard said.

Landon inclined his head. "I cannot thank you enough for coming along, Lady Druscilla. Your presence as a witness will go a long way."

The door to the tavern opened and Sheriff Bartholomew Howard entered. He glanced about and then came to where their group was seated.

"Are you ready?" he asked gruffly, his white, shaggy brows moving with a life of their own.

"Aye," Landon responded, glad to have a court official with them as they challenged Lord Reynard and Collin Campion.

Landon had discovered as they'd traveled closer to Briarwood that Howard was the sheriff for this county and, as such, the king's chief officer of law. Though the sheriff had the authority to summon a jury, which handled mundane issues such as trespassing and disorderly behavior, Howard also had the power to refer more serious matters to the royal court. Landon had met with him for over an hour the night before, laying out his case against Payne and Campion. It would be up to Howard whether or not he referred the case to the royal court or passed judgment himself. Either way, the sheriff assured Landon that he would sleep in his own bed at Briarwood as the Earl of Briargate by the time the sun fell again.

As Barnard collected their horses from the inn's stables, Howard asked, "What happened with Tarquin Grosbeck? I know he was in service at Briarwood for several years."

Landon frowned. "I won't give you details regarding his treachery. I'll only say that his lies and disloyalty caused Lady Cassiana to ban him from the estate. Why do you ask?"

The sheriff replied, "He showed up at this very inn, drunk and belligerent, bemoaning his fate. When those present had enough of his ranting and demanded he settle down or leave, Grosbeck picked a fight with the wrong man—a dockhand twice his size. Grosbeck kept coming at him and the dockhand killed him in self-defense. I ruled on the case and wanted to satisfy my curiosity."

Howard's words didn't surprise him. Grosbeck was volatile. Knowing the knight was dead brought Landon some peace of mind.

They rode out from Stony Eastbridge, the fishing village to the east of Briarwood. Lady Druscilla had proven to be an excellent horsewoman. Barnard was an adequate rider, while Stephen had been enthusiastic during their entire journey north.

Landon caught sight of the castle and prayed that all was well, especially with Cassiana. As they turned off the main road and traveled along the one that led directly into the castle, he saw the gates opening. Several dozen riders poured through, all male. Signaling for his party to stop, Landon waited to see what group was leaving Briarwood and why they'd been present.

He picked out Lord Tormund near the front of the group, a nobleman with an estate twenty miles to the southwest of Briarwood. The baron had been present at Landon and Cassiana's wedding. As Landon's eyes skimmed over the approaching riders, he recognized many more who'd been invited to the wedding.

Lord Tormund motioned for his group to halt. Landon noticed that everyone averted his eyes, not daring to look in his direction.

"What's going on, Lord Tormund?" he demanded.

The baron, who'd been quite friendly during his stay at Briarwood and played two games of chess with Landon, looked sheepish.

"We are the rejects, Sir Landon. Men summoned by the new Earl of Briargate as potential husbands for Lady Cassiana."

"Campion's already trying to marry her off?"

"Aye. There's not a man present who didn't like and respect you, my lord, but Campion made it clear that he would never allow you to wed his half-sister. He issued an invitation for all unwed noblemen throughout Northumberland to return to Briarwood and seek her hand. He's narrowed down his choices to three men and will negotiate to let the highest bidder wed her today."

"What?" Anger erupted from Landon. "He's *selling* her?" He could only imagine the humiliation Cassiana must be feeling.

"He is." Lord Tormund glanced to the sheriff. "Do you have some word from the king that will stop this, Howard?"

The sheriff smiled enigmatically and glanced to Landon, who replied by shouting out so the entire group could hear his words.

"I invite all of you to return with me to Briarwood as witnesses," knowing they would spread the word of today's events throughout Northumberland and beyond.

Landon spurred his horse and rode to the gates, which were about to close. Looking up to the gatekeeper, he greeted him by name and said, "The entire group is returning. Keep the gates open until every rider comes through."

The gatekeeper grinned. "I hope you're home for good, my lord."

Riding through the outer bailey, Landon shouted for everyone present to head to the great hall. He rode past the training yard and bellowed at Sir Adam for the men to cease their exercises and come to the keep. By the time Landon arrived at the keep's entrance, the inner bailey had begun to fill. He dismounted and helped Lady Druscilla to the ground.

"You have an impressive estate," she commented. "No wonder Collin wanted it for himself."

"Wait until you see my future wife," he countered. "Then you'll understand everything I do, I do for her."

He escorted Lady Druscilla up the stone steps, Howard, Barnard, and Stephen following closely behind. They passed two men known to him and Landon invited them to turn around so they could witness what would soon unfold. He figured them to be part of the trio who'd tried to win Cassiana.

Messina met him, a bewildered look on her face. "My lord, what are you doing here?"

"I've come to reclaim what is mine," Landon told the faithful servant.

"Lord Collin just left the records room with Sir Garth Atwood. They have gone to the solar to negotiate the wedding contract between Sir Garth and Lady Cassiana. I'm to bring them food and drink."

"Then do it, Messina. But not a word of my presence."

She looked distraught. "Once the contract has been drawn up, Lady Cassiana will be legally bound to wed Sir Garth."

"Not if the contract was completed under false circumstances," Sheriff Howard interjected.

Messina nodded, beginning to understand. "I'll tell Cook to send out ale to everyone coming into the great hall." She hurried off.

"You're certain about the contract?" Landon asked.

"If Collin Campion is not the Earl of Briargate, he has no say in the lady's fate. Circumstances would revert to the king's command—that you wed Lady Cassiana," Howard assured him.

"Good."

Landon funneled everyone into the great hall and climbed upon the dais. The room fell silent.

"In a few minutes, Sheriff Howard and I will speak to the man falsely calling himself the Earl of Briargate. I have brought witnesses to speak up in the manner. If you'll be patient, we'll begin soon."

Landon returned to his party. "Now, we wait. The trap is ready to be sprung. We only need the mice to appear."

CHAPTER TWENTY-FOUR

C ASSIANA OPENED THE chest where she had hidden Landon's clothes. She would need to instruct Messina to send its contents and Landon's armor to Northmere. Nicholas and Katelyn would make sure Landon received his possessions.

She lifted the forest green gypon resting on top and buried her face in it, inhaling the wool's scent. Memories of Landon flooded her. Tears welled in her eyes and she blinked them away. There was no sense in thinking about him anymore. Landon was lost to her. Everything was lost to her now—but in losing Briarwood, at least she saved her people. No harm would come to anyone because she would go through today's nuptial mass with whatever groom Campion provided to be her husband.

Refolding the tunic, she bent to replace it in the trunk and saw a small bit of parchment. She traded the gypon for the parchment and opened it. It contained the official order from the king, proclaiming Landon de Blays the new Earl of Briargate, awarding him the earldom and lands associated with that title. She stared at the bold writing, wishing things could have been different. As she rolled it up again, the door behind her slammed open. Hastily, Cassiana slipped the parchment up her sleeve and closed the lid of the chest. Turning, she faced her half-brother and saw Garth Atwood accompanied him.

"What were you doing?" Campion demanded.

"I was looking through my trunk to find something to wear to my wedding."

"Wear what you wore to the other one," he ordered.

"Nay. I assume I'm to wed Sir Garth. If so, 'twould be a disservice to him to see me clothed in what I wore as I pledged myself to another man. If you'll give me two days, Collin, I can finish sewing a new cotehardie, even better than the one before."

"No delays," Campion said firmly. He turned to his companion. "You don't mind Cassiana wearing the same wedding gown?"

"Not at all, Lord Collin," Sir Garth said easily. "She won't be wearing it for long." His smile turned her belly sour.

"Then if you gentlemen will excuse me, I need to send for hot water so I may bathe before the ceremony."

"You may forego that, as well," Campion said. He nudged Sir Garth with his elbow. "In fact, I'll have hot water sent up after you wed. You and your lady wife can enjoy bathing together."

Atwood's eyes lit up with the suggestion. He gave Cassiana a hungry look. Her cheeks flamed in embarrassment as both men laughed heartily.

"Come along, Sister," Campion instructed. "Let's go downstairs and to the chapel. I'll send for the priest and we'll conclude this business. By this time tomorrow, you'll be on your way to your new home, your marriage consummated."

Without warning, her half-brother stepped up and embraced her. In her ear, he whispered, "Gasp when his cock enters you. While he sleeps, cut your finger and dribble blood onto the bedclothes. He must think you a virgin."

Campion pulled away and gave her a benign smile. In that moment, she made a choice. She would not let her people see her cowering. Instead, Cassiana raised her head high and walked proudly past both men and into the corridor. She made her way down the stairs, every step one that led her further away from the life she'd dreamed of with Landon. Reaching the bottom, she turned.

And saw Landon.

He stood in the doorway to the great hall. She froze, wanting to rush into his arms but knowing if she did, it would lead to trouble.

Collin Campion pushed past her and came to stand before Landon. Cassiana saw the waves of anger emanating from her half-brother as Landon stood confidently, his arms crossed over his chest, looking down upon the shorter man.

"What are you doing here?" Campion shouted. "I banished you from Briarwood."

"I have come to speak with you and Lord Reynard."

"I've already sent my uncle away. Guards!"

Several knights appeared behind Landon. He glanced at them and nodded. They moved as a group and surrounded Campion.

"What are you doing?" the earl cried, turning in a circle and seeing no means of escape.

"We are to escort you inside. Sheriff's orders," Sir Baldwin said as he took hold of Campion's arm.

Her half-brother tried to throw the knight's hand off but another soldier moved in. They latched on to the nobleman and dragged him into the great hall, followed by the remaining soldiers. Atwood raced after them, leaving Cassiana and Landon alone.

He closed the gap between them but did not touch her. "All will be well," he promised. "Do you believe me?"

"Always," she replied. Though she didn't know what would unfold, she trusted him implicitly. For the first time since Collin Campion stopped her wedding, hope filled Cassiana.

"Come with me."

Landon slipped her hand through his arm and led her inside. It startled her to find the room crammed with people. Not only were Briarwood's soldiers and servants present but many of their tenants and, from the looks of it, every man who had come to woo her this past week. As they approached the dais, Cassiana saw the county sheriff sitting at the center of the table, along with a noblewoman she did not know and a man who looked vaguely familiar.

"Greetings, Sheriff Howard."

"And good day to you, my lady," he replied. "Come and join us. I think you'll find the proceedings most interesting."

He indicated a seat to his left. She took it and Landon sat in the one to the sheriff's right. Collin Campion now stood before them. His jaw dropped as he seemed to recognize the others on the dais. Since he'd ceased struggling, the knights released him. Conversation in the great hall came to a halt.

Then Atwood rushed to the front of the room, pausing in front of the dais. "Sheriff Howard, I am Sir Garth Atwood, recently betrothed to Lady Cassiana. I fear what may occur today will be most upsetting to her. I ask your permission to remove her from these proceedings."

He placed a sheaf of papers before the sheriff. "Here is our marriage contract." Atwood stepped back.

Howard glared at the nobleman. "That contract is void."

Atwood said firmly, "No, it was signed by all parties. I intend to leave with Lady Cassiana and wed her immediately."

"Are you serious, Atwood?" Campion shouted.

Landon spoke up. "Sir Adam, have this man escorted from the great hall and removed from the grounds."

The captain of the guard stepped forward. "With pleasure, my lord." He signaled and two knights moved to obey.

Atwood backed away as the soldiers approached him. "But I have a contract," he shouted.

Howard picked up the papers and tore them in two. "And I told you the document is invalid."

He tossed the pieces to the floor as the knights took hold of Atwood and dragged him from the great hall.

Sheriff Howard rose. "Shall we try this again?" His gaze skimmed the room and he seated himself. Looking to Campion, the lawman said, "Let the prisoner make himself known to those present."

"Prisoner?" scoffed Campion. He threw back his shoulders. "I am Collin Campion, eldest son of the deceased Lord Darwin Campion, and the current Earl of Briargate."

"So you say," Howard said succinctly and sat. He turned to Landon. "My lord?"

Landon came to his feet. "As those gathered know, I was awarded the earldom and the estate of Briarwood by King Edward the Third."

Cassiana slipped the parchment from her sleeve and stood. "Here is the document that proves your words, my lord."

Howard stuck out his hand and she handed it to him. He unrolled the paper and quickly read the contents before placing it on the table before him.

"I'm satisfied as to its authenticity," he said. "I have seen the king's hand many times. 'Tis his words and signature."

"That means nothing," Campion said angrily. "I am Lord Darwin's last living son, from his first marriage to Lady Juetta Payne, my mother."

Landon held a hand out and the woman next to him took it. He helped her to her feet and then sat.

"Sheriff Howard, I am Lady Druscilla Payne, wife of Lord Reynard Payne, the brother of Lady Juetta. While it's true that Collin is Lord Darwin and Lady Juetta's son, no marriage occurred between them. My husband drugged Lord Darwin so that Lady Juetta might lie with him. He left Newfield less than two weeks after their encounter and never returned. No one contacted the earl and so he never knew about this bastard son."

"That's a lie!" cried Campion, as those gathered began murmuring.

"Is it?" the man seated next to Cassiana asked. He now stood and she recalled where she'd seen him before as he began to speak.

"I am Barnard Lovell, assistant steward at Newfield. Lord Reynard forced me to come with him and Collin Campion and halt the wedding between Lady Cassiana and Lord Landon. Lord Reynard demanded that I pretend to be the priest who'd married Lord Darwin and Lady Juetta.

"I am no priest. No wedding occurred. The parchment I carried that day was a forgery." Lovell sat as the gathered crowd gasped.

Lady Druscilla added, "My husband and Collin also told another falsehood to the people of Briarwood. Lady Juetta . . . is alive."

Now, the great hall erupted as people began talking all at once.

"Silence!" called out Sheriff Howard. He looked to the noblewoman. "Why didn't Lady Juetta herself come today and share this truth?"

"Because my sister-in-law is mad. Ask Collin. As a boy, he used to visit her in the turret tower where she's lived all of her life. Separated from others because she easily turns violent. Collin was afraid of her and asked never to visit her again. He said his mother was dead to him. My husband and I have raised Collin. I'm afraid to say that we haven't done a good job of it, since he lied his way into being the Earl of Briargate."

"Thank you, my lady," Sheriff Howard said and Lady Druscilla seated herself.

Cassiana watched Collin Campion wilt before her. His shoulders slumped. His head hung in shame.

The sheriff stood. "Since no marriage took place between Lord Darwin Campion and Lady Juetta Payne, any issue from their coupling is legally a bastard. As a bastard, Collin Campion cannot inherit anything from Lord Darwin." He scooped up the parchment before him. "Since King Edward awarded Sir Landon de Blays the title Earl of Briargate and all lands that accompany it, I proclaim him, now and forever, the rightful earl."

Cheers erupted throughout the great hall.

Landon stood and shook hands with Howard. The sheriff asked, "What would you have me do with Campion? And Lord Reynard? I can have them sent to the king since they conspired together and committed fraud."

Cassiana rose. Her gaze met Landon's and he nodded.

"I think justice has been served, Sheriff," Landon said. "Lord Reynard is on the edge of losing his estate to gambling debts. He and Campion will suffer humiliation and poverty. That is punishment enough. Are you in agreement, my lady?"

She nodded. "I am, Lord Landon." It felt good calling him by his title again.

"Then my work here is done. I'm needed in Berwick-upon-Tweed to settle two cases. I hope we meet again, Lord Landon, under much better circumstances." The sheriff left the dais.

Cassiana turned to Lady Druscilla and Barnard Lovell, who'd joined them. "I can't thank you enough for testifying on Landon's behalf. We will be forever grateful."

The noblewoman took Cassiana's hand. "I hope you and Lord Landon have a very happy marriage and are blessed with an abundance of children."

Sir Baldwin came to stand in front of them. "Lady Druscilla, your escort awaits you."

Landon lifted her hand and kissed her fingers. "Lady Druscilla, I hope you have a safe and pleasant journey and enjoy your new life with your daughter and son-in-law."

"Come visit me sometime, Lord Landon. I would like that."

He smiled. "I would, too."

Sir Baldwin handed her down and led the noblewoman from the great hall, several soldiers falling into step behind them.

Landon gestured to Barnard. "Lady Cassiana, Barnard and his son, Stephen, will now reside at Briarwood. I thought it best for them to stay."

"I think that's a fine idea," she declared.

Barnard bowed to them and jumped from the dais. He went to a young man who stood nearby and embraced him. Cassiana thought it must be his son.

Now, only Landon stood in front of her, drinking her in.

"Would you still be interested in wedding me?" he asked, a twinkle in his eye.

"I thought you'd never ask," she teased.

Then she was in his arms, his mouth on hers, and the world around them faded away.

Stomping and clapping finally made her aware that others surrounded them. Cassiana eased her lips from Landon's and looked around the great hall. Beaming faces stared back as those present rejoiced in the return of their liege lord.

Father Peter fought his way through the crowd until he reached them. "The people are demanding your wedding take place immediately."

"Now?" Landon asked.

The priest nodded.

Landon looked to her. "What do you think, my love?"

Cassiana gave him a brilliant smile. "That we should change into our wedding finery and please our people."

Landon returned her smile and then faced those gathered in the great hall. "Lady Cassiana and I will be wed in an hour."

"Why not right away, my lord?" cried a loud voice.

He held his arms wide. "Look at me. I have the dust of the road on me from racing to Briarwood. The least I can do is wash and don the beautiful cotehardie my future wife sewed for me."

"I'll see to the hot water," Cook called out and everyone laughed.

Cassiana found herself swept away by Messina and several other servants. As they turned the corner, she waved at Landon as others took charge of him. In her bedchamber, her wedding attire was laid out and she allowed herself to be dressed in it. Messina unplaited her hair and combed it until it shone before she placed the gold circlet from Katelyn atop Cassiana's head.

A part of her wished that Nicholas could have been present to escort her to Landon and that Katelyn might have witnessed her brother marry. They would have to venture to Northmere soon and share their saga in person with the couple.

Everyone left once she was ready except for Messina. The long-time servant watched Cassiana with tears in her eyes.

"You look lovely, my lady. Happiness radiates from you."

"I feel I am the most fortunate woman in the world, Messina. I'm marrying the best man I've ever known."

Messina wiped away the tears that began to spill. "God has also favored Lord Landon, my lady, for he is lucky to wed you."

Someone rapped on the bedchamber door and Messina answered it. Sir Adam entered.

"My lady, I would ask for the opportunity to escort you to your wedding to the Earl of Briargate."

"Thank you, Sir Adam." Cassiana slipped her hand around his arm and they left her room.

Once more, she traveled the familiar path from the keep to the chapel. Musicians again played a merry tune as she approached the crowd assembled for the ceremony. Then she caught sight of Landon and her heart flipped twice over. The slight breeze caught his dark hair and his emerald eyes glowed as she approached. Everyone else faded from view as she reached him and he took her hands in his.

As if in a dream, Cassiana listened as Landon made his vows to her and she repeated the same to him. He slipped on the simple band that he had purchased for her and she gazed at it sitting on her finger, knowing she would never remove it. Father Peter ushered them inside the chapel and said mass. At the end, he proclaimed them to be man and wife.

Landon cradled her face in his large hands and bent to kiss her. Anticipation made her heart flutter wildly. Then his lips tenderly brushed hers. Her arms went round his waist and he deepened the kiss, drawing her close. Wild emotions raced through Cassiana—but the one that rose above all others was love. A deep, abiding love for this good man poured from her into their kiss and she clung to him, never wanting to let go.

Her new husband was the one to break the kiss. He rested his forehead against hers.

Quietly, he said, "The sooner we leave the chapel, the sooner we can hurry to our solar." Landon smiled. "I think you know what awaits us there."

Cassiana's hand found his and they raced from the chapel as their people looked on in approval. Once outside, Landon swept her up in his arms and ran the rest of the way, through the bailey, into the keep, and up the stairs to the solar. Their solar. The room that would always be their private retreat. A place where they would spend long hours with the children they would make together. In love.

Landon set Cassiana down, his hands encircling her waist.

"I love you, Cassiana de Blays. You are my wife and my life. Everything I am or will ever be, I owe to you." His mouth met hers.

Landon tasted of love. Their love. Which would last a lifetime.

CHAPTER TWENTY-FIVE

L ANDON AWOKE WITH Cassiana nestled in his arms.

His wife . . .

He could only give praise to the Virgin Mary for seeing them safely through such a turbulent storm. When he thought of what his life might have been like if he'd lost this beautiful, caring woman, only a black void came to mind. Landon would have spent the rest of his life lost. Bitter. Unhappy.

He pressed a kiss to the top of her head, savoring the scent of lilac that wafted from her. In this moment, he knew utter contentment.

She began to stir and then opened her eyes. Her lips curled into a smile.

"Good morning, Husband."

"Good morning, Wife."

Landon kissed her. "I'm sorry to have kept you awake half the night."

"Are you?" Her eyes twinkled with mischief.

He cupped her cheek and she flinched.

"What's wrong?"

"Nothing."

He reached for the candle that had almost burned out and brought it between them. The left side of Cassiana's face was bruised and swollen and her eye blackened. He couldn't imagine their love play having caused such injuries. Then it realized who was responsible.

"Campion," he said, low and angry. "I'll kill him."

She clutched his shoulder. "Nay. He is out of our lives now, Landon. Collin Campion is the past." She paused, toying with the hair on his chest. "I'd rather focus on our future. Better yet, the present." Her smile grew wide and then she pressed her lips to his.

Landon loved her sweet and slow, covering every inch of her in gentle kisses as he caressed her body, her skin like silk beneath his fingers. Cassiana returned the favor, kissing him in places that he'd never known could be so sensitive to touch. Her hand trailed down his chest to his manhood. As she stroked it, he knew he couldn't wait any longer to be inside her.

Lifting her by the waist, he settled her above him and then lowered her until she sheathed him completely. Buried in her velvet softness, he closed his eyes and sighed.

"Oh, my. This is new."

She wriggled and he groaned.

"Hmm. I rather like this."

Landon opened his eyes. "I thought you might." His hands squeezed her waist gently.

Slowly, Cassiana began to move, finding a rhythm that suited her and then the both of them. They came at the same time, each calling out the other's name, and she collapsed against him. They lay entwined for some minutes and then she raised her head.

"I think we should go to Northmere today."

He frowned. "I've only just returned to Briarwood."

"Katelyn and Nicholas must be worried sick about you. We must let them know all is well. That we are wed and you are once more the Earl of Briargate. Besides, you should return Nicholas' horse to him.

We won't be gone but a day. We can leave once we break our fast and be there in less than two hours. That would give us plenty of time to visit and then we can depart for home tomorrow morning."

"It would please Katelyn to see us," Landon mused. "All right. Let's dress and make our way downstairs—before I decide to keep you in bed all day."

Cassiana readied herself for the day. As she started to fasten the amber pendant around her neck, Landon stopped her.

"I have something else I'd like you to wear today."

He opened his palm and revealed an ornate brooch composed of rubies.

"Is that a dragon?" she asked, curious where this piece came from.

"Aye," he confirmed. "I have another confession to make. You already know of my father's transgressions. I also have another disreputable ancestor. My great-grandfather, Godwin de Blays, was a pirate. They called him God of the Seas."

Cassiana burst out laughing. "A pirate, truly?"

"Aye. Father used to tell us stories about Godwin as we sat on the bank and fished. He was the son of an earl who was sold to pirates as a boy."

"Sold?" Shock filled her.

"I'm fuzzy on the details but I remember Father telling me his grandfather took Lady Melisent captive on the high seas. They wound up marrying and Godwin learned of his origins. He returned to Blackwell and became its earl. Father said that Godwin loved Melisent so much that he gave up pirating for her. This brooch was his gift to her since he captained a ship called *Dragonstar*."

Landon pinned the brooch to her cotehardie. He grew serious.

"Moments before the king's men arrested Father, he pressed this into my hands and told me to give it to the woman I loved." Landon kissed her. "That's you, my love."

Cassiana fingered the brooch. "You have given me two pieces that

I'll treasure. Thank you." She kissed him, wondering how else he would surprise her over the years.

They entered the great hall and Landon spoke to Sir Adam, advising the captain to select a guard of half a dozen men to see them to Northmere.

Once they'd broken their fast, Cassiana gathered a small bundle to attach to her horse with fresh clothes for the next day and they made their way to the stables.

"Why don't I ride Orion to Northmere?" she suggested. "Then we can ride on him together when we return tomorrow."

Landon thought it an excellent idea and asked a groom to saddle Nicholas' horse while he prepared Orion for the trip. He led the horse from its stall and saw Cassiana in the one opposite. She'd laced her arms around Tressa's neck and wept into the horse's mane.

Entering the stall, he softly asked, "Is something wrong with Tressa?"

She ran a hand down the horse's nose and then kissed her before turning away.

"Nay, Tessa is fine. It's just that Campion threatened . . . he threatened . . ." She dissolved into tears again.

He enfolded her in his arms and let her weep. Her half-brother must have discovered how much Cassiana cared for the horse and used the affection she felt against her. It was merely another reason that if Landon ever saw the bastard again, he would strike him dead.

She pushed away and wiped her sleeve across her reddened eyes. "Let's go."

Once outside, he helped her mount Orion and then took his place on Nicholas' horse. The assembled guard did the same and their party galloped through both baileys and the gates, heading north toward Berwick-upon-Tweed before they turned west for Northmere.

The gates opened as they approached and Landon knew those on duty had recognized the banner of the Earl of Briargate. He glanced up at it dancing in the breeze and was overwhelmed by a moment of wonder that the banner represented him. His house. The ones who'd come before him and the children which would follow him.

The group made straight for the keep. As Landon suspected, Katelyn awaited them outside, her face flushed with color. He helped Cassiana from Orion and they greeted his sister. She embraced him for a long moment and then kissed him soundly. Katelyn turned to Cassiana and lifted her hand.

"You're wed!" Katelyn cried. "Oh, I'm so happy for you." She hugged Cassiana tightly and then fell into Landon's arms once again.

By now, Nicholas joined them. "Forgive me. I was in the training yard. I would greet you but I'm filthy."

"Come inside, Nicholas," Katelyn urged. "You can train any day with your men. We need to celebrate Landon and Cassiana's being married."

Nicholas' face lit up. "You are?" He slapped Landon on the back. "Well done, my friend."

The two couples entered the keep. Katelyn called for hot water to be brought up for Nicholas to rinse with and for their noon meal to be delivered to the solar. She quickly nursed Ruston and gave him to a servant so the boy could nap.

Soon, the four sat around the large, oak table as Landon and Katelyn took turns relaying the events of the past week.

"I can't imagine how you felt, having all those suitors lined up to inspect you as if you were a horse they might buy," Katelyn told Cassiana. "And to think Campion wanted to sell you like a slave to one of them."

"I realize they were, for the most part, good men. In search of a bride."

Landon lifted Cassiana's hand to his lips and kissed it tenderly. "You are a prize, my love. Any man would vie for the opportunity to take you to wife."

Her amber eyes glowed with affection. "I was only meant to be one man's wife. Thank the Christ it came to pass."

"Do you think Collin Campion merely greedy in trying to falsely claim Briarwood? Or do you think he might be touched by his mother's madness?" asked Nicholas.

"There's a strong possibility his mind is tainted," Landon said. "Lady Druscilla admitted that her husband spoiled him as a boy but I got the feeling that she'd grown somewhat afraid of him as he grew older."

"His temper was volatile during my time in his company," Cassiana confirmed. "The least thing set him off. I spent the week he lived at Briarwood trying to placate him and keep others out of his way."

Katelyn looked at her sympathetically. "I can see you suffered under his hand."

Cassiana self-consciously raised a hand to her face. "It wasn't until the end that he struck me. I'll admit that I provoked him."

Landon tightened his fingers around hers. "If I ever see him again . . ." His voice trailed off.

"I doubt you will," Nicholas said. "From all you shared, he will be doing what he can to survive. If Lord Reynard's gambling debts are called in and he loses his estate, both he and Campion will be homeless."

"Thanks be to God that Lady Druscilla—and Barnard Lovell— were willing to speak the truth," Cassiana said. "At least she will be safe at her daughter's. Landon was kind enough to give refuge to Barnard and his son. They will remain at Briarwood."

Suddenly, Katelyn's cotehardie moved with no one touching it. She began to laugh. "The babe is awake again."

Nicholas placed his hand over her belly and rubbed it affectionately. "Should we take a walk? That usually seems to calm her down."

"You believe it a girl?" Landon asked.

"I do." Nicholas grinned. "She'll probably be even more beautiful than Kate and have everyone at Northmere wrapped around her tiniest finger. Including Ruston."

"I think as an older brother, Ruston will be protective of the babe, be it a boy or girl."

Nicholas offered his wife a hand and helped her to her feet.

"Would you care to walk with us?" he asked Landon and Cassiana. "The babe seems to enjoy that. I have a new horse I purchased two days ago that I'd like you to see."

The couples exited the solar and went outside. The late October afternoon was sunny but chilly.

"I would like to rub some hyssop on your face to alleviate the bruising," Katelyn told Cassiana. "I'm running low, though. Instead of visiting the horses, would you like to join me to pick some?"

Cassiana agreed and they parted from the men. She strolled with Katelyn through the gates and they ventured outside the castle's walls.

"I noticed your brooch," Katelyn said. "Melisent's brooch."

"Aye. Landon gave it to me this morning. He told me about his pirate great-grandfather and the woman he took captive that became his wife."

"Mother abhorred that story," Katelyn confided. "Father would tell us pirating stories only when we were well out of her sight." She pointed. "The meadow lies just over there. I can usually find hyssop at the edge of the woods. We won't need much."

She watched Katelyn's cotehardie wiggle again. "Does it hurt?"

"Not now. As I grow larger, it's a bit uncomfortable. I have to relieve myself frequently. The last month when I carried Ruston, I found it a little hard to breathe. And sleep was difficult because my belly had grown so large. No matter how I lay, I couldn't get comfortable."

"What about childbirth?" It was something Cassiana dreaded, having watched her mother give birth. Those screams still haunted her dreams.

"It hurts a great deal," admitted Katelyn. "I'll not lie to you about that. But it's as if the memory of labor dissolves once your babe is placed in your arms. A blanket of pure love wraps around you and your babe and you forge a powerful connection with one another."

"My mother lost several children while giving birth. The last time, she also died. Her babe did not survive."

Katelyn shrugged. "'Tis part of being a woman. To me, a babe is an expression of the love I bear for Nicholas. The love we have for one another." She cradled her belly with both hands. "I would die for the child within me—and I haven't even met it yet. Come, here we are. Let's cut through the meadow."

They crossed the wide space and Katelyn told Cassiana to keep an eye out for the hyssop, telling her it would be both blue and pink.

"I see some," she said.

"I do, too," Katelyn added. "Let's each pick some sprigs."

Cassiana knelt and plucked several strands of the herb. Her face hurt a great deal but she would never have told Landon. She knew bruises healed quickly. Once they'd faded, there would be no more reminders of her half-brother.

Rising, she asked, "Do you think this is enough?" She raised her fist, which clutched the hyssop—and then dropped it.

Collin Campion held Katelyn against him, one arm wrapped about her as his hand held a knife to her throat.

"Come here," he commanded.

Cassiana moved toward them. Katelyn's eyes were large but surprisingly held no fear.

"What do you want?" she asked Campion.

"My *life* back," he hissed. "I was supposed to be the Earl of Briargate. The liege lord of a vast estate. Wealthy beyond my dreams. Until Landon de Blays took it all away. A man stained with the mark of his father's treason. Why should he be granted a vast estate?" Campion glanced down and started. "I see a wedding band on your hand, Sister.

I suppose you married him so that you could keep running Briarwood as you did before."

"We are wed," she confirmed, thinking this man's mind and blood were corrupted by the madness that ate away at his mother.

"I wonder which one of you de Blays cares more for? His sister? Or his new wife?" mused Campion. "We'll soon find out."

Keeping the knife to Katelyn's throat, he said, "Approach slowly. Pick up the rope lying on the ground."

Cassiana walked in their direction, knowing if she made any sudden move to free Katelyn or disarm him, he would plunge the dagger into her sister-in-law's throat.

"Tie your right ankle to her left one," he instructed. "Knot it several times so that I can see that it's firm."

She positioned her leg beside Katelyn's and then squatted, tying the rope around their ankles, binding them together.

"Rise," Campion instructed. "Loop it around her waist and yours."

Cassiana did as commanded, dread filling her.

"Hold your right hand out," he ordered. "Lady Katelyn, your left."

The women raised their arms and touched hands then allowed their fingers to entwine. Quickly, he wound the rope around their wrists and tied it off. Stepping away several paces, he assessed them.

"Walk to me."

The first step proved awkward. They had to launch their bound ankles together and then swing their free legs around. After a few tries, they figured out how to move more smoothly as Campion backed away and they continued to walk toward him. Cassiana realized there was no way they could successfully outrun him, being tethered together, especially since Katelyn was with child.

"What is the point of this, Collin?" she asked.

"The point will be to see which of you de Blays saves."

Her belly soured at his words. Cassiana had no idea what Campion intended. Her fingers tightened around Katelyn's.

"Walk through the meadow until you reach the road. I'll be right behind you."

The two women looked at one another. Cassiana saw determination filled Katelyn's face. She took strength from that as they set out. As they walked, they found a rhythm between them and it became easier. They reached the road that dead-ended at Northmere's gates and Campion told them to halt when they reached the center.

"Face the castle."

They did. Cassiana looked over her shoulder and saw the dagger clutched in his hand.

He waved it menacingly. "I said to look at the castle, Sister. If you turn around again, I'll cut Lady Katelyn's child from her bulging belly and then her throat."

Quickly, she whipped her head around, knowing this monster would make good on his threat.

She didn't know how long they stood there. She could see activity on the wall walk and knew those on duty must be alerting Nicholas as to something strange occurring. They were within reach of an archer firing an arrow but Campion hid behind them, their bodies offering him protection from harm.

Cassiana glanced to Katelyn and saw her sister-in-law's right hand cradled her growing belly. She remembered that Katelyn had said she would die for her child. Cassiana hoped it wouldn't come to that.

Movement on the ground caught her eye. A man emerged from the gates and slowly walked in their direction. She realized it was Nicholas who headed their way. It took him several minutes before he stood before them, his arms wide open.

"I come unarmed," he said. "I ask for you to take me as hostage instead of these women."

"Who are you?" Campion demanded.

"Lord Nicholas Mandeville, Earl of Northmere."

"Where is Landon de Blays?" shouted her half-brother. "I want de

Blays here. Now. He is the one I will deal with. I want *him* to be the one to make the choice."

"What choice is that?" Nicholas asked calmly, his arms still wide.

"Whether I gut his sister or his wife."

Cassiana swallowed. She squeezed Katelyn's fingers, trying to reassure her.

"I know I won't have time to kill both of them. But I want de Blays to suffer. As I have suffered. He stripped me of everything. The least I can do is return the favor and take something precious from him. Let him watch as either his sister or wife bleeds to death before his eyes."

"Neither Kate nor Cassiana have done you any harm," Nicholas said. "I told you—take me. I will go with you willingly."

"I don't want to *go* anywhere!" Campion roared. "I have nowhere to go. This is the last play of my game. I will take de Blays' sister or his wife with me. I know the moment I slice open one, I am a dead man. An archer will fire upon me. Or the man in front of me will pounce and kill me with pleasure.

"I want that man to be Landon de Blays, Lord Nicholas. Not you. Fetch him. Now. I want him to make the decision of which lady dies with me and which one will live."

"Nay," Cassiana said, not daring to look at the fiend. "I'll make the choice. Not Landon. Take me, Collin. We belong together. We are of the same blood. We did not live together but we can die together." She paused. "Lady Katelyn already is mother to one child and will soon bear another. Please. Let her live. Let her be a mother to them. Take me, Brother. Now."

Katelyn gasped as Cassiana steeled herself for the thrust of Collin's knife.

It never came.

Instead, she heard a grunt and then a loud, long keening, the sound so unearthly that she shivered. Then Nicholas was before them, tugging them toward him, pulling their heads into his chest.

"Don't look," he warned as he withdrew a blade and began cutting their bonds.

Cassiana ignored him and lifted her head. She twisted around and saw Landon standing behind Campion, his sword jammed straight through her half-brother's torso. Blood bubbled from Campion's throat as he groaned in agony. Her husband ripped his sword out and then swung it with all his might, slicing through Campion's neck. The head sailed several feet away as the body swayed and then crumpled to the ground.

Their gazes met as Nicholas sliced through the last rope binding her to Katelyn. Landon flung his sword away and dashed to her. Cassiana fell into his arms. He kissed her over and over and ran his hands up and down her arms.

"Are you all right?" he asked hoarsely.

"I am now that you are here."

He kissed her again, hard and possessive, and she clung to him. Then she thought about Katelyn and pulled away. Her sister-in-law was weeping as Nicholas brushed her tears away.

Then Katelyn called her name and Cassiana ran to her. They embraced one other, their hearts beating wildly so much that the other could feel it.

"You were willing to die for me," Katelyn said.

"You had your children to live for. I could not have taken you from them."

Landon slipped his arms around her from behind and she leaned into him. Nicholas did the same with Katelyn.

"I kept him talking as long as I could," Nicholas said. "When we recognized Campion from the wall walk, Landon immediately headed for the sally port. He sneaked through it and hurried around the woods so he could attack from behind."

"I was afraid I would be too late, knowing how unpredictable he was."

Cassiana lifted a hand to stroke his cheek. "You weren't. You saved us from a madman."

"We both did, Nicholas and I," Landon proclaimed. "We are a good team."

"Good friends and now family," Nicholas said. "I love each of you but most of all, my precious Kate." He turned his wife in his arms and kissed her.

Cassiana maneuvered in Landon's arms so that she faced him. Her hands went round his neck and pulled his mouth to hers. Their kiss celebrated life—and love.

ΕPILOGUE

Briarwood Castle—June, 1343

CASSIANA OPENED HER eyes slowly, luxuriating in her favorite part of the day. It was when she awoke each morning in Landon's arms. Having him cocooned around her made her feel safe and brought a peace that she'd never known existed—until this man came into her life and changed everything.

She lightly stroked the forearm locked around her waist, knowing how important today was to her husband. King Edward would arrive at Briarwood on summer progress, the first time the monarch had ventured this far north with his entire royal court and family in tow. England's forces had conquered most of Brittany last autumn and the king wanted to celebrate the victory, while also showing support for his northern nobles.

Landon stirred and then nibbled on her neck enticingly.

"We should probably rise and dress," she said.

His tongue teased the soft spot just behind her earlobe and Cassiana shivered in anticipation.

"I'm not sure there's time for love play, what with your cousin arriving soon."

Landon's teeth sank gently into her earlobe. "There's always time for love play, sweetheart," he murmured.

She abandoned any protest and gave herself over to him, reveling in each pass of his hands over her. Soon, they joined together as one, their spirits soaring higher than the Heavens before they gently drifted back to Earth.

"Now, we can dress," Landon proclaimed and rolled from the bed as he stretched his arms high over his head. "I am proud to wear what you sewed for me for I know every stitch was completed with love. Mayhap, I will be better dressed than the king himself."

He came around to the other side of their bed and offered her a hand. She took it and looked around, trying to remember where she'd placed everything. Landon had told her it was custom for the host to give up his solar for the length of the king's visit. Fortunately, Edward was only going to spend two days and nights with them. Cassiana had decided they should sleep in a guest bedchamber last night so that she'd had time to prepare the solar for the royals the day before. She would look in once more this morning to make sure everything was as she wished.

"I'll go fetch Gavin so you can nurse him," Landon said once he'd dressed.

Their son would turn two late in August and was a great delight to them. He'd walked early and now talked constantly, asking questions all day long. Landon had already started placing Gavin in the saddle in front of him as he rode about Briarwood and called upon their tenants. Love washed over her every time she saw father and son sitting together atop Orion.

A wave of nausea came and went as she bent to retrieve her comb. Cassiana thought a moment and discovered her courses should have come two weeks ago. They'd always been regular, both before and after Gavin's birth. She realized her breasts had felt tender when Landon made love to her a few minutes ago but had thought it was due to her courses coming soon. She lifted one and it seemed heavier than usual. She placed a hand against her flat belly, wondering if new life grew within her again and hoped that it did.

Landon returned with Gavin as she finished with her hair. He handed the child to her and Gavin greedily sucked on her teat. He was already eating solid foods but Cassiana cherished this time with her boy. Once he'd been fed and burped, she returned him to his father and they left the keep to attend mass.

After they broke their fast, Cassiana met with the servants inside the keep, going over everyone's assignments while the king and queen were at Briarwood. She'd hired extra hands from Stony Eastbridge to help with the cleaning and cooking and several of them would help serve in the great hall today as the biggest feast Briarwood had ever seen would be laid out.

Her last task was collecting fresh flowers for the solar. She asked Justin to accompany her. The squire had sprouted several inches over the last year and now towered above her, almost as tall as Landon stood. She could tell by the look on his face that watching his countess pick flowers wasn't what he had in mind but Landon required her to be with protection whenever she left the walls of the castle. Nicholas did the same with Katelyn. Even though Collin Campion was long gone, Landon told Cassiana that she was much too precious for him to lose. He would rather her be safe and a little inconvenienced than find herself in danger as she had once been.

She found the exact flowers she wanted, burgundy sweet peas and bloody crane's-bill. Returning to the castle, she trimmed the stems and arranged the two different bunches together, interspersing dark and light artfully. She placed one arrangement on the oak table and the other beside the bed, stepping back to survey her work and finding she was pleased with it.

Returning downstairs, Messina hurried toward her.

"The king's banner has been sighted, my lady. They'll arrive within the quarter-hour. Sir Adam said the entourage is beyond comparison."

"Where is Lord Landon?"

"Right here, my love."

Landon came toward her with Gavin in his arms, looking more handsome than he did a few hours ago. It thrilled Cassiana that she fell in love with this man over and over again, sometimes when she least expected it.

Her two men accompanied her outside so they could greet the king and queen. Landon had wanted Gavin to be present but he wisely handed the squirming boy over to Messina, who would await nearby.

Riders swept into the bailey, the king's banners flying merrily in the breeze. She estimated a good hundred or more men-at-arms entered the castle walls, along with the king and his family and various nobles. Thankfully, the majority of those on summer progress would set up tents outside of Briarwood, though they would all be welcomed in for the feast and entertainment later today.

She spotted the king immediately. Landon had told her his cousin would now be two and thirty and she thought the monarch both handsome and dignified. He dismounted and immediately went to assist his wife. Queen Philippa was a year shy of thirty and richly dressed. The royal couple approached them and Cassiana swept into a low curtsey as Landon bowed.

"Get up, Cousin," ordered the king, a bit of exasperation in his voice. "You, too, Lady Cassiana."

Edward warmly embraced Landon. "It's been too long since we've seen one another."

The queen's eyes lit up as she looked at Landon. "We have missed your company, Landon."

He took Philippa's hand and brushed his lips across her knuckles. "I need to meet your new children, as well as introduce you to my wife."

He took Cassiana's elbow and brought her closer. "My king, my queen, this is the love of my life, Lady Cassiana de Blays."

The king smiled benignly. "I knew your father well, my lady. You favor Lord Darwin. I've been told you also kept Briarwood running smoothly during his last few years and are a true asset to Landon."

"Thank you, your majesty."

The queen took Cassiana's hand, surprising her. "I am delighted to meet Landon's wife." Her eyes grew mischievous as she said, "I'd hoped he might wait until one of our girls grew older so they could wed. Lord Landon is my favorite of the king's many cousins. You are a fortunate woman to have him by your side."

Cassiana laughed. "I couldn't agree more, your grace."

"I hope you won't be telling my sister that I'm the favorite cousin," Landon teased the queen. "I know you go to Northmere to visit Katelyn and Nicholas once you leave here."

"Show me your son," the king commanded.

Cassiana motioned to Messina and she brought Gavin forward. She started to hand the child to Landon but the king swept Gavin from her hands. Startled, the servant froze a moment and then slipped away.

"He's a handsome one, Landon. Even-tempered?"

"Gavin is, your majesty," Landon shared. He looked around. "Where are your children?"

A young lad the very image of the king stepped forward. "Do you remember me, Sir Landon?" he asked eagerly.

"Lord Landon," the queen gently corrected. "Remember, your father rewarded Landon with a title and this lovely estate, Edward."

"Lord Landon," the boy corrected.

Landon bowed and then thrust out his hand. "How could I forget you, your grace? You have grown taller than weeds since I last saw you. Are you ten and three now?"

"I was last week," the prince said proudly. He looked to Cassiana and swept up her hand in an elegant motion, kissing it. "Your husband was my first friend, my lady. He taught me to ride and how to swing a sword and mace."

"I hope he was a good tutor, your grace," Cassiana said, impressed with the prince's poise.

"He was. I would like to return the favor to him someday." Prince Edward held out his hand to Gavin, who seemed perfectly at ease in the arms of the King of England.

Gavin took the younger Edward's hand and pulled on it, forcing the prince closer. Gavin patted Edward's cheek. "I like you," he proclaimed.

"And I you, Master Gavin," the prince said. His gaze returned to Cassiana. "If it pleases you, my lady, I wish for your son to come to court to foster."

"While no mother looks forward to the day her young son must leave home, 'twould be an honor if my Gavin fostered at the royal court, your grace," she replied.

Gavin held his arms out to the prince and Edward lifted the boy from the king and held him close. "Don't worry," he told Cassiana. "I've had plenty of practice entertaining all my brothers and sisters."

"Enough talk. My belly is rumbling," the king complained good-naturedly. "Show us to your solar so we can rest a bit and have something to eat before the festivities begin."

"This way, sire," said Landon, leading the king into the keep, followed by Prince Edward and Gavin. A small boy ran from the crowd and scampered after them.

"That's Lionel, our five-year-old son," the queen commented before she spouted a few orders.

Immediately, two girls came forward, each holding the hand of a young boy.

"This is Isabella on the left, who has John, and Joan, who carries Edmund," the queen informed Cassiana. "Let's go to your solar. Come along, girls."

She accompanied the queen and the four children as the bailey behind them buzzed with activity. Messina hurried to her side.

"Refreshments in the solar at once."

"Aye, my lady."

The two families gathered and enjoyed something to eat and drink with all of their children. When Landon suggested they leave so the royal family might rest, the king waved the notion away.

"I haven't seen you in ages, Landon. Stay, so we can talk. We have much to catch up on."

The men remained at the table, while Prince Edward pulled out several wooden soldiers and distributed them to John, Edmund, and Gavin. The boys gathered before the fire and began playing as the two princesses took out needlework. Cassiana and the queen retired to chairs on the far side of the room.

"You've made the solar so welcoming, Lady Cassiana. I'm very fond of fresh flowers. I'm sure Landon told you that."

"He did, your grace. We have many varieties throughout the estate. I thought you would enjoy these."

The two women soon chatted as old friends. Finally, the queen asked, "When will your babe come?"

Cassiana sensed her cheeks heating. "How did you know? I only realized it this morning."

Philippa smiled. "After having eight children, I know the signs. You have a radiance about you. I assume you haven't told Landon yet?"

"Nay. I'm still getting used to the idea myself. I've only missed my courses once. I suppose the babe will come early next year."

The queen glanced to Landon. He and the king had joined the boys on the floor and now acted out some battle, with shouts of warning and glee.

"I meant what I said earlier. Landon is a true gentleman and a favorite of ours. He looks very comfortable as a father."

"He is," Cassiana assured the queen. "And he's also a wonderful husband."

"You love him?" the queen asked pointedly.

"With all my heart."

"I love the king," Philippa confided. "As all royal marriages are, ours was arranged. It took some time but love blossomed between us."

"I can see how much he loves his children, too. Landon told me he wanted me to get to know his cousin as a man during this visit—and not as a monarch."

"Edward thinks the world of Landon. He feels as if they are true brothers." Philippa smiled graciously. "He will be most happy to know that Landon has found love with you."

"My love?" the king called out. "The boys are becoming cranky. They need a nap. As do I," he added.

Landon scooped Gavin up. "This one is irritable, too. Let us leave you to get some rest."

Cassiana accompanied her husband and son from the solar and found Messina lingering in the corridor.

"Do they need anything else?" she asked anxiously.

"Only a little peace and quiet," Landon said. "Would you take Gavin and put him down for a nap?"

The servant took the boy. "Come along, my lord. It's to bed for you. You can play with the little princes later."

Cassiana led Landon across the hall to the bedchamber they were using and closed the door.

"Are we also due a nap?" he asked, his eyes twinkling.

She laced her fingers with his. "I like your cousin quite a bit. And the queen is lovely."

Landon smiled. "I'm glad we were able to spend some time alone with them. In truth, they are just people, like you and me. They both mean a great deal to me."

He kissed her softly. "You mean a great deal to me, too. You and

Gavin. My heart is filled with love for the two of you. For our family."

Cassiana gazed up at him. "Do you believe you have more room in your heart?"

She watched his confusion turn to understanding and his fingers tightened about hers.

"Are you . . . with child again?"

"I am. Come the New Year, we should have another little de Blays in our lives."

Landon's eyes filled with tears as he smiled at her. "I found myself when I found you, my love. You are my life, Cassiana." He bent and pressed a kiss to her belly and then rose, his mouth covering hers.

In his kiss, she knew the promise of all the good days to come.

THE END

About the Author

Alexa Aston's historical romances use history as a backdrop to place her characters in extraordinary circumstances, where their intense desire for one another grows into the treasured gift of love. She is the author of Medieval and Regency romances, including *The Knights of Honor* series.

A native Texan, Alexa lives with her husband in a Dallas suburb, where she eats her fair share of dark chocolate and plots out stories while she walks every morning. She enjoys reading, watching movies, and can't get enough of *The Crown* and *Game of Thrones*.

Made in the USA
Coppell, TX
25 April 2021